PRIVATE TIMOTHY FERGUS CLANCY

A NOVEL OF THE GREAT WAR

BY

WILL R. BIRD, MM

CORPORAL,
42ND CANADIAN INFANTRY,
THE BLACK WATCH OF CANADA

CEF BOOKS
2005

Library and Archives Canada cataloguing in Publication

Bird, Will R. (Will Richard), 1891-1984.
Private Timothy Fergus Clancy: a novel of the Great War/ Will R. Bird.
ISBN 1-896979-45-9
(Special limited edition reprint series; #5)
First ed. Published: Ottawa: Graphic Publishers, 1930.
1. World War, 1914-1918 - Campaigns - France - Fiction. I. Title. II. Series.
PS8503.I67P7 C813'.52 C2005 - 900241 -7

Published by: CEF BOOKS
PO Box 40083.
Ottawa, Ontario,
KIV 0W8, Canada.
1-613-823-7000

Titles in the Special Edition Reprint series (Available 2005):

1) **Scouting Thrills** by Captain George B. McKean,VC, MC, MM; 14th Battalion, C.E.F. (Original 1919)
2) **The 116th Battalion in France, 1914-18** by The Adjutant. (Orig 1921)

3) **The 2nd Canadian Mounted Rifles in France and Flanders, 1914-18** by G. Chalmers Johnston. (Original c.1922)
4) **Private Timonthy Fergus Clancy** by Will Bird, MM. (Original 1930)

5) **Not Mentioned in Despatches; A Memoir, 1914-1917** by Fred W. Bagnall, 14th Battalion, C.E.F. (Original 1933)
6) **Prisoner Five-One-Eleven; Memoir of a P.O.W.** By Harry Laird, 4th Canadian Mounted Rifles, C.E.F. (Original 1919)
7) **Mopping Up!** by Lieutenant Jack Monroe. P.P.C.L.I. (Original 1918)

8) **Shrieks and Crashes; a Memoir of 1917** by Wilfred B. Kerr, C.F.A

9) **Arms and The Maple Leaf; a Memoir of 1918** by W.B. Kerr, C.F.A.

10) **From Thunder Bay through Ypres with the Fighting Fifty-Second** by W.C. Millar. (Original c.1919)

Cover Design by Sean Horton, Manotick, Ontario. Text work by Lachlan Christie, Alexandra Christie and Clayton Robichaud.

Introduction to the 2005 Limited Edition

Will Bird wrote two of Canada's classic First World War books; *Ghosts Have Warm Hands* (1968, a revised version of *And We Go On*, 1930) and *Thirteen Years After*, a series about revisiting the Old Battlefields Will wrote for Maclean's Magazine in 1931.

Will's writing career started in the 1920s, when after returning from the war, he had to find a way to make a living. It was not easy and his early successes were primarily articles he wrote on his war experience and veteran's issues. It was during this period he wrote *And We Go On* and *Private Timothy Fergus Clancy*. By 1930 the public was getting tired of war books and titles published in a small market like Canada had a hard time at the best of times. Quickly both books vanished from sight. But Will persisted in preserving war memories, and promoting the rapidly-forgotten sacrifices of Canada in the Great War. He wrote for newspapers and magazines throughout the world and often would give slide presentations to veteran's groups across the country. He was a one man remembrance program. In 1931 his collected Maclean's articles were published as *Thirteen Years After* and in 1933 he privately published a collection of his articles, entitled *The Communication Trench*. By the 1990s these books had became exceedingly rare collector's items.

In the 1940s and 1950s Bird wrote historical novels about Nova Scotia, travel books, Regimental histories, short stories and articles on many different subjects. But he rarely revisited his own war, with the exception of *Ghosts Have Warm Hands* in 1968, a revision of his 1930 memoir *And We Go On*. It was published on the 50th Anniversary of the End of the Great War. But it too quickly vanished.

In 1997 CEF BOOKS decided to bring back Will Bird's important contribution to Canada's First World War literature and republished *Ghosts Have Warm Hands*; in 2000, *The Communication Trench* was revived and in 2001, *Thirteen Years After* was resurrected.

Bird's rarest book is his lost novel of the war, *Private Timothy Fergus Clancy*. Originally published by Graphic Publishers Limited of Ottawa in 1930 the book is so scarce that copies often sell for more than $400. It is one of Will's early runs at fiction and follows a scandalous Irish-Canadian soldier, Private Timothy Clancy of the 5th Canadian Mounted Rifles, 'The Mudhounds'.

On an historical note, The 5th Mounted Rifles were raised in Quebec's Eastern Townships and served in the 8th Brigade of the Third Canadian Division. (Bird served in the 42nd Battalion (The Black Watch) of the 7th Brigade in the Third Division.) They came to France as dismounted cavalry in 1915 and never got their horses back. They were used as infantry from 1916-1918, participating in the major Canadian battles of Mount Sorrel, The Somme, Vimy, Passchendaele, Arras, Cambrai and Mons.

There are many parallels with Will's own experience in the war throughout the story. Bird did serve with an unusual Irishman in the 42nd, and in his memoirs he recounts many of this 'Clancy's' escapades. Sadly Bird's original Irishman, Timothy Flinn of County Cork, was killed at Passchendaele in November 1917.

And now, after an absence of 75 years, here is Will Bird's lost novel.

Norm Christie
Ottawa, Ontario
January, 2005

CONTENTS

PROLOGUE

As the years go by our memories of the Great War grow dimmer. That is, we more and more forget the lesser parts, but each veteran carries with him pictures that will never fade, remembrances that are his priceless possessions. At will he may go back to battered sections of the line and there again live through a zero hour or a trench raid, visualize uncanny hours spent in an isolated listening post. It is impossible ever to forget or omit the horror attendant on those old battle grounds, the grimness of war, the sordid wretchedness of trench life in the Salient or on the Somme. But woven through the existence of the soldier ran a thread of humour - ragged and frail enough at times - that proved the saving grace of the situation, in all our poignant memories that touch of humour lives. Its presence spelled largely that by - word of all our staff officers - morale.

At this time, when the edges of memory are beginning to wear thin, I feel it would be a splendid thing if some time-rusted episodes of the trenches were brought up from the dugouts of experience and burnished for a general inspection. Humorous bits, the bright rays that helped one through dreary routine or death-laden hours, should be re-told. In this tale of Timothy Clancy I have made an effort to do such work, and the hope that has been with me in its writing, is that here and there through the narrative the reader who is an ex-serviceman may find incident or setting that will sweep back to him echoes of merriment from some billet or dripping, rat-haunted dugout.

Clancy was but a character found with almost every platoon of front-liners. He was always doing the unexpected, creating suspense and turmoil among all authority, and yet, at critical hours, in hard-won corners, a mighty warrior and faithful unto death. Behind the lines, his care-free swagger and contagious good humour entwined him in many romances and kept his paybook conspicuous with red ink. His kind were the salt of the trenches and only irritant to the wounded pride of the parade-ground cockatoos.

The Mudhounds were any front line battalion in any brigade, and all reference to the Fifth Canadian Mounted Rifles is but for the purpose of giving a realistic touch to the story.

Some of Clancy's adventures are so near the truth that they will be easily fitted to the unit to which they belong, but I feel that this will only add to their interest. That is all I have to say to you.

Parade! - 'shun! Carry on with your reading!

NOTE: The author is indebted to the editor of the Toronto Star Weekly for permission to use, as chapters, certain of Clancy's adventures which they published as short stories.

CHAPTER ONE

THE DISMOUNTED MUDHOUNDS

PRIVATE Timothy Fergus Clancy peered into the murk of a Belgian dawn and growled his blessing on the day. His tent was on an "island" in a sea of mud, and the island was gradually submerging. The tent itself was a sad and soggy affair, draped from a crippled pole. In the distance there were many others of its kind and, floundering through the mud, visiting each in turn, was the tall form of 'D' Company's Sergeant-Major. He was a red-faced, red-necked individual with a ramrod back and an exceedingly caustic tongue. His very presence rasped Clancy like sandpaper.

"Stir out there, you thick-heads," he shouted as he saw the tent flap open. "Breakfast's ready. Fall in at seven for a working party."

"Another av thim hell-blistered wurrkin' parties. By th' crown av ould Ireland, what kind av a mob is this I'm joined up with?" asked Clancy savagely as he sat up in his damp blankets and felt for his boots. "In th' nixt war I'll be joinin' with wan av thim labour battalions an' have an aisy time av it."

"Quit your grousin'," grunted a sleepy voice from the dark interior of the tent. "Don't you know it's an honour to belong to the Fifth Canadian Mounted Rifles?"

"I do not," snorted Clancy. "Yer Fifth is half av th' Sixth, ye have every race but th' Jews, and th' Colonel thanks Hiven that there's enough av th' Irish to make ye a fightin' mob, and th' only horses ye have iver seen has been thim transport mules. Mounted Rifles! Dismounted Mudhounds is all ye are, and I'm sorry I let mesilf be enticed to joinin' the same."

It was a topic that never failed to stiffen the hair on Clancy's neck. He hated the muddy trenches and the ground-hog game of war, and made no attempt to conceal his dislike. The very sight of spurs and riding breeches was enough to double his fist, and every time he heard the word "Mounted" he was ready to hit the nearest man.

"Is Clancy there?" The Sergeant-Major roared the query as the working party was falling in, and Clancy shambled forth. "Ah, there you are. Put your cap on your head, man, don't slip it on your ear. Go over to Major Pike's tent and report to him. You're a runner for a couple of days."

"A runner. Holy cats! Runnin' in this glue." A dozen chuckled comments eddied to Clancy's ears as he plodded through soupy mire to the driest ground about the "Duck Pond," as the camp had been dubbed. He made no answer to them; his mind was occupied with wondering just what the duties of a runner were.

Major Pike, unshaven and gruff, looked up from his plate of eggs and toast. "You the runner?" he demanded. "Brush your tunic, man, and straighten your belt. You're in the Fifth Mounted Rifles, not a construction gang."

Clancy saluted and swallowed his wrath. "Yis, sir," he answered.

"Take this message over to brigade and give it to Captain Bull. You may have to wait for him, but see that you deliver it. Get going."

"Yis, sir," said Clancy.

Outside, out of earshot of the tent, Clancy collared a weary-looking batman. "Where is brigade?" he demanded.

"At some place they call 'Bellaloo,' or something like that," came the answer. "It's a little two-dog place with an estaminet in the middle."

An estaminet. Clancy licked his lips. "An' how far is it?" he asked.

"Oh, three-four kilos, I dunno exactly. Take that road where the lorries is runnin' and go left and you can't miss it."

Clancy went forth on his errand. He found the road to be better than he had hoped, a fairly broad cobbled way, and as he dodged motor traffic and passed slow-moving limbers, he comforted himself with thoughts of refreshments ahead. On his arm was the red band that was his passport for the area and a document in his pocket allowed him to go places barred to the ordinary foot-slogger. There was a hint of privilege attached to this runner occupation. And then he entered a village.

It was well along in the morning and the sun had decided to shine for an hour or so. Its warmth brought forth swarms of officers of every rank and figure and Clancy became a human windmill as he saluted those he could not avoid. "Hell's bells" he grunted, as his arm got draggy. "Ivery monkey that's schemed his way into a Sam Browne is out for air this mornin' and headin' for this village. "Tis a long four kilos to this Bellaloo." Then he stopped to ask questions of a muddied

A.S.C. man. "How far is it to Bellaloo?" he inquired.

"Bellaloo. Never 'eard of it, myte. I cawn't sye."

"Is that so, "snorted Clancy. "Well, thin, where are we now?"

"This plice? Bli'me, there's a sign up at the corner, myte, but I never read it. Yer cawn't miss it."

Clancy left him without another word. He tramped to the corner and read, spelling laboriously. "To Essex Camp." A finger pointed the way he had come.

"What is it, my man? Lost your way? Have you a pass?" A burly, blue-chinned M.P. blocked Clancy's path.

"I am not," said Clancy. He hated M. P.'s. "And I have. Where is Bellaloo?"

"Don't try to be funny with me?" blustered the M.P. "I don't know any Janes by that name. Where are you goin'?"

"I'm lookin' for brigade that's at Bellaloo, or some sich name," said Clancy, smothering his ire.

"Bellaloo? Hummm. There's a place where there's a brigade staff about three kilos ahead but I think it's 'Bellaval'."

Clancy slipped by as the M.P. reached for a soldier without a belt. He went on and on, gradually leaving the traffic, and then saw that the road divided, right and left. Which branch should he take? On a chance he risked the right. He came soon to a shell-wrecked village, with only a few houses remaining intact, and then saw huge shell craters in the middle of the highway. Only two other soldiers were in sight and they were making furtive speed along a path that paralleled the road. At sight of Clancy they waved and shouted to him, but he paid no heed. It was a relief to be able to trudge along without dodging mules and motors. At the far side of the ruin he sighted the village he sought. He was sure of it, for he saw sentries in front of a sand-bagged building, and a flag drooped over the entrance.

"Is Captain Bull in there?" he asked the sentry.

The sentry frowned on him, glared, and continued his beat. "Divil take ye," said Clancy, and he went in at the open door. A Sergeant met him, a man who seemed in a tremendous hurry. "Is Captain Bull in there?" Clancy repeated his question.

"He is not," said the Sergeant. "There is no such officer in the Third Brigade."

"Third" said Clancy, and he gulped. "Th' Third. Where in th' devil is the Eighth?"

"It's some place three kilos to the left there," the Sergeant pointed vaguely toward the shell-ruined village through which Clancy had come. "It's a place called Saint Bellavoo."

Clancy wiped his forehead with tunic sleeves and turned about. He was hot and tired and thirsty. "Kin I get a drink av somethin' about this place?" he asked. “I'm so dry I'm blistering me innards."

"You cannot," said the Sergeant, "and...

Before he could speak further, an officer came rushing out. "Glad I caught you, Sergeant," he panted. "You'll have to take this message along with you. It's for the Eighth Brigade at Bellasaint, or some such place. You'll find it if you inquire."

"This man is a runner from the Eighth and he's goin' there now," interrupted the Sergeant eagerly. "Just give. . . "

"Thank goodness," said the officer. "Here you are, runner. Hurry like a good chap. This is important."

Clancy took the paper. His brain was seething, but what could a private say in the presence of a red-tabbed Captain? The Sergeant had saluted and mysteriously vanished in some inner passageway.

Outside, the sentry paced to and fro, glaring at Clancy as he passed. "Kiss me foot, ye owl-eyed safety-first," said Clancy. He felt that he must let loose his ire on someone or sizzle into flame.

He entered the war-shocked village again, and eyed the ruins as he passed. Halfway through he paused, stepped across the ditch, and stared. It couldn't be true, but it was. There, in a shed that had one end torn away, lay a bicycle, a real bicycle, with wheels and sprocket intact and in working order. He pulled it from the debris and examined it. It was a rather high machine, adjusted for some long-legged rider. The seat was loose and two bolt heads were ugly projections at the rear of the saddle. He pushed the bicycle out on the road and tried to mount. The ascent was too steep. He got a few bricks and built himself a stepping block, pushed the saddle over the bolts and got aboard. Once mounted he found that the machine pedalled easily, and his heart warmed. What were three kilos on this bicycle? Brigade would welcome the messages he carried and this Captain Bull was a queer fish if he would not offer a hard-worked soldier something to eat or drink.

Whee-eeee! Crash! Bang! Crump! Smash! Shells, salvos of them. They crashed into the ruined houses; they detonated on the street ahead of him. With one wild swoop he circled a broken pump in a yard and raced back the way he had come. Crash! Bang! Two shells hit directly in front of him. He understood now why no one travelled through the village. To his dismay he discovered that his machine had no brakes and there did not seem room to make another turn. Bang! Bang! At the last second he saw a by-way leading from the street and shot up to emerge into another lane. It led back up the village, and, egged on by bursts of overhead shrapnel, he pedalled madly up the road he had just abandoned. Far ahead he saw an M.P. waving and signalling to him. "To th' divil with ye." he grated between his teeth. "I'll be out av this before ye can blink yer eyes."

He shot into a squared area and narrowly missed a deep crater. Crash! Crash! Two shells hit not fifty yards behind him. Clancy put weight and muscle on the pedals and fairly soared down the roadway. He spun around a corner at a dizzy speed in order to avoid passing the traffic officer and grazed a pompous Sergeant-Major who was bellowing orders to a group of recruits. A swerve, and he was beyond the danger zone of that immediate locality, and the voice of the enraged and outraged parade-ground lord came faintly on the breeze. Then he was on a cobbled road again, a road that led down a gentle slope.

Hilarious with his success in evading all collisions, he tried to calculate how far he would have to break to the left in order to reach his brigade headquarters. Far over, distinct in the sunlight, he saw the glittering bayonet of another sentry, and knew it must be the required haven. He saw, also, that he was but going farther from his destination and tried to slow his steed. This was difficult to do at once, so he threw his weight on the pedals in a retarding motion. Something ground with a crunching sound, gave, and he jolted roughly on his seat, so that the two bolts came through to tender flesh. Clancy groaned loudly, tried to wrench free from them, and found that his breeches were impaled. At the same time he made another important discovery - the bicycle was running away with him. Some bit of mechanism somewhere had slipped and he was careering downhill at alarming speed.

A bit farther and he shaved a lorry by inches, the driver yelling wild abuse. Then he nicked the heels of a sad-faced horse ridden by a lady-like officer who squeaked commands for Clancy to halt. Another burst of speed and he jumped and cleared the tracks of a railway, looped a water main and was splitting the atmosphere between him and a mule line. Apparently he was off the travelled way again and he was in a perfect labyrinth of mules before he could change direction. He hurdled a bale of hay and knocked a Corporal into a mudhole before the final crash came as he ran full tilt into a G.S. wagon. It all happened in a heart-beat, but the wild rider had wits enough to make a desperate, spread-eagled Right as he crashed. He wanted to avoid head-on contact with the wagon and descended on a bony, moth-eaten, evil-minded mule!

Whether the mule had just broken loose or whether the Corporal had untied the animal and was about to lead it away, Clancy never knew, nor went back to find out. One thing he did know and that was that this mule had no steering attachments and that he had amazing speed for one of his despised tribe. Clinging with hands and legs, Clancy shot out of the lines and took a ditch as if he were riding to hounds. A chorus of yells drifted after him but he was soon beyond them. It seemed as if the mule was crazed by his visitor's sudden arrival and he did a few hundred yards in nothing flat, to stop as suddenly as he had started. Clancy, however, kept going. He alighted in a morass of filth that saved broken bones but demoralized his language, and when he crawled forth on the bank he did not look back at the mule.

Beyond was a sort of a road and it led to the headquarters he wanted. There he could scrape off the thickest mud and have some nourishment. The sentry at the building rolled his eyes alarmingly as Clancy passed and seemed to want to signal him, but the Irishman was past warning. He strode direct to the entrance to the imposing billet and entered without knocking. A Sergeant met him.

"What and who the devil are you?" he blurted. "You're not fit to be seen. Get out of here."

"Is this th' Eighth?" asked Clancy grimly.

“It is,” said the Sergeant. "It's the Eighth Brigade headquarters, Field Artillery. Who do you want?"

"I want the Eighth Brigade av dismounted mudhounds," said Clancy, and he said it bitterly. "I have travelled this country backwards and forwards an' divil a bit kin I advance. Is this place Bellasaint or some such name?”

"It is not," said the Sergeant. "There is a Bellewarde Lake a couple of miles from here, and there’s a Bellamer over to your right a few kilometres. Keep on this road and you can't miss it. You'd better hustle, soldier, for one of the officers of the M.P.s. is in here right now."

Clancy went out into the sunshine and wearily plodded from sight. He saw, in a village not too far away, a few houses that were not total wrecks, and resolved to find rest in one of them. Captain Bull, and all other bulls could go to blazes for the rest of the day. Lagging, dragging, he made the grade and in the nearest place that held a roof slumped down. Scarcely had he settled before he was up again. To his nostrils had come the delectable odour of a browning steak!

The next billet was a sand-bagged affair, and in the big room that held no windows a greasy cook was busily engaged. He looked up at sight of Clancy and swore violently. "Who in sivin divils are ye, and what are ye after?"

"Kin yez beat it?" exclaimed Clancy, his heart beating his joy. "An Irishman at last. Me name's Tim Clancy and I'm a runner from th' Fifth. Niver a bite have I had since last night and niver a drap av anythin'. Kin yez not save me from starvin'?"

Half an hour later he rose with an effort from the packing case he had used as a seat and table. He groaned. His muscles were sore from his unusual exertions on the bicycle and mule, and his stomach was crowded to a bursting point. "Niver will I fergit ye," he said heartily. "Good luck to ye whereiver ye go." "Now I'm on me way to Captain Bull."

"Ye'll have a divil av a trip to locate him." came the answer. "He was hit by a shell this mornin', and what's lift av him's in a hospital."

"Kin yez beat that!" said Clancy. He stared and spat, then looked around. "How do I git back to me crowd?" he asked.

"Where are yez at?" queried the cook. "I dunno anyway.

Clancy thought of the message he had from the other brigade, the one that was so important. What the devil ... ? Did they think he was runner for all His Majesty's Forces? He went out and once clear of the place shredded the message to fine bits. Then he started to find his camp again.

A runner passed him, a soldier with the insignia of the C.M.R's. "Hold a bit," yelled Clancy. "Where are you headin'?"

"For the Duck Pond," snapped the fellow. "Why?"

"Jist wanted to know th' direction meself," panted Clancy as he caught up to him. "Ye see I'm a runner."

"Are you from the Brigade?" asked the stranger. "No - well there's hell to pay about some message that hasn't come through from the Third. It was given to some runner of the C.M.R.s. And Captain Bull was hit this morning, he was the guy that did the Intelligence stuff."

"About what time was he hit?" Asked Clancy.

"Round ten o'clock," answered the runner. "Why?"

"Nothin' at all," said Clancy. "Jist wanted to know."

He saluted Major Pike snappily and handed back the message he had received so early in the morning. "Captain Bull's been hit, sir," he said solemnly, "at ten o'clock, so you see I couldn't deliver yer message."

"Hit? At ten o'clock?" barked the Major. "Well, where have you been since then? It's only five kilometres there and back."

Clancy felt a tremor steal over him, and then he took a wild plunge. "Sure an ye told me to deliver it to th' Captain himself and I tried to catch him at th' dressing station, sir."

Major Pike rose slightly in his chair and peered at his man. Clancy, mud-splattered, clothing torn, puttees loose, sweat-streaked, looked as if he had crossed Europe. "By th' pipers, man, that was a fool thing to do but it showed you have pluck and initiative. It's hard to get that among runners. Go get something to eat and I'll try you again."

"Thank ye, sir," said Clancy, and made his legs carry him from danger.

At the cook wagon he argued some cold tea, biscuits and cheese from the dixie washers, and then heard the prevalent rumours. The battalion was to go in to relieve some outfit of the Third Brigade, but orders had not come through. The officers had told everyone to stay by their tents and the hope was that the line could be reached before it was too dark. A night march into the salient trenches was as cruel an ordeal as could be imagined. Clancy thought of the paper he had destroyed, their moving orders?

The rest of the afternoon he stayed by his tent listening to the grousing of the men. All blankets had been handed in, all packs made up, everything was in readiness to move, and yet the last remaining hours of daylight slipped away and they still sat in the mud. One hour after dusk the news came. Some runner had failed to get his message through, and the Third had not known, now everyone must march as rapidly as possible in order to make the relief at a reasonable hour.

Clancy, in the rear of his platoon, wading pools and stumbling over debris, sweated and toiled. It was a man-killing march, without rest, and he wished a thousand times that he had not destroyed the paper, and when curt summons came for him to double to the front of the company he knew that the consequences were coming his way. "We are at support lines of the Third," said Major Pike, his voice rumbling like a bulldog's in the darkness. "Go along Canary Trench on your right and give this messaqe to Captain Tooke of 'C' Company."

"Beg pardon, sir," said a voice nearby. "But isn't Canary Trench to the left?"

"Perhaps it is," rumbled Pike. "Anyhow the runners should know. Move quick, man, and see that he gets it in time to arrange his posts."

"Yis, sir," said Clancy. He thrust the paper into a breast pocket of his tunic, slipped the strap of his Lee Enfield over his shoulder and wheeled into the yawning black of a sap, advanced ten ankle-deep paces and fell head-first into a water-filled crater.

When he arose, he spit forth water and filth for several minutes and during that time the rest of his company filed by the sap end and he was left alone with the darkness and muck. With Irish vim he loosed a flood of profanity into the dark regions about him and then plodded along. Ten yards on was a second crater. He did not fall into it, but slid in gracefully like a swan, and did not go above his belt. The water was cold but his temperature was rising. He was in danger of bursting a blood vessel, and with drastic resolution he climbed out of the ditch that served in lieu of a trench and started overland. Three paces on and he fell over old barbed wire, tearing one of his puttees from his leg. Again he strained his vocal cords with a hectic flow of language. Then he quieted. Where how far was this headquarters of 'C' Company. "Go along Canary Trench" - how far along? Of all fool orders to give a man!

He got over the wire and went several yards before the earth gave way beneath him, and he did a mad side-slip into a trench, landing in the pancake style approved by airmen. Only the mud in his mouth prevented him from scaring the Hun with his language, and when he rose he was a rebel. He refused to do anything more for his country or his King. But a man must rest when he quits work, and so Clancy tried to find a spot on which he could sit without sinking. He went around a corner and then around another and found a trench floor. It was fairly dry, but his groping hands connected with loose earth. Some big shell had erupted a baby volcano in the trench itself. He climbed out, anxious to get around it, for the trench floor suggested shelters beyond and he intended to crawl into the first one he found and there repose until the war became more sane and business-like.

The big crater bordered on another, and a third extended from it. Clancy skirted them all -and couldn't find the trench again. Then he heard a voice somewhere. It was calling. "Hullo, hullo," yelled Clancy "where are yez?"

"I'm here," came the answer. "Who are you?"

"The Crown Prince," shouted Clancy. "Where are yez?"

He was answered by two voices, from different angles. Foot by foot he advanced, call answering call, and at length met with two sagging figures. "Who the devil are yez?" asked Clancy, "and where's Canary Trinch?"

"I'm a Fourteenth man," said one. "Do you know which way Three platoon went?"

"I do not," snapped Clancy. "Who are yez?" He asked the question of the second man.

"I belong to 'A' Company of the Fifth C.M.R.s he said shakily. "Do you know which way their batmen went."

"To th' divil is where all av thim kind belong." retorted Clancy. "Are yez both lost?"

“We are," they chorused.

"Thin stay where ye are till daylight," he grated and plunged by them. He walked blindly in one direction and in a short time stepped into a trench so heavily that he bounced his nose on his knee. His steel hat came down over his eyes and his rifle-bolt caught in his equipment. After a few crude words in his cramped position he straightened and tested his frame and went on. His hand touched a wooden post. It was at the entrance to a partly dry shelter. He lighted a match and saw a table and two bunks. Into one he crawled. dripping water, oozing mud; and in three minutes was fast asleep.

He was awakened by cursing, soaked, angry men who crowded into the dugout and. commented luridly on the system used by the ruling staff of the battalion. "Who are yez?" asked Clancy, sitting up. "Are yez th' Fifth?"

"We are," growled the Sergeant. "What are you doin' here?"

“Waitin' for 'C' Company," returned Clancy. "Have you seen thim?" He sensed the difficulty of his position and forced himself to be polite.

"We are 'C' Company," shot back the Sergeant. “What do you want?" His voice was cold with suspicion.

"Yer Captain Tooke is th' man I'm wantin'. I've orders for him," said Clancy calmly. He exulted within himself. Luck was with him.

Some voice called into the dugout, and the Sergeant hastily lighted another candle. “There's the Captain now," said one man. "Gee, I'm glad we're some place for the night."

Captain Tooke looked as if he had come through the Slough of Despond. He was tall and thin and his legs seemed to want to buckle under him. "What is it?" he asked wearily and slumped to a chair before opening the paper Clancy produced.

He read, and then his wan features grew more pale. "By the lovely sweet-say, Sergeant, we've got to move out of here. This is from Major Pike and he says orders are changed, that we are to take over Mustard instead of Canary Trench." Then he looked up and groaned. "What trench is this we're in, Sergeant?"

"I've no idea, sir," said the Sergeant, "but there was some of the Fourteenth in the other end, sir, and I thought it would do till daylight."

"No," said the Captain, climbing to his feet. "We must find Mustard. Wait a moment," he added, scribbling a note. "Here," he handed it to Clancy, "take that to Major Pike."

"I will, sir," said Clancy,

The Captain went out into the damp void, and after baleful looks at Clancy his men followed him. Clancy grinned, winked at the candle the Sergeant had forgotten and swung back into his bunk. "Tis the luck av th' Irish," he chuckled. "Divil take this war."

An hour or so later came more tramping feet, muttered curses, wet exhausted men, but this time he knew them, and as the leader came into the candle light, Clancy gasped. He was looking at the brick-red features of Major Pike!

"What in blazes are you doing here?" blared the Major. He was mud to the waist, his tunic was torn, his eyes were red-rimmed with fatigue.

"Sure an' I was waitin' for yez, sir, I have a message for yez from Captain Tooke."

"Tooke! Where did you find him?"

"He was - in a wrong trinch, sir, but I located him and delivered yer message, sir."

Major Pike snorted unbelief, but his attitude changed as he read the missive. Then he looked at Clancy carefully. "How long have you been here?" he demanded.

"Not long, sir," said Clancy, his courage reviving as he realized that he held the advantage. "Not more than half an hour, sir."

"But why did you crawl in here when you should be looking for me?"

"Sure, but isn't this your dugout, sir?" asked Clancy. "I stayed here so as not to miss you, sir."

"By the pipers, your legs and boots are nearly dry. You've been here hours, man. I don't believe you ever found Tooke."

"How ilse could I have the message, sir?" asked Clancy.

"Well, how far is it from here to where he was?" roared the Major.

"Not far when ye know the way," said Clancy. "But he isn't where he was at, sir."

"What do you mean?" raged the officer. He seemed fed up with the night and the war in general.

"Well, ye see, sir, I found him in th' wrong place and he wint to where he's at, sir. I wasn't there because I come here whin I knew ye wouldn't go ayther av thim places. It's hard to go from here to there, sir, but it was aisy to find where he was at." Clancy was much in earnest.

"I believe," said Major Pike, "that you are an expert liar. Anyhow, you can get back to your company. Everything's gone wrong since you started carrying messages."

"Thank ye, sir." said Clancy. He went out into the darkness. Along the trenches he bumped into hurrying figures, trod on toes, and made the usual progress a soldier made in an unknown trench. Fourteen, he learned, was well along at the far end of the sector. Twice he fell into mudholes, and once he banged his head terrifically on an abandoned gas alarm, but at length he was among his own. His Sergeant heard his voice and straightway handed him a shovel. "There's not enough room here for all hands," came the chilling tones. "'Dig a sap out to that crater behind. It's dry and it will make a good bomb store."

Clancy dug and dug. He hacked through old wire and bits of a trench floor. He blistered his hands and skinned his knuckles but kept on, knowing that when he finished he would have a dry place to lie down. And then, at the finish, a tall figure loomed above him, coming overland along the trench. "Get down, ye fool," said Clancy, "Can't ye see..."

The man got down with amazing speed. He overstepped the safety zone and came down on all fours, burying his head in the soft ooze where Clancy had last dug. "It serves ye right," said Clancy. "This whole blistering outfit is cuckoo, blast thim all. Niver mind cussin', ye don't have anythin' to cuss about," the man had raised his head and was making gargling, strangling noises. "How would you like to be me? Old Pike sinds me with fool messages to men that's in hospital and ivery fool place in Belgium is a Bellyloo or Bellydoo or Bellycoo. Niver did I hear such fool names. Ivery man I meet up here is lost, and but for my intowishin I'd have been lost mesilf. I've fell in every pond on this front, I've been wurrkin' twinty hours out av twinty-four and now ye've caved in the side av this hole and that fool serg'int will come and yell his head off if I don't shovel ..."

He ceased. A match flared, cupped in his visitors hands, and he saw the grim turkey-cock features of the Sergeant-Major.

"Beggin' yer pardon, sir," said Clancy. "I-I," he thought furiously, "but did ye iver have a bad fall? I hit me head tonight and it's made me talk delirious like."

The Sergeant-Major still coughed and spat and his voice was queer and strained as he spoke. "You'll be delirious before I'm through with you, Clancy. Show me where the Major's dugout is and don't forget that I heard every word you said. If you make any trouble this trip, you're for it."

Clancy sadly wended his way the tortuous length of the trench and then came back to find that someone had salvaged his shovel. Before morning he had finished, however, and wrapped in his greatcoat tried to shiver himself to sleep. Then a soldier stumbled over his feet and stood staring at the distant flares that rose and fell endlessly and the red flashes of gunfire. "What place is this we're at, Tim?" he asked.

Clancy grunted. He was too tired to kick the fellow out of his den. "It's Bellyache!" he growled huskily. "Git out av me sight."

The fellow did, and then another figure loomed in view. 'What outfit is this?" it asked.

Clancy knew, as he pulled his ear out of the mud, that the inquirer was an engineer, probably after a working party. He ground his answer bitterly. "Tis th' Dismounted Mudhounds, a branch av the Foreign Legion."

The figure gasped. Probably he was newly out, and lost. "Oh! all right, all right," he said, and disappeared into the night.

Next day the Fifth became, by voice of Fourteen platoon, unofficially the "Dismounted Mudhounds." It seemed a lucky name.

CHAPTER TWO

TRENCH FEVER

THE Dismounted Mudhounds had come to the Somme. After a lengthy sojourn at the Salient they had come through the peaceful rural districts of France that certainly were "sunny." Long, glorious days they had trudged through dust-laden sunshine and waved gaily to the mademoiselles and portly madames who smiled at them from their cottages and gardens. But for the nightly reminders of blistered toes and peeled heels, the battalion would have had a gay holiday, and as it was no one complained - save Timothy Fergus Clancy.

The Irishman now considered himself a war-worn veteran and deserving of all the breaks that were conceded as the rights of the private with long service, therefore his blood was hot and his temper vile as he contemplated his duties at the end of their march. He, was to be a batman to a brand-new officer who was to join them at Albert.

He would have rebelled had there not been grim reasons for this turn of affairs. There had been a night of celebration before they left the Salient and when festivities were at their height, Clancy had conceived a real Irish touch for the occasion. He had proposed and seconded the motion that they capture the nearest military policeman and make him confess that cowardice prevented him from going "up the line." Some of the bolder spirits added encouragement, and Clancy led a foray that ended in a one-man attack. His zeal led far toward the accomplishment of his purpose, but the M.P. was the first to receive reinforcements, and so the next morning there was a solemn half hour at battalion headquarters. "Private Clancy," said the Colonel. "I have punished you by fines and imprisonment and it seems to do no good. This time it will be a different matter. I sentence you to one month's service as batman to the first new officer to join your company. We'll see how a taste of polishing and shining will suit you."

Clancy had made remarks that in his opinion the only thing lower than a batman was a worm in the ground. After a rain-soaked three days at the Brick Fields they arrived at Albert. Clancy feared the worst but no haughty six-weeks' wonder awaited him. He found a dry shelter and slept peacefully. In the morning the Sergeant roused him. "Git over to the officers' billets and find yer man." he ordered. "He's a beaut and his name's Lieutenant Lucien Biggar. Go to it, you loafer, and you'll learn a thing or two about mixin' with M.P.s."

Clancy slung on his clothes and sallied forth. One month as a batman was just thirty days too long, and he racked his brain to find a way to avoid serving his term. And then, before he well realized it, he was at the abode of "Lucy" Biggar. "Good morning, soldier. Are you Private Clancy?" piped a mild voice.

"Yis, sir," said Clancy, and that was all he could say. Lieutenant Biggar had a small pink face and serious blue eyes, small hands and feet and a bird-like voice. "Well, there won't be much for you to do this morning, Clancy," he said, and the small pink face was wreathed in the friendliest of smiles. "We'll just get acquainted. You see I thought that you'd be tired after such a long march and I've shined all my leather and made my bed and - well, everything. Come in and see my equipment."

Clancy still speechless, went in. He saw the bed and table and three-legged chair in apple-pie order. "Lucy's" leather and brass were glistening. On the table was a wondrous array of hair-oil, tooth-powder, mouth-wash, and various bottles, with French names, that were horribly like perfume containers. On a shelf lay an army revolver, a large pair of binoculars, house slippers, a collapsible cup, an alcohol lamp, a silver plated thermos bottle, a lunch kit, insect powder, countless articles that were sold in London as "trench necessites." "Now Clancy, I wish you would tell me what is really necessary for the trenches." said "Lucy," beaming again. "You see, I know nothing whatever about this war and I want you to tell me everything. You be my instructor, won't you?"

"I will, sir," said Clancy, and he hardly knew he said it. He was stunned, horrified. It seemed to smack of child murder to send this immaculate, smiling little man to the cruel, muddy trenches, and his appeal to Clancy choked the hardened trench pirate. A bullying "know-all," who would curse him hourly, would have been to the Irishman's taste, and such a man Clancy would have battled to the gong. But this dapper canary bird, this wistful little fellow, wanting so much to make friends and doing all the work on account of him being tired the first morning, well -. He gulped, scratched his head, hastily adjusted his own belt and tunic, and then spoke with gruff huskiness. “Mister Biggar, jist lave iverythin' to me. Don't yez listen to any wan ilse. I'll tell ye all there is to know about this trinch business and I'll put yez wise to the Colonel. I'll be back in ten minutes, if ye'll excuse me ..."

"Certainly, most certainly," said "Lucy." "There's plenty of time."

Clancy said not a word to anyone as he returned. He got his razor and soap, and afterwards his button stick and polish. When he went back to his officer he was shined and scrubbed to a finish. "My!" gasped "Lucy". "You are very quick foer a big man."

Clancy's chest swelled. There was only a roll-call as a morning parade, and he had plenty of time to exchange confidences with his ward. He learned that "Lucy" was the only pride of a widowed mother, that he had tried for two years to get into the army and had succeeded only through the influence of a family connection who was a bit of a "Blueblood." At this acknowledgment Clancy unfolded some of his past. He kept secret the fact that he had left Killybegs at Donegal Bay for the good of Ireland generally, but announced grandly that he had a lineage of his own that extended back to the time the Irish used to win their wars, and then stated honestly that Biggar was the "firrst rale white officer I've met with."

When the platoon to which Biggar was assigned came on parade Clancy was in the ranks. There was no need of it, and the Sergeant roughly said so, but "Lucy" mildly said that it was Clancy's desire. The rear rank was chuckling audibly as they sized up their new commander when they caught a throaty growl "Lave off yer fool cacklin' or I'll bloody yer noses."

There was no mistaking that challenge, and Clancy had proved his prowess with bare knuckles too many times to be lightly taken. The snickerings ceased, and "Lucy" was accorded a surprising respect and docility. When parade was over it was Clancy who addressed the platoon, and though his expression were not in K. R. and O. he was understood. "Lucy" was his charge, and the boys could think what they liked but they must treat him 'white.' Clancy meant what he said.

Their first trip in the line at the Somme was a comparatively easy one to those that followed, but ,"Lucy" had a strenuous time. He was located in a damp, slightly underground retreat that fairly squirmed with red worms. He caught sight of one crawling into his can of condensed milk and was dreadfully sick for a time, but Clancy comforted him and finally found him quarters that were more confined but freer from wriggling occupants.

On the first night in, the Hun laid down a small barrage on the C.M.R. line as a sort of welcome, and "Lucy," apparently, thought his hour had come. He became white instead of pink and his limbs trembled. "When will they attack?" he shrilled in Clancy's ear.

"Niver, if they know th' Canadians are in front av thim," said Clancy. "'Tis but a bit av a shoot an' if ye sit tight in yer dugout nothin' will harm ye."

But "Lucy" insisted on viewing the bursting shells from an honourable position in the trench and he stayed there until things were normal again and only looping flares lighted the jungle between the wires. On the second night the new officer was on duty during the weird midnight hours. His duties compelled him to visit every post on the company front once an hour. On the left the mud was almost impassable but he pluckily waded and crawled to his objectives and talked with the sentries in his piping, shaky voice. Clancy missed him on his last round and made frantic search. It was some time before he found him coming up an abandoned sap with the tail of his shirt extending from a tremendous gap in his breeches. "I-I missed my way," said "Lucy", "and I got on some wire. Oh dear, this is a frightful war."

But the hour was not over. There was a great outburst of flares from the German lines. Beautiful red rockets, blazing green stars, sizzling streaks of orange, reds over greens over reds, gave lustre to the night. Clancy, crouched in a post with his officer, repeatedly stated that it was nothing but "thim Heinies on a bust," though he secretly expected everything from a general attack to the exploding of a gigantic mine Then word came that a shell had struck an enemy flare store and all was serene once more. "Lucy" expressed his relief. "How long have we been in, Clancy?" he asked plaintively. "I've lost count of the days."

"Ye are but one day and two nights at prisint," said Clancy softly. "Th' time'll go quicker whin ye are used to it."

Yet the Irishman worried. He knew his charge was not fitted for such service, and he cursed bitterly the powers that had permitted him to go to France. "Lucy" would not even take his "issue". I promised I would never drink rum," he piped to Clancy when the matter was mentioned. "But that Major Pike made me fill my water bottle. Will you empty it for me, please."

Clancy did so - into his own bottle, but for the first time in his memory received such an offering unwillingly. "Ye should have a drop to hearten ye." he urged. "Jist a spoonful would put ye in shape."

"Please don't. Clancy," pleaded "Lucy". "You see I promised I wouldn't." And Clancy subsided.

At dusk of the third day he found the little officer actually happy, "By Jove, Clancy," he chortled. "The day went so quick I had to ask the Sergeant-Major about my watch. I'll be all right now, if we have candles."

"Candles!" said Clancy, "What do yez mane?"

"Come inside and I'll show you. You see, Clancy, I'm something of a poet I make verses and that sort of thing, and this awful place should inspire one, shouldn't it? Let me read you what I've composed this afternoon."

Clancy's sunburned hue deepened. Poetry - in the trenches. Then he peered anxiously. "Have yez a bit av a faver?" he asked. "Do yez feel hot?"

"No", said "Lucy". "I never felt better, and if you don't mind I'll read this."

Clancy settled into a comer between the brazier and, bedroll. "It's entitled 'Here and There', continued Lucy". He cleared his throat and read with dramatic fervour:

"I love the larks in the sunny blue,
Singing their merry lay.
The thrush at dawn in a leafy bower
Greeting the break of day.
I smell the rose just burst in bloom.
The scent of new-mown hay;
And with such charms to lure me on
Nothing my step can stay.
But here my ears are filled with din,
And stenches foul hold sway.
I hate the howl of a heavy shell And the...."

"That's as far as I could get. I've tried the words that rhyme with day and hay. There's 'bay', and 'ray', and 'way,' but what will go with them? I thought of noise around the bay,' but there isn't any, and 'the guns across the way' sounds as if I were cowardly, doesn't it? I am really timid but I don't want to put it in a poem."

"Mister Biggar," said Clancy, "There's a faver in th' trinches that's dangerous. Won't ye please go back to th' M.O.'s place an' let him take your pulse?"

"No, indeed," said "Lucy", "but I'll tell you what I'll do. I'll give you a Bradbury if you'll finish this line for me. I've worked at it all the afternoon."

"I'll see what I can do," Clancy promised, "if you'll go to the M.O."

But "Lucy" would not. He firmly contended that his health was perfect and now that he had hit on composing to pass the hours, he was glad he had come to France. Clancy went into the trench and hunted up the Sergeant. He never had had any use for any soldier with stripes on his arm but his anxiety forced him to overlook trifles. He explained "Lucy's" symptons. The Sergeant heard him through and then grinned in a way that set Clancy's teeth on edge.

"I knew that guy was nuts as soon as I seen him," came the unsympathetic reply. "Let him scribble his stuff, for it'll keep him out of the road. His head's too small to have more'n one idea at a time so you may as well let him be. Anyhow it's no good to see the doc. You can't inoculate for that sissy's troubles."

"Sissy me eye!" snorted Clancy. "He's worth a dozen av yez jailbirds. Ye don't know class and a gintleman whin ye see wan."

"Not so free with yer jaw," growled the Sergeant, or we'll have you dig a latrine."

"Arrrh!" grated Clancy. "Ye make me sick."

"You'll be sicker next trip in," came the retort, "and you better get that mama's boy of yours to stay home. We're going over near Regina Trench, and you know what that means."

Clancy made no answer. He knew his limit with Sergeants, and the words of the non-com gave him a strange sensation in the spine. Whatever would he do with "Lucy" in a general attack? In the mud, with the Germans fighting grimly for an inch of ground, it would be tough going for the hardiest soldier, and for the canary bird, plain suicide. He tried his best to plot some means for having the little officer detained but fate seemed against him, and when the Dismounted Mudhounds returned to the trenches after a two-day rest. Lieutenant Lucien Biggar marched or rather waded at the head of his platoon. He did until merciful dusk hid him from his men, and Clancy was able to assist him as he would a boy, boosting him up muddy banks and dragging him from wallows, keeping him going long after every atom of strength seemed drained from his fragile form.

Zero hour was at six in the morning and "Lucy" was at his post on time, his slight frame shaking with the dawn chill, his voice tremulous as he shouted to make himself heard above the clamour of the guns.

There came a deafening, blasting roar of gunfire, a final five minute barrage. Smoke drifted over the trench tops and mingled with the mist. Men coughed and strangled with the reek of explosives. Machine guns raved and chattered as they penetrated the din, and then, came the cutting shrillness of a whistle. The signal was for "over the top."

Men clambered out of their sticky ditches, shook mud from their rifle barrels, clawed it from the ammunition pouches, waded, plunged, struggled forward, going at a snail's pace, white-faced and determined. The mud was as great an enemy as the men in grey. Clancy placed one big hand at "Lucy's" rear and pushed him up on the parapet with a single heave. Then he scrambled up beside him and they went forward. They were at a point where the Hun was not far away and won the angry whine and snap of bullets told their danger. With a quick, jerk he forced "Lucy" to a crouching position and squatted beside him, peering into the murk. He could see livid sheets of flames, bomb bursts, where the fighting was hardest, and then came the murderous rapping of a Maxim. A trio of CMR's just at their right went down as one man as the rat-tat-tat suddenly swung toward them.

"Lucy" struggled to his feet and drew his army revolver. He plunged ahead, going to his knees at every step, and Clancy, perspiring, with fear for his protege, tore through the mud to get ahead of him. A shell explosion eddied the curtain of smoke and mist so that he could see through it and his heart jumped. Four Canadians were battling desperately to reach the Hun machine gun, and as he looked he saw a tall German cut one man down from behind with his bayonet. The remaining three turned back to back and fought desperately, slashing, jabbing, thrusting, slugging with rifle butts, but soon another man went down. Clancy aimed his rifle but dare not pull the trigger, for the men moved so fast that he was as likely to hit friend as foe. Then he yelled like a wild man. He had forgotten "Lucy" for the moment and there was the little, fellow, plunging forward. every step an effort, closing in to get a shot with the big pistol which seemed too heavy for him to aim.

Bounding like a kangaroo, puffing entreaties to "Lucy" to "git back". Clancy reached the melee. One close-in shot downed the nearest Hun. His bayonet spewed another but so terrific was the lunge that attacker and attacked bowled into the slippery mud and the rifle was torn from his grasp. He rolled over a dead body, driving a terrible kick into the groin of an enraged Hun he came in contact with, and then rose up in front of the man and wreslted his weapon from him. It was a precarious situation. A bayonet missed him by a hair as it came from behind. An evil face grimaced at him through the mist as another German tried to shoot him with an empty rifle. Clancy drove forward, locking bayonets, holding and striking, using feet and hands, taking a blow that skinned his cheek and at last wrenching free his captured rifle in a way that permitted him to drive the butt into the hateful countenance that leered into his. Simultaneously he felt the hot breath of a man close behind him as a German stumbled bodily against him. It was another assailant who gripped a wicked-looking trench knife and who would have driven it home had not a vicious pink-cheeked terrier, sobbing with exertion and excitement. fastened him round with a desperate clutch. One fling by the German and "Lucy" was hurled clear, but in that breath Clancy swung his rifle like a club and crunched the helmet and skull. Other rifles were swinging near. Panting, gasping, slugging, stabbing men were an about them. To one side yawned a crater, not large, as craters go, but large enough to shelter a small man. Clancy reached over and picked up his officer by the middle and with one great heave sat him down solidly in the deep mud at the bottom of the crater. He was reasonably sure that "Lucy" would never free himself and there the little man would be safe until the worst was over.

There was a temporary lull. For the moment the CMR's were in possession of the trench, and they sought the best cover in preparation for the inevitable counter attack. A man beside Clancy oiled his rifle bolt, another turned over a dead comrade and took from him his field dressing, a third anxiously counted his rounds of ammunition. Then a Corporal with a bloodied bandage on his head called out a sharp warning as he looked over the make-shift parapet. The Huns were advancing. Clancy set the rifle sights at point-blank range and fired until the barrel was hot. He saw the pot-helmeted figures pitch forward, drop sideways, in spins, in strange writhings, but others plugged doggedly on until they were within yards of their objective. Then, finding themselves without leaders, the survivors suddenly turned and shambled for shelter in grotesque panic.

Clustered "golden-rain" flare signals shot up from the German side, and shortly came shrapnel fire, searching the occupied territory. One huge white puff burst directly over the hole where Clancy had planted "Lucy" and the Irishman plunged over to see the extent of the damage. He found the little officer queerly bent and huddled. He had managed to tug himself almost clear. and was wounded in the thigh, a gaping cut that Clancy bound with awkward haste. "I'd try and git ye out now," he told the little man who was now watching him with the startled, frightened look of a hurt thing. "but 't would be askin' for it. If ye kin jist be still in wan av these places till it's dark, I'll git ye out safe."

"Lucy" nodded. "I'll trust it all to you, Clancy." he said and grinned feebly.

A machine gun in the German lines began a leisurely tapping fire as it swept the ground to the left, and the tattoo rose to deafening sharpness as the bullets sang directly over the crater. "There, that sittles it." said Clancy. "Whin they start shootin' that way they're through with comin' over. I'll git ye a Heinie overcoat that's in th' trinch an' make ye a bed as soft as a crib, Now hold yersilf while I put some iodine on yer hurt."

He emptied a bottle over the wound and "Lucywriggled and gasped but did not cry out. "Ye have th' guts av two men. Mister Biggar. " said Clancy. "Now jist kape yer mind aisy an' we'll be all right."

"I'll try," said "Lucy" weakly. "I'll be thinking of the last line for my poem. Clancy." He closed his eyes and said softly:

"But here my ears are filled with din.
And stenches foul hold sway.
I hate the howl of a heavy shell,
And the..."

He opened his eyes again. "Clancy," he piped, "can't you find a finish for that line?"

"I'll try, sir," came the promise.

Clancy got the greatcoat crawling back to the crater while snipers raised little spurt of earth close beside him as they shot one by one the hours dragged by. The guns on both sides thundered and stormed the line of battered trench and shell holes was; consolidated to some extent but for the most part the men lay or crouched under cover, numbed by fatigue and a sense of the appalling casualties the battalion had suffered.

At dark a chill drizzle began to soak the ground and add to the misery of the wounded. Clancy waited until the rattle of rifle and machine gun fire had become spasmodic and then got "Lucy" on his back and staggered out of the crater. It was a nerve-straining suspense after the first move. He could not hurry, he could not see. The shell fire was haphazard, and therefore much more dangerous. The glare of a Verey light froze him in a stooped position and he had to order "Lucy" to be still. The little man had cried out and tried to slide to earth.

They met parties of men moving in, reinforcements. blundering through the dark, calling to each other, and twice Clancy fell over a stiffened, sprawled figure. Overhead stray shells whined and rumbled, and behind them the Verey lights rose and fell intermittently lending Clancy a guide-he kept his course straight from them. At last they came to a semblance of a trench, and there "Lucy" reclined while his carrier recuperated. A clump of men was not far away, men of a brigade, and with them was another stretcher bearer. Clancy asked his to have a look at the officer's leg, but got a gruff respoitse. 'I can't do nothin' for him Where'd I get a light? Anyhow, there's work up ahead for me as soon as were arrested, and I'll be lookin' after the men first."

"Is that so," hissed Clancy. "'Tis on me mind that ye'll be hidin' in this ditch till daylight, or ilse a serg'int boots ye out."

The men with the stretcher bearer were evidently too tired to take sides in the argument and so the Irishman retreated with full honours. He was worried, however, by the way "Lucy" slumped down and begged to be let alone. The little man was giving in. After a long wait they left the trench and went on, pushing farther away from the flares, and by endless labour, wallowing in the watery darkness by circuitous routes, with constant rests that grew longer each time, they reached an abandoned battery position by daybreak. The rain had ceased and morning brought the sun with heat enough to rouse myriads of flies. "Lucy" ate ravenously of bread and jam which Clancy had found in a dead man's haversack during the night and drank three bottles of water, more booty salvaged from the dead. He slept till noon and then became slightly delirious, reciting again and again the lines he had composed. Always he finished with almost childish pettiness. "Why don't you tell me the last line Clancy? I want something to rhyme with 'sway'."

Time dragged more and more heavily and at four o'clock Clancy's patience was exhausted. He got "Lucy" on his back and crawled towards a ditch he had made out not far away. Breathless, and bathed in sweat, he made the shallow trench and found it led, wriggling fashion, to the rear. Then began an ordeal that tried him to the limit. The little officer seemed much heavier than before, he was getting more and more difficult to manage, and the way seemed endless. Then big shells began to erupt near their route, showering them with filth, filling Clancy's heart with dread that some caprice of Fate should undo all his labour. It was just dark when he rounded a turn and saw ahead of him a deeper trench close-packed with wan, bandaged men. It was a regimental aid post and with eager, joy he pushed forward, elbowing his way to the door of a sandbagged shelter. All the wounded had been dressed and ticketed and the medical officer was merely keeping his eye on the worst cases and waiting for the dark and the Red Cross men. He gathered in "Lucy" with gentle strength and stared at Clancy as the Irishman crowded in to the candle-lit shelter. "Where did you bring - him from?" he asked.

"From th' front," said Clancy briefly, then thought of "Lucy's" showing. "He was wounded up in th' trinch we took from the Heinies; and I've lugged him back. He's not much for size but he's a wildcat among th's quareheads. Ye should have seen him..."

"You mean to say that you've brought this man on your back from that cutting near Regina Trench?" broke in the M.O.

"I did that." said Clancy proudly, "and I'd do it again for an officer like him..."

"Does he know what you did?" the medical man interrupted again, looking at "Lucy's" closed eyes and drawn features.

"He does not," snapped Clancy. "And there's nothin' to tell him. I jist did it because I liked him, an' it's me own business."

The M.O. pursed his lips and whistled. "Well, hold your horses, man. I don't mind if you save a Brigadier. Listen, what was that?" A "pinning" echoed -sharply from the corrugated iron roof of the shelter. "Ah! I know. It's just a ricochet. They were whining over here this morning. They're from Heinie's lines all right."

He applied the needle to "Lucy's" arm and the little officer awoke and stirred fretfully. Perspiration was beading his forehead. "Hummm." said the doctor, "this chap seems in fever, more than he should be. Was he sick before he was hit?"

"He was that, I believe." said Clancy quickly. "He was in his shelter overnight thryin' to make up some poetry, and ye know he must have been light to do that."

"Hummm, Poetry! Queer enough, but then men do queer stunts in this war. You can't go much by that. Still, there's quite a bit of trench fever."

"I hate the howl of a heavy shell, And the... Clancy, Clancy, can't you get that line?" It was "Lucy's" voice, weak and fretful.

Clancy bent over the little officer, then started and stared defiantly at the doctor. "By th' crown av old Ireland, I kin that," he exclaimed. "Ye put the line in me mouth. Listen, Mister Biggar. How does this go? 'And the whine av a rickoshay!"

"Lucy's" countenance lost its fretful curves and a smile stole over it. He looked up at Clancy and the fever was not in his eyes. "You got it," he murmured. " 'The whine of a ricochet.' Remarkably clever." Then his eyes closed again, and his deeper breathing told that he slept like a child.

"There, you've quieted his nerves, whatever was the trouble," said the M.O. "He'll be right as rain now and the ambulance men will have him in before midnight."

"Then I'll be goin'," said Clancy, but at the door of the shelter he halted. "Would ye mind writin' down thim words for him?" he asked. "Ye could put thim on th' card or somethin' to slip in his pocket. 'Twill kape th' faver from him."

The medical man looked up sharply, then nodded and reached for a tag. And on it he wrote:

"I hate the howl of a heavy shell, And the whine of a ricochet."

"Ye kin spell th' 'shay' out plain so's to rist his mind whin he sees it." said Clancy. And as he went out into the dusk to seek him a trench corner in which to sleep for hours through all the ravings of guns and shells, he carried the look of a satisfied man.

CHAPTER THREE

A PERSONAL MATTER

THE Somme was a matter of history and the Dismounted Mudhounds had come to the Vimy sector. They had been out to Bruay for a rest and now were marching back to the front. The night was misty dark. Rain had made the going slippery and the men were weary to the point of rebellion. They had had nothing to eat since noon and rumour said they were due for the support line before morning.

"They used to put cuckoo guys in asylums," muttered Private Timothy Fergus Clancy, giving his pack a vicious hitch. "But now they give thim a Sam Browne and sind thim to France, an' ivery blasted wan av thim heads for th' Fifth CMR's. May th' divil take th' whole wu-urks."

"Fall out on the right!" The order was barked sharply.

There was a scuffling of feet, a bumping of laden bodies and equipment, snarling curses, thudding sounds as men dropped heavy to earth regardless of their landing.

"Time somebody had a brain wave - Where in hell's th' cooks - Get to blazes off my feet - Old Pike talks like we wuz horses." Bitter and caustic were the remarks that eddied in the dark.

Clancy slipped his pack and stood up. "Some wan lind me a drink av water," he spoke into the shadows. "I'm chokin' dry."

No one answered him or offered relief. "Well - this soldier is goin' after wan," he announced grimly. "Ye kin tell th' army to wait fer me."

As he spoke, a shaft of light split the night, then vanished. Someone had opened and shut the door of a lighted building not far from where the battalion rested. Clancy blundered through the darkness till he found a path leading to the door he sought. He opened it without ceremony and entered - to stand dumfounded. Here was heaven on earth. A cheery fire crackled in the gate. Officers reclined in easy chairs. There were framed pictures on the walls, rugs on the floor, a gramophone and piano. The nearest man grinned a welcome. "Rotten night, old top. Tough on the P.B.I. Got a message?"

Clancy was primed for trouble, but the friendliness of the speaker was disarming. "I wuz chokin' fer a drink and saw yer light." he stated.

"Drink! You come to the right church! Hey, George, give this fellow some coffee."

"George" proved to be a freckle-faced orderly who beckoned from an inner room. Again Clancy stood aghast. He faced a table covered with spotless linen, glittering cutlery, china, and all the good things that tickle the stomach. At each plate stood a delicate tumbler. Here and there were tall bottles, sealed and crowned with tinsel. The label of each bore the figure of a mounted knight, white against a green background.

The orderly handed Clancy a cup of steaming coffee and placed a tray of sandwiches at the end of the table.

"Nawsty night," he said politely. "'ave a sandwich."

The Irishman wolfed half a dozen and drained his third cup of coffee. "What outfit's this?" he demanded, wiping his mouth with his tunic sleeve. "Does Haig kip so clos't to th' front?"

"'Ardly," said the orderly, still grinning. "This is the mess of the Ninth Squadron. You've 'eard of the Foofums aerodrome?"

Outside, a whistle sounded loud and clear. It was the fall-in signal. "How about wan av thim tall byes?" asked Clancy. tensed to go. "They'd never miss it." His mouth watered at the thought.

"Lumme! soldier. Yer cawn't mean it. Them White Knights is donated. Yer cawn't buy them-haighteen and haighty-one they be."

Clancy realized the futility of argument or attempting forcible possession and sped back to his company. As he plunged into the drizzly night again he carried with him a picture of the comfort and luxurious plenty he had seen. He had filled his eyes and ears and nose with the joy of it all. Now he was back in the wet blackness and slippery roads. But the men were jostling each other excitedly. A row of buses, gigantic in the gloom, had ranged alongside, and the men were swarming on board. Clancy had difficulty in finding his pack and the delay cost him an inner seat. He was forced to perch at the rear end of a crowded truck, receiving full benefit of the drizzle.

For a space they rode in silence. Then someone's rifle jabbed someone else and the usual grousing began. Clancy had heard it all before, with variations. He hunched miserably in his exposed position swearing deep and long at every hard jolt.

At midnight they were set down. Then came a toilsome journey up a sunken road blocked more or less with mules, to arrive at last in cellars vile with smoking coke. Clancy crawled into a chicken-wire bunk.

"'Old 'ard, me lad." said the Sergeant. "Yer booked fer gas guard. Out with yer and keep awake. Two hours."

It was the last straw. Clancy went, but behind him trailed smoking maledictions on the army and its officers; their pedigrees and mental deficiencies were mixed with a fervent desire that they be a cross-piled in the hottest corner below. There were no interruptions in the torrid flow as Clancy climbed the steps and his last sulphuric wishes were broadcast at the blanketed dugout entrance. Then he caught his breath. A darker blot in the trench meant some listener, and he knew instinctively he had placed his head in a noose. "Your name and number," hissed a voice with an edge like a knife. "Do you belong to 'D' company?"

"Yis, sir, to Fourteen platoon," Clancy's reply was tinged with humility. "I've had a bit av a faver, sir, an' wu-urds slip out I don't mane, sir."

"Your name and number." Sibilant and more threatening than the hiss of a snake came the rejoinder.

"Timothy Fergus Clancy's me name, sir, an' me number's..."

"Never mind it." The words came like pistol shots. I've heard of you before - too many times. You're the worst malingerer in the company -you never would soldier, but by the nine black pipers, I'll put you in place yet. Report to me at noon."

"Yis, sir, very good, sir," said Clancy, and swung up his hand to salute. In the darkness he knocked it smartly against a long angle iron that served as a gas alarm. He could not restrain a howl of profanity. "I hit me hand, sir," he explained hurriedly.

The blur in the trench remained immovable for a long minute. Then came the sharp rasping voice. "Clancy, this is going to be a personal matter. Remember - at noon."

Some time after the blur had gone out of range the gas blanket was pushed aside and the Sergeant stepped into the trench. "Put yer blinkin' foot into it that time, me lad," he chortled. "Old Pike won't skin yer, not 'arf. Which wye did he go? Some bloke lost the rum comin' in and he'll be worse nor poison come noon. Make yer will afore yer goes up."

Clancy hated the Sergeant as cordially as he did all "Limeys," but he felt he must talk to someone to regain his composure. "What's th' name av this hole?" he asked. "Where are we?"

"This is Neuville St. Vaast," said the Sergeant evidently anxious to display his superior knowledge. "Rotten 'ole, too, me lad. Tunnels and caves all over. They sye as 'ow the froggies had runs underneath to go back to Mont St. Eloi, to Arras, h'up on the Ridge h'and everywhere. An engineer bloke told me. 'any ‘ow, yer'll find out more about it. Pike'll 'ave yer changin' the geography with a shovel and sand bags. 'Appy dreams!"

"Wait a second." Clancy was desperate. "I'm a sick man. Can't ye put in a wu-urd fur me? I'm reporting to th' doctor in th' mornin'."

"Yer barmy if yer tries that gime. Yer'll only get a number nine h'and duty. I'd hadvise yer to keep yer eyes h'open till yer relieved, too. H'old Pike is no piker."

"And further" - Major Gillington Pike thrust his red jowls close to Clancy's - "further, I’ll see to it, personally, that you soldier for one trip. You'll do your bit this time if I have to do nothing but watch you. You're a disgrace to your Company, a discredit to the C.M.R.’s, the worst malingerer in the C.E.F., but you're going to soldier. Take him out, Sergeant, and me that he digs a latrine at that place alongside Dead Alley. I'll be around to see the job before stand-to.”

Clancy climbed the dugout steps as if on his way to meet an executioner. During his turn on gas-guard he had imagined all sorts of things, from firing parties at dawn to a two-year trip to Rouen. When relieved, he could not rest. The cellar was cold, rats scampered everywhere, and he could think only, of the ordeal that awaited him. Major Pike, an old bulldog with a row of service ribbons, was the one man in the C.M.R.’s who could awe Clancy to dumb obedience, and the verbal deluge that had descended on the prisoner's head had equalled the Sergeant's prediction. Furthermore, he pondered, as he trudged in front of the Limey N.C.O., there would be no rum until evening, and the longer the Major was without his beverage the more irritable he would become. The latrine must be finished before he arrived.

The site selected for the excavation had been chosen by the Major and reflected his thoroughness. It was in the chalkiest, most difficult to be got at place along the trenches. In all that graveyard swamp of mud and slime, it represented the one area requiring picks and tremendous labour. Disdaining the lead forget-me-nots that whined about Clancy risked a look over the clay embankment that bordered the latrine site and saw that he was working in the garden of some former resident of Neuville-St.Vaast. Back towards Mont St. Eloi the hollows were shrouded with white mist and the mud wall beside him oozed green slime that was thick and greasy to touch. Ugh! Clancy shivered as he set to work.

"Put some beef on that shovel," ordered the Sergeant, who was acting as guardian angel at Pike's request. "Four feet deep and six feet long. It'll be yer grave when h'old Pike comes. 'Op to it."

Clancy hopped. He picked and spaded as he had never done before, and all the while his brain raced to evolve some scheme of escape. Not for naught had he gained the name of 'D' Company's champion dodger. "They brought in some labour outfits h'at the rear lawst night." commented the N.C.O. as he lighted a cigarette. "but I 'ears as 'ow they is goin' back again. Private Clawncy will furnish the workin' parties in this sector. 'Op to it."

Clancy made no reply. He had discovered that one end of his excavation was mysteriously easy to dig. It was composed of loosely packed earth and chalk. and he sunk the pit with a rapidity that astonished the Sergeant. "Bli' me, Tim, but yer a wonder h'at diggin'." he remarked. "Yer shovel must be 'ot."

There was no reply. Clancy was unusually impervious to sarcasm, but there was a reason. A last downward thrust with his shovel had uncovered the side of a bottle. Clancy had always had a keen interest in such glassware and now, in such an odd place, he was doubly interested. Yet he was far too clever to let the Sergeant know of his discovery. When that gentleman was not looking he cleared away enough earth to see the label on the bottle. It was that of a mounted knight, white on a green background. "Yer cawn't buy them, haighteen and haighty one, they be," the words came back distinctly, and the briefest inspection proved that the seal was intact. With a last turn of his shovel Clancy banked it neatly from view.

"There's yer hole," he remarked calmly, as he drew himself up in the trench. "What's nixt on yer program?"

The Sergeant spat and scratched himself. "Blawsted if I knows," he ejaculated. "Stay 'ere a bit. One thing I does know is...?"

"Is Clancy there? What - finished! Not deep enough by a damn sight. You'll finish it when you get back. Nonsense-four feet? I said five feet. Get your rifle and take this message to 'C' Company headquarters, and get back as quick as you know how. I'll be waiting for you." There was grim portent in that last sentence.

Clancy hurried up the trench. The misty afternoon was closing early and already the light was fading. It was fully three hundred yards to the front line, and another hundred to 'C' Company headquarters If the Sergeant jumped down to find the reason of Clancy's quick work, or if the sanitary corporal came nosing around, the precious White Knight would be uncovered. The very idea caused the Irishman to perspire.

He halted, torn by conflicting desires. Should he hurry on and deliver his message, trusting to luck that the bottle would remain hidden, or should he nip overland to the excavation and make sure of it? The trenches snaked in such zigzag contours that he knew it was only a short distance to where he had been working. Peering closely he deciphered the message he carried: "Brigade wants a prisoner. Will you try for one or shall I send out a party? G. Pike, C.O. of 'D' Company."

Phew! The paper shook in Clancy's hands. Too well he knew who one of the raiders would be, should Pike's company receive the detail. Luck was all against him. He thrust the message in his pocket and scrambled out of the trench.

The early dusk was in his favour. Occasional sniping shots whined overhead but he wriggled along to a cellar, crawled through an old wire entanglement. and found himself looking down into the new latrine pit. In less than three minutes he had unearthed one dozen of the long sealed bottles. Four bore the picture of a white mounted knight, on four the rider was dressed in scarlet, and the last quartet had golden uniforms. Clancy took them through the wire and went back to pat earth in the cavity the bottles had occupied. Steps sounded, coming his way, and he took the parapet as a frightened cat takes a backyard fence, to lie, scarcely breathing. close to his precious find. Major Gillington Pike passed by, tramping angrily and striking at the trench walls with his cane. It was plain that the officer was in very bad humour.

Very carefully Clancy made his way back to the cellar he had crossed and there interred his "knights". It would be foolish not to sample their contents before leaving, and so he knocked the neck from a green and white. The gurgle that followed was pleasant and sustained. Clancy wiped his lips and settled back. Away up in front he saw a Verey light soar and burst palely in the gloom and the guns over on the Somme commenced their evening "hate". There was another prolonged gurgling and Clancy forgot the urgency of his errand. He lay back contentedly and began to plan a series of excavations in the gardens still traceable about Neuville-Saint Vaast. Why, in this cellar he occupied there might be...

He sat upright with a jerk and tried to peer into the depths of a well-like cavity beside him It was too dark. After much fumbling he found and struck a match. The hole revealed extended through a ragged aperture in masonry into a second cellar. In its corners were many candle ends. Very carefully he smoothed the grave of the eleven remaining "knights" and then slid down the opening. Within him burned the lust of a treasure seeker. The proposed raid could wait its turn.

Clancy found himself in a clammy underground chamber. Its walls oozed moisture. and dirty mould clung everywhere The atmosphere reeked of decay. He threw light on the wall and rounded ceiling and looked toward the other end of the room. He stared in amazement-there was no end, the vault extended into the dim shadows. Clancy took another drink.

He went forward ten steps - and saw no barrier. He was in a tunnel, and remembered dimly, as he took another drink, that the Sergeant had said they branched in a directions. This one might lead toward the front line. Suppose it were to open into 'C' Company's trench, wouldn't he be putting something over the runners? The thought tickled him so that he took another "Irish nip". Then he recalled that he had left his rifle by the wire entanglement while after his knights, but there was no need of it in this place.

The tunnel stretched endlessly. In places the air was foul. Here and there water seeped through the walls, but in places, the stonework was dry. Under foot was a loathesome fungoid film, slippery to the tread. At one point an explosion overhead had driven in a portion of the ceiling, but there was room to squeeze by the fallen pieces. As he halted for another drink he had a bright idea. He tore the message into shreds, resolving to make his orders verbal. He should tell the officer of 'C' Company that brigade requested a prisoner before morning, and make no mention of the proffered assistance. Clancy lighted another candle and toasted his cleverness.

Ahead the passage was partly blocked. One side of the tunnel had been blown in by explosives. The Irishman tried to think clearly but the "white knight" had befuddled his brain. He still remembered that he was en route to the front line, but he did not know where he was supposed to emerge. Had he been told, or not? His difficulties increased. A jam of broken timbers and shattered masonry almost blocked him. He drained the last of his refreshment and kissed the bottle before tossing it to one side. Then came a sound that roused him to wariness. From somewhere just beyond a man coughed.

With visions of 'C' Company's staff speechless with surprise, Clancy clambered over the debris. A wall of coloured sandbags confronted him and as he gazed at this barrier the hidden individual coughed a second time, a wheezy cough that trailed off into a snore. This person must be on the other side of the bags.

Clancy set his candle in a niche and tugged at a yellow bag until it came clear of the barricade. No one on the other side spoke or objected, and the Irishman pulled away more bags until he could push through the opening.

To a certain extent Clancy was drunk, for he had lost his fear of consequences. Yet he knew enough to reach with cat-like quickness for the bomb that lay beside the sleeper in the little dugout, for the bomb was a potato masher, and the sleeper a stout, middle-aged Hun. He had a very florid, full-moon face, and in his outstretched hand lay a letter bearing a blue censor-stamp. Evidently the Germans had had mail this evening.

Clancy crept in beside the fellow and stood up. He was in a sort of pit, stocked on one side with coloured packages. A brief examination proved them to be flares. On a ledge was a flare pistol, loaded and ready. Clancy seized it and at that second heard a heavy tread above. The heavy steps passed by and receded in the distance, and the invader knew that he was very near a trench. For a moment he struggled to solve the problem, then gave it up. Somehow he had blundered into the German lines, but he was positive there was a trick in it somewhere, and that 'C' Company had not played fair. Then he smiled and wished he could pat himself on the back. Brigade wanted a prisoner. Here was one all ready to deliver, only needing to be escorted to Major Pike. Would they give him a Military Medal or ten day's leave - he would ask for the leave. But first he must push aside the gray blanket that hid his exit and have a peek at the Huns. Maybe he could pinch a machine gun, a Heinie officer or some trophy. To a certain extent, Clancy was drunk.

He picked up the letter that lay in the sleeper's moist hand and stowed it in his pocket. It might contain valuable information. Perhaps he would get both leave and medal. Then he paused again. Right at the doorway, by the blanket, was a neat stack of potatomasher bombs, and on a shelf was a tin box. Clancy investigated. It held a small brush and various glass jars, labelled with German inscriptions. A yellowish, wax-like substance that glimmered in the candle light drew his attention.

He stuck a finger into it and the digit glowed in the dark. He had discovered the luminous "dope" that Heinie used sometimes to mark wire "lanes" for his patrols. And what splendid stuff it would be for him to use in marking graves for future "knights". Clancy placed the lump in his pocket and pushed the blanket aside.

The stairway up to the trench was shorter than he expected, and too late he remembered the candle. He blew it out with a mighty puff. The resulting darkness enveloped him like a coverlet. The mist was still falling. He could not see a thing and his groping hands touched sand-bagged parapets exactly like those the Canadians built. Undecided, he stood and listened. There was a slight movement somewhere in the black void and he thought he heard a whispering. After a long wait he heard a step, quite close, and a distinct whisper: "Wer ist das?"

With a jerk of his arm Clancy pointed up his fare pistol and pulled the trigger. The Verey light shot up with a hiss and burst into a brilliancy that the mist silvered. Ten feet away stood two Huns. One was tall and wore the uniform of a German officer, the other was a short fellow with a nasty little face embellished by a stubby beard. Clancy bore him an intense dislike at the first glance, and sprang forward to make full use of the all revealing light. He lashed a vicious left at the tall Hun and at the same time made an overhand swing with his pistol at the shorter missionary of Kultur. His lefthander missed its mark, but knocked an automatic from the officer's hand. The pistol butt landed fairly amid the features he disliked and one of the enemy was "kaput". The tall Hun, however, exhibited unexpected activity. He drove a fist into Clancy's right ear and encircled his neck with a long arm. Then he bawled Teutonic orders into the night.

The blow on the ear worked miracles. It roused Clancy from the spell the White Knight had cast, and with skill acquired from many rough-and-tumbles, he kneed his man and broke the hold that threatened to choke him. Then with an adroit shift he stooped, picked the man bodily from the trench and carried him to the door of the flare pit. Another flare shot up from somewhere nearby and with a heave he sent his struggling burden down against the gas blanket, ripping it from its holdings. The stout sleeper was rudely awakened. His bellow denoted that he must have been dreaming of the Fatherland and heroism galore, for he tackled his countryman with delightful zeal.

Clancy would have dearly loved to allow them to complete the round, but guttural shoutings and a clamorous machine gun demanded speed on his part. He still held the flare pistol and as the light died he plunged down the stairs of the pit and seized two bombs. Turning back, he hurled one to the right and one to the left. The shouting ceased abruptly. In the dugout the battle still raged. He struck a match.

It flared just as the tall Hun, on the floor astride his opponent, produced a flashlight. The Irishman seized a potato masher and menaced the men in the gray as he snatched the electric torch. They scrambled to their feet, hands over their heads, and the stout man whined "Kamerad! Bitte, Kamerad!"

"Git through that hole thin, ye scum av the Kaiser!" roared Clancy, pointing expressively. "Move quick or ye are dead corpses."

The stout fellow turned and dived into the aperture Clancy had made, scuttling from view like a frightened pup. The tall Hun hesitated. "Git after him, Hindenburg or ye are sausage," yelled Clancy, with a half swing of his bomb.

He saw that he was dealing with one of those arrogant, supercilious Prussians, and his anger grew. The German turned sulkily and followed the fat man. Voices rasped again, just outside. Clancy hurled his bomb up the stairway. Then he caught up the flare pistol he had dropped to seize the grenade and thrust it into his pocket, accompanied by a handful of flares. In a split second he had another bomb ready and was plunging through the vent in the sandbagged wall. The narrowness of the space immediately beyond made it impossible for either of the Huns to ambush him, but by the rays of the flashlight he saw the officer trying to wrench a club from the refuse further on. Clancy flashed his light back into the pit. A German was just entering, his bayonet held ready. The Irishman threw his bomb and the next instant came a terrific explosion.

The force of it drove Clancy backward in cartwheels, like a professional tumbler, and saved his life. For the passage was closed entirely by the fall of debris. Too late, the Irishman had remembered the stack of potato mashers by the stair. So great had been the explosion that a portion of the tunnel roof dropped in, barely missing Clancy as he struggled to his feet. Glancing up he saw a myriad of lights illuminating the heavens. There were red ones, green ones, gold ones and bright orange. Red-over-green-over-red, and all the rest. They were like monstrous shooting sparks - the flare store had ignited.

Just in time Clancy turned to his prisoners. The officer had freed a long, splintered stick and he lunged savagely, but missed. The Irishman aimed his flare pistol directly at the Prussian's features.

"Drop that stick, ye black-hearted divil," he yelled, "an' git back."

It was doubtful whether he was heard or not, as a perfect bedlam awoke overhead. The crackling of rifle fire blended with the rattle of machine guns, and the roar of whizz bangs added to the din. It sounded as if the entire front were in action. But whether he heard or not, the German evidently sensed Clancy's determination. He dropped his weapon and went sullenly down the tunnel. The stout man was well in advance, his hands still over his head.

Clancy studied his capture intently. He preferred the common or garden variety of the Hun, and felt that the easiest way to deal with the Prussian was to let him swallow a Verey light, but changed his mind as he recalled that such officers were rarely captured. This feat might land him a job at the base. Then he had an inspiration; he would lessen his chances of sudden assault. "Take off yer belts, ye sausage grinders," he shouted. "Let loose thim 'Got Mitt Uns' toot sweet."

The fleshy Hun swung around. He was perspiring freely and plainly did not understand the order. The Prussian glared like a tiger and Clancy believed he comprehended English. "Tell yer man." he snapped, "or ilse ye'll have a flare in yer teeth."

The German spoke harshly, and immediately the fat man unfastened his belt and cast it from him. As a result his baggy trousers sagged enough to reveal a dirty shirt, and came to rest so precariously that Clancy knew any quick movement would tumble them about the fellow's heels.

"Rip off yer own, we bye," he spoke again, his voice grim with determination. "Ye have list wan second more to make up yer mind."

"'Schwein," muttered the Prussian. but he stripped his belt and grasped his trouser tops.

"Ye'r learnin'," said Clancy, contemptuously. "Now travel, me son."

The Prussian marched stiffly and his slippings on the slimy floor of the tunnel made his performance grotesque. "Why don't ye try yer fool goose step?" sneered Clancy. "Ye are a swate pitchoor, I don't think. Niver did I see a Heinie what could sojer."

The flashlight's beams weakened, and Clancy worried until he had an idea. "Halt-th' pair av ye," he commanded. "Ach-chung!"

The fat Hun came to attention with remarkable alacrity, but the Prussian resented Clancy's juggling of the "Mother tongue" and stood slouching holding his breeches.

Clancy carefully placed the flashlight on the floor, tilted so that it threw light in his direction. Then, holding his pistol in readiness, he walked up to the officer. I don't like th' colour av yer dial." he remarked carelessly. "So jist hold still while I do a bit av decoratin. Kape yer fins on yer breeches if ye want to 'hoch der Kaiser' again."

It was a dare-devil stunt, but then to a certain extent, Clancy was drunk. He saw the Prussian's eyes on the trigger of the flare pistol and purposely tightened his grip. The least fraction more would discharge the weapon. And so his movements were almost deliberate as he produced the luminous substance he had found in the flare pit and massaged the German's face. Then he stepped back. his gaze meeting the Prussian's with a cool challenge, and ordered him along the trench.

The fat man received similar treatment and the result lived up to Clancy's expectations. He switched off the light a second and two faces, one of the full-moon variety, seemed to float in the darkness. "Now, ye sauerkrauts" he chuckled. "I've got me a target if th' light does go out. Stip along, me lucky lads. I've an appointment with th' Major."

They came to the blown-in roof at last, and light flashes played down the opening. The din overhead had abated but there was still considerable shelling. "Git up th' hole, Heinie," Clancy yelled, pointing. "Up with ye, Von Klucker!"

The fat Hun wriggled and squirmed up the opening until his heavy boots disappeared. Then came Clancy's problem. How was he to keep the Prussian in control. The tall officer seemed to be of the same mind, for he scrambled quickly after his fellow prisoner and was almost above before the Irishman could seize his legs and drag him back. In the struggle that ensued the flare pistol dropped and Clancy fared badly until he had struck a terrific blow with his only available weapon, the flashlight. It was smashed to junk on a hard head, but the officer was out for the count.

A round new moon looked down, from above. Clancy seized the inert German's tunic collar and raised him. "Git hold av this dog meat," he panted. "Pull him up."

The fat Hun tugged and grunted and between them they hoisted the officer into the top cellar. In another moment Clancy was up beside him. Flares were going up all along the front and there was a faint odour of heavy explosives. The night was not so dark as before but the two luminous faces stood out sharply.

Clancy felt about the cellar until he found loose earth. There was a clink of glass and pleasant gurgling sounds. The contents of the "Knight" fired Clancy anew, warmed his veins and loosened his humour. He took another long pull and then placed the neckless bottle to the glowing "full moon". There was a gasp of alarm. "Hold steady, Otto," said Clancy. "Ye are a half-dacint Hun. Have a rale drink fer wance in yer crooked life."

He tipped the bottle and the stuttering protest ended in a gurgle. Clancy was forced to stop it. "Aisy, me beauty, " he chuckled. "Ye are a haythen camel."

"Gut, ja!" said the German.

The Irishman had another drink and then uncovered three more of his cache, placing them inside his tunic after tightening his belt, then he and the fat Hun half-dragged the unconscious Prussian toward the wire tangle by the newly-dug latrine. They were nearly there when Clancy heard voices and thrust the "moon" to cover. Men passed along the trench, talking loudly. "That fool, Clancy, will be crucified when old Pike gits told of him," said one. "ne old boy's like a hon tonight and that Irishman's never come back from 'C' Company."

"Yes," responded another voice, "he's in for it. And it beats all that the rum had to get smashed in that shelling. Gosh--old Fritz threw over everything he had for a bit. I wonder what started him. D'ja ever see such a shower of lights as went up before the shellin' begun?"

"There wuz more'n lights." came a rejoinder. "A mine or somethin' went up. Old Pike's so mad he kicked his batman out of the dugout jist fer laughin'."

"An' they say the Brigadier's on his way up to find out where's his prisoners he ordered," added a last speaker as the party filed away in the distance.

Clancy drank long and deep from the bottle he was nursing. Then he helped slide the Prussian into the trench. As he alighted the officer groaned and sat up. "Shut up," ordered Clancy. "an' git up on yer pins."

The Hun stood up. His breeches had been pulled down and yanked up again with his shirt outside, and he was holding his head with both hands. Clancy passed the bottle to "Moon-face". "Impty it, old kid," he said gaily. "To hell with bad luck an' th' Kaiser." He pushed the Prussian along, jabbing him with the flare pistol. "Wan slip from ye an' I pull the trigger." He threatened. "Yer in th' trinches av th' CMR's."

The gas sentry at 'D' Company's dugout uttered a wild yell and - tumbled headlong downstairs to fall into the lap of the visiting Brigadier. Major Pike sprang up, incoherent with rage. "You-you blasted -."

"I seen them -I seen them," yelled the man 'They're comin'. Heads - floatin' in th' trench - heads." He was wild with fear. The Major rushed up the dugout stairs, murder in his heart. Had any blankety-blank fool been playing tricks? ... He paused, reaching blindly for the automatic he had left below. Not far away in the gloom a strong voice broke into song, a song not heard in the Canadian trenches. "Deutchland, Deutchland uber alles," it caroled, and a husky baritone with an unmistakable Irish flavour tried to join the melody.

The Brigadier and his aide emerged from the dugout, to step promptly behind Pike. "Kape in stip, ye long string av misery," said a rough voice as the song ceased.

Major Pike stiffened and clinched his fists. "Hey, Clancy, you devil," he shouted. "Where are you?"

Silence - except for the guns along the front. "Come on," yelled Pike. "I saw you, and by the nine black..."

He was interrupted. There was a sharp "pop" and into the night looped a German Verey light, soaring high and bursting perfectly. The picture it revealed is legend in the ranks of the CMR's. A tall Prussian officer, his face glowing like nothing on earth, was endeavouring to tuck his shirt-tails into his breeches. Behind him was a very stout Boche, bunching his trouser tops in one hand, the other thrusting through the arm of Timothy Fergus Clancy. The Irishman was wearing the red and grey pill box favoured by Fritz, and the Hun was crowned with Clancy's steel lid, rakishly over one ear. And their affection for each other was touching to behold.

The flare sizzled out. In the darkness were two floating faces, one very full. Pike found his voice first, and after a long minute. "By-by the nine pi-pipers-Clancy, what have you done?"

"Halt in front! Mark time! Private Timothy Fergus Clancy, sir, reporting with two captive Huns taken alive on C' Company's front according to orders. Wan is a long streak av Prushinnism, divil take him. Th' other is a dacint sort, an' beggin' yer pardon, a fair singer. I hope ye'll see fit to..."

"Silence!" The Brigadier's roar proclaimed his recovery. "I shall want a very full report on this, Major. Send these prisoners along at once."

"I'll see to everything, sir!" There was a world of portent in the Major's reply.

To a large extent, Clancy was drunk.

"Where is your message from 'C' Company?" the Major snapped the instant they were below.

Clancy tugged at his pocket, then gravely presented a folded paper.

The Major opened it, stared, turned it over and stared again. Then he turned to a signaller who nursed a telephone. "You read this cussed German," he said, sharply. "What's this?"

The signaller held the paper to the light. "Dearest Heinrich," he read. "The news is good. The Englanders are starving and Paris will be taken. Our pig is doing well but Otto has a cough. I hope you come home soon and with an Iron Cross. Gott Strafe England. Your loving Bertha."

Silence - ominous and painful. Major Pike seized a pen and seated himself at his box table. "Private Clancy," he said grimly. "You have come to the end of your rope. I told you this would be a personal matter and by the nine black pipers you'll find I'm a man of my word. I'm putting you down for court martials on three counts. First, you hurt the morale of the company; second, the Brigadier asked me to investigate; and third. the honour of the regiment is involved. What have you to say?"

Clancy felt his heart pounding, but outwardly remained steady. "I missed me way in th' dark," he stated, "an' wandered into the German trinch unbeknown'st to mesilf. Havin' a bomb with me I charged wan av their posts, rememberin ye wanted a prisoner. I mislaid yer message, but - iverything's all right An' there's three rale reasons why ye should reconsider yer wu-urds." He paused dramatically and fished a tall bottle from his tunic. It bore a white and green label. "Fu-urst, here's a hilp, to yer morals; sicind, this'll square the Brigadier." He jerked forth a red and green. The Major sat bolt upright, his eyes glistening. "An' this, gentlemen, will square th' honour av Private Clancy." A third bottle appeared, bearing a Knight in golden attire.

Major Gillington Pike leaned forward and feasted his eyes. "By the nine ... it's genuine chasseur brandy." he blurted. "Eighteen and eighty stuff. You've more, you say? Two bottles? Clancy... I..."

He looked at the signaller, the third man in the dug-out. "Go, get me a runner," he ordered, "and don't rush yourself."

When the fellow had gone, he stuck out his hand. "Clancy," he said, kindly. "We all make mistakes up here. I'll report this matter - fully - in your favour. You're excused duty for twenty-four hours and I'll ask no more questions. Good-night and good luck."

Clancy had barely reached the dugout steps when he heard a bottle neck crack. The Major had not stopped for corkscrew or glass.

In the trench he met the signaller. "What did yer git?" quavered that individual. "Isn't he an old tiger?"

To a certain extent, Clancy was still drunk, but his answer was dignified. "I'm not," he said, solemnly, "accustomed to belittlin' me betters. nor to hearin' th' same av others. An' our transactions, me lad, are a personal matter."

CHAPTER FOUR

THE LUCK OF THE IRISH

ONE month had gone since the episode of the bottles and the Boche. Major Pike, after a week of tolerant humour. had resumed his bear-like attitude and had become as hostile toward Clancy as ever, until the Irishman figured that either he or the Major had had a lapse of memory.

They were in the front line, on the crater posts. A chill, soaking drizzle enhanced the dreary dawn. Not for years had France known such weather as ruled this Vimy sector in early '17. Night-long working parties toiled to keep the trenches clear of the mud that oozed up through the duckboards during the day, to re-build parapets that kept sliding inward.

Clancy came slowly along the crater line that was 'D' Company's front. A hectic six-hour stretch on duty had left him in a sour frame of mind. He was absolutely fed up with the whole game of war. Mud, rats, lice, dirt, discipline and discomfort had worn his nerves threadbare.

Stamping half-frozen slush from his legs, he glanced over the dismal waste of mud that hemmed him in from every side, and shuddered. " 'Tis wan hell av a pitchoor," he muttered.

He descended slippery steps into a large dugout. It was crowded with chilled and blasphemous humanity, surly over an issue of scanty rations. Clancy elbowed his way to his chicken-wire bunk and reached for his mess tin. He had tied it to a beam with a cord, so as to be out of the way of rats. Only the string remained on the post. The rodents had gnawed the kit loose; it had fallen to the mud floor and opened, and only a tin of bully remained. "By th' sivin pipers," snorted Clancy. "Ye can't beat the luck of th' Irish. Not a crust lift, not a crumb! May ivery blasted varmint av thim die av belly ache!"

Someone wedged through the steaming, swearing men who milled up and down the passage, and came to the end bunk beyond Clancy's. The Irishman was aware of a rank odour peculiar to goats. Then a sputtering candle was placed on a ledge and he beheld a dour-faced individual who looked anything but a soldier. A wet woollen balaclava draped over one ear but managed to reveal a bald red skull; a muddy and bedraggled goatskin jerkin, offensive alike to eye and nostril, draped over bony shoulders; the puttees that wrapped his bowed legs were filthy with trench mud.

The newcomer reached to a beam above and released his mess tin from where it hung. Clancy saw the reason it had been rat-proof. It had been fastened with wire, not with a cord. Then the stranger reached to an inner pocket and produced a large newspaper which was carefully unfolded and spread on his bunk. Followed the appearance of a ration of bread and cheese, and the usual hardtack. Clancy stared anew as he saw the rations devoured with evident enjoyment. The spread paper caught every crumb and fragment that fell and these were gathered and licked off a wet and dirty forefinger.

"I'll make wan guess," grated Clancy, unable to keep silent, "an' that is that ye are a Scotchman."

The last crumbs were flicked from view before the dour face was raised. Its owner surveyed the guesser with maddening deliberation. "Aye," came the answer, "and prood tae be one. I tak' that you are Irish."

"I am that," retorted Clancy. "Is there any nade av wearin' that goat hide among dacent men?"

"Donal MacClaverty is as decent a mon as any in this platoon," was the calm reply, "and this jerkin o' mine frees me o' many deeficulties."

"Well, ye can take th' word av Tim Clancy that it'll git ye into many difficulties if ye kape it in this dugout." came the hot rejoinder.

MacClaverty refolded and stowed his paper, then from his puttee drew a flat, whittled stick which he ran under the collar of his shirt and guided expertly, giving grunts of satisfaction all the while. The operation stirred Clancy to an attack on his own person. "MacClaverty," he hissed, "yer as lousy as a pet coon an' ye should be barred from dacent sojers."

"Aye-there's no doot I'm lousy the noosin' sleepin' wi' sic' comrades," came the quiet admission.

The stick was withdrawn and restored to its keeping as the gas curtain parted and an officer stepped into the dugout. He blinked in the candle light and then beckoned to MacClaverty. "Here you," he called, "I want you to come with me to the Stokes pit. They've had trouble up there."

The rest of the platoon disappeared into their bunks, and snoring issued. No man just off duty, wished to be added to the party. The

Scotchman obeyed without a murmur and brushed close to the officer at the gas blanket. The lieutenant sniffed - and gasped. "You - I guess I'll change you for that other chap next bunk," he stammered. "Come along, fellow. Hurry."

Clancy was the "other chap," and he ground his teeth as he went. Very clearly he recognized the value of the scorned "goat hide" in getting its owner out of "deeficulties."

They located the Stokes pit. It was in an exposed position and they were forced to crawl up the battered sap that led in. A white-faced gunner sat nursing a bandaged arm from which blood dripped. "Me mate's out there yet," he said huskily. "We was clearing the rubbish from in front so's we could use a periscope when Fritz opened with a machine gun. He got me through the elbow an' Jim's hit in both legs. If you crawl up the ditch you can reach him, but keep low."

Clancy had shed his steel hat and gas mask as the fellow was speaking, and a moment later was worming his way up a vile ditch. In peering around the Stokes pit he had observed the day's rations of the gunners still untouched, and his stomach yelled out loud. He got the trench mortar man in after several narrow escapes from a sniper, and then assisted in getting both casualties to the main trench. A stretcher party took charge, and Clancy saluted the officer. "Is there anythin' more ye nade?" he inquired.

"Nothing - except your name," was the answer. "You acted like a very brave man."

" 'Twas nothin' at all," said the hero, expanding his chest. "Me name is Timothy Fergus Clancy, av Fourteen platoon, sir."

The officer was barely around the bay before the Irishman was crawling up the Stokes gap. In the pit he spread a two-man ration of bread and cheese beside him and prepared to enjoy himself.

Cruruump! The soul-shocking crash of a minnenwerfer! Clancy was pitched head first into sandbagged walls. Mud and debris showered outside. Smash! A heavy lump of frozen earth drove through the roof of the shelter and obliterated every trace of the hard-earned rations. Clancy, choking with the acrid odour of high explosives, regained his feet. Ruefully, he surveyed the scene, the gaping hole above him. " 'Tis the luck av th' Irish," he gritted. "I inherited th' same from me old man. Divil take ivery blasted Heinie on this front. May th' blisterin' lot av thim be..."

Cruruump! Another shower of filth. He made rapid retreat down the battered sap.

Back in the dugout he borrowed hardtack and lay in his bunk gnawing at it until he fell asleep. He was awakened by a roar that would have roused the dead. MacClaverty was dancing about the passageway as if reason had forsaken him. "Where's the thievin' wretch that stole ma jerkin?" he yelled "I'll hae his heid in a sling. Did ye tak' it, Clancy?"

"I did not," rasped the Irishman. "But I hope ye niver find it. 'Twas an unsanitary thing to bring among sojers, an' ye know it."

After fruitless questioning the Scotchman subsided. He was jeered by a dozen sleepy voices and found no sympathy. "Juist the sam", he announced grimly, "I'm goin' ta hold ma suspeecions aboot the mon wha' took it. There'll be mair aboot this later."

It seemed to Clancy that he had no more than got to sleep when his name was shouted by a runner. "Who in th' divil wants me now?" he snapped, kicking off his blanket.

"Old Pike wants you down at th' War Office." chuckled the messenger. "Wha'cha been doin'?"

The C.O. wanting him at his dugout! Ah-ha! The Stokes officer had handed in his report of Clancy's bravery. The hero pictured the battalion orders that would be posted when they were next out at rest billets: "Private Timothy Fergus Clancy is awarded the Military Medal for conspicuous bravery in rescuing a wounded comrade. R.O. 22-M-L.

"An' Private Donald MacClaverty is wanted, too. Is that guy down here?"

"Aye," rumbled a burry voice. "What is ut ye want?"

"Come along with Clancy," flung the runner. "Jist follow him, Jock."

The Irishman did not wait for his proposed company. If possible, he would leave the Scot in the lurch and let him search for the War Office. But Clancy halted as he rounded the first bay. A familiar odour had reached his nostrils. Just over the parados lay the despised goat skin-and MacClaverty would be sure to find it. It must not be. He reached for it and found it had caught on strands of barbed wire. He tugged mightily and the jerkin came loose just as the dour Scotchman panted into his rear. "And sae I find ye wi' ma jerkin!" There was grim triumph in the words.

"Hand ower. Gin ye ken ony Irishman that could trick a Scot? There'll be a feenish to this, dinna doot."

Clancy realized the futility of argument and tossed over the garment without comment.

Major Gillington Pike ruled "D" Company with an iron hand. No despot in the days of Rome swayed destinies more dramatically than this red-jowled veteran of the regulars. He abhorred the society of his subalterns to such an extent that he dined with his batman and a signaller in a foul, unsafe cellar under the ruins of a shattered cottage midway between the first and second line trenches. This hole was dubbed "The War Office" on account of the drastic decisions that originated in its depths.

Clancy ignored the sentry in its sap and pushed aside the gas blanket at the bottom of the short stairway, to confront the Major, flanked by three officers. The Irishman saluted and made way for MacClaverty who wheezed into place beside him, still muttering imprecations.

"Hell's bells and lights out!" roared old Pike. "Where did you get that goat hide? Take it off, man, tear it off. Throw it outside. Blast you-you are worse than the goat. He had to wear it."

MacClaverty's deliberate ways were hastened by a second outbreak, and Clancy felt a wave of joy sweep over him as he heard the sentry outside pitching the jerkin far into the mire behind the dugout.

The officer on the Major's right was a staff Captain from brigade. Beside him was the Lieutenant who had investigated the Stokes pit. And on Pike's left was the most insipid looking specimen the Irishman had ever seen, in a Sam Browne, a languid. effeminate fop, whose upper lip was decorated with chicken-down.

“This man," saw Pike, speaking to the staff Captain, and pointing at Clancy, "will make another of the raiding party. This Stokes officer has recommended him, but he needs the like to square his conduct sheet."

Clancy shivered. So this was his reward for lifesaving. "Another of the raiding party!” Ugh-th' luck av th' Irish!”

"And this freak," - Pike stuck a finger at MacClaverty, “was wished on me by 'B' Company. You can have him. Men," the Major's tones changed to knife-like sharpness, "you are going out for three days to train for a special raid. Brigade wants a prisoner and is going to have one, whatever the cost. If you acquit yourselves like real soldiers, I'll see that you get treated right, if you bungle the job, you'll dig latrines till duration. Get me?" He Pushed back his cap and turned to his left. "Lieutenant Willoughby," he drawled sarcastically, "take your party. I -I wish you luck."

It was nearly dawn. Fourteen heavy-footed men straggled along a muddy trench that led to the road behind Vimy Ridge. Here and there were slimy mires that almost engulfed an unwary stepper and into one of these slid the man in front - Lieutenant Gerald Willoughby. A moment he flopped like a hen in a puddle and then implored assistance in a high-pitched treble. "Help, you blighters," he called. "Pull me out of this bally hole."

There was a low murmuring in the dark, the squelching of boots in soft mud. "Step on 'im - walk over th' boob," said a raucous voice in the rear. But someone lent a hand and pulled Gerald to safety. "What blighter spoke back there?" he demanded squeakily, as his breeches dripped slime.

"G'wan, shove on," said another rough voice.

Gerald peered near-sightedly, then turned and plodded.

They were established in a barn loft and issued rations. Gerald came around in the afternoon, resplendent in a clean uniform, and ordered the raiders to assemble in a field behind their billet. There they stacked rifles and listened to his elaborate mention of the honour and glory attached to their mission, the expectation of the British army in regard to results of their venture, and lastly, his dislike of a soldier who made remarks under cover of darkness. He closed with the information that they would receive all instructions from Sergeant Binks, who was due from the trenches, and that he, the officer, would only give service by spiriting their charge into the fold of the enemy.

Clancy had small use for "Limeys," but he was glad when he saw Binks enter the barnyard. "How in th' divil did that Willie iver get put down fer a raid?" he queried desperately. "'Tis murder for ivery wan ay us if ye don't watch him. Niver did I have sich luck."

"'E's got a family tree wot's 'ung with 'igh blokes." said Binks, despondent as the Irishman. " 'E sure is one 'oodoo if yer ask me"

The spot chosen for the raid was among the craters northeast of Neuville-Saint Vaast, where the fronts were less than one hundred yards apart. Between the craters the chalky soil had been so upheaved by shell fire that only certain lanes could be used, but there was no deep mud to hamper, and the uneven ground would give some cover from flanking fire. Binks explained this as he taped the field for dummy trenches.

Seven men were to go each way, under the leadership of either Binks or the Lieutenant. A box barrage would be laid on their immediate front, so as to prevent the enemy from getting assistance, and a barrage of rifle grenades would clear the first post. One man was to accompany the leader, the first couple would be bayonet men, the second pair bombers, and the last two would carry Stoke mortars to be used in demolishing dugouts. A hot argument arose over the different positions. No man wanted to be carrying the big explosives or to be a leading attacker. Binks took charge. He marked the positions on paper slips and each man drew.

In Clancy's crew a bomber howled as he found he would use a bayonet. Another cursed the luck that gave him a bomb slip. Clancy opened his paper and swore fearsomely. He had drawn "Stokes carrier." He glanced about him. MacClaverty held his paper in his bony fist, unopened. Minus his goatskin and balaclava, shaven and washed, he looked more gaunt and grim than before.

“I’ll trade ye, MacClaverty," said Clancy softly. "an' I'll give ye a franc fer yer kindness."

The Scotchman raised his eyebrows. "Ye are unco' ceevil juist noo." he remarked. "Why should I trade ya ma slip?"

"Jist a notion av mine," said Clancy, smothering rising anger. "I'll give ye two francs to stop yer questions. Are you willin'?" The Irishman was distrustful of Stokes; he hated them.

MacClaverty looked at his folded paper and shook his head. "I dinna ken yer game, mon," he stated solemnly," but if ye want the bit of paper, t'will cost ye five francs."

It was all the money Clancy had and they would be out for another day, yet his aversion to the trench mortars conquered. "Take th' money, ye old Shylock," he grated... "an' Hiven trate ye fer a Scotch robber," he finished with a wild yell. "This paper is the same as me own.”

"Aye," agreed MacClaverty, producing a stubby day pipe, "it couldna be onything else. The ither laddies had shouted theirs without namin' a Stokes."

"An' ye knew it! An' I'm teamed with ye! By th' sivin pipers, 'tis th' luck av th' Irish, 'tis what I inherited. I-I-" He could not speak further.

MacClaverty tamped a neat filling in his clay and struck a match. "I was wunnerin’," he remarked between puffs, "just what ye would call it."

All the way into the line Clancy bemoaned his luck. As a mate of the Scot he feared the worst. The party was halted at the "war office” and there each man was asked two grisly question - his religion and next of kin - and divested of all regimental markings. "T’is like preparin' fer yer grave," groaned the Irishman after his turn. "I kin see an R.I.P. over me now."

He groaned again when two stretcher bearers, bandage-laden, fell in at their rear. "There's jist th' three kinds of cases," said one, "stretcher-walkin-an' sandbag, an' I hope we gits walkin' or bags. It's blasted tough carryin' a stretcher out of these trenches."

"Will ye shut up?" hissed Clancy, swinging around, or ye'll be usin' wan av yer own stretchers."

Zero hour was at nine a.m. At eight forty-five the barrage opened and the rushing of shells overhead drowned all conversation as the raiders huddled in a tunnel entrance quite near the jumping-off exit. The Lieutenant's face assumed a pasty pallor as he pushed forward to their sally post. There he gave final instructions in a trembling voice-and took charge of the party Clancy was in. "I knew it," muttered the Irishman. "I inherited th' same."

Gerald's arm waved the signal, but he faltered. Binks rushed up the sandbagged steps, revolver in one hand, a Mills bomb in the other, and dashed through the lane in the wire, the raiders at his heels. Rifle shots came sharply and Clancy saw chalk bits fly from under his feet. Bang! Bing! Crash! Three cylindrical stick bombs came looping from the German trench and exploded to one side.

Pinnng! It was the metallic smash of the Sergeant's bomb. There came a frantic shout in German, and they were in the Hun line. Gerald sprinted by the Stokes carriers and ducked into the haven of the trench. Clancy just had time to note the poor construction of the parapets, the timbered saps that honeycombed the front, then he swung left at MacClaverty's heels. Immediately there came a rattle of shots ahead, more smashing reports. The men in front were stopped. They backed. "What's th' matter?" yelled Clancy, elbowing by those in front of him, regardless of his burden. Lieutenant Willoughby was huddled in a corner. "There's - a hundred Germans - in this trench," he gasped.

"Arrrh! Give me thim bombs," Clancy was raging. "Take this Stokes, somewan," he roared, and charged around the bay to hurl a grenade with exact precision into the centre of a Hun garrison that blocked the way. Pinnng! Guttural shouts-cries of pain. A flash of steel as the two bayonet men found courage in the turn of events. "Take me out - I'm hit - I'm hit!" It was Gerald's shrill squeak, and with the plea he flung himself into Clancy's arms, knocking the Irishman's steel hat over his eyes.

The Irishman gripped the pleader, shook him from him and dropped him over the neck of the Scotchman who edged near. "Take this beauty, jock," he howled exultantly.

Back he rushed to the fray. Four dead Huns lay in the trench. He glimpsed the bayonet men in hot pursuit up a C.T., the bombers racing along the post line. "'Tis ivery man fer himself," he panted, and tore up a sap, to find it ended in a latrine. "Blast th' iver lastin' luck," he yelled. Craassh!

A potato masher just missed him. "Ye dirty spalpeen!" Pinnng! Clancy had retaliated with a Mills bomb. He rushed back into the main trench to find an inert enemy who was beyond trouble, while a second Hun was just disappearing down a C. T. The Irishman pursued. This was a grand game and he was hilariously happy. He saw the German, a long-legged fellow who ran like a deer. Clancy heaved another bomb but it fell short and added to the fugitive's speed. The chase doubled back front again and it was evident that the Hun was winded, for he slowed up as Clancy made a valiant spurt. Then a shot rang out and the German fell like a stone. Gerald sat hunched on a fire-step, revolver in hand, his countenance a ghastly yellow.

"Oh! Thank heavens, I'm saved." he quavered. "Not another shot in my revolver. Carry me, you blighter, I'm shot in the leg. Hur-rry!" The officer's request ended in a scream. Bombs were going merrily in another quarter and the morning seemed full of war. Clancy paused only to glance at Gerald's wrist watch. There was yet five minutes before recall, five minutes in which to capture a ten-day leave.

He ran up another sap, ducked to his right and saw MacClaverty alone, methodically depositing Stokes mortars down each dugout entrance. Clancy took a turn left. There came a thudding of heavy feet, and he wheeled about. A giant in Bavarian blue, armed with rifle and bayonet, was plunging into the front trench. Clancy leaped out to cut off possible retreat and dodged back.

The Hun might find Gerald. Grimly hushing his conscience he scrambled over a barricade, and a small Hun started from cover like a frightened hare running overland. Clancy gave a wild whoop and followed. Bullets hummed around them and they dived into the front line at the same time. The German bolted up trench and upset MacClaverty in his lunge, then ducked out into No Man's Land.

Clancy hurdled by the Scot. The barrage was slackening and from the Canadian side came the clear notes of a bugle - the recall. Fritz was coming to life and his artillery was answering the S.O.S. Shrapnel burst overhead and salvos of whizz-bangs erupted small volcanoes on the C.M.R. front. The fleeing Hun doubled and raced in an effort to escape barbed wire. Clancy exerted himself to complete his capture and at that moment came MacClaverty's bellow for help.

The Irishman paused. Every second was precious, but he could not desert the old Highlander. The Scot had carried on as coolly as when in practice and now, perhaps, was being overwhelmed by numbers. Clancy raced back. At the trench he stopped only to snatch a rifle from a dead Hun; then he plunged on. MacClavverty was on his knees just where he had been bowled over. "Where are ye hit?" shouted Clancy.

"Gie ower yer cackle," snapped the Scotchman. "I juist found it." He rose triumphantly, exhibiting his clay pipe. "Gin I get ma hands on the Hun that bumpit me I..."

MacClaverty's threat was drowned in a crash of potato-mashers. A dozen coal-scuttle helmets bobbed into view around the corner. Bang! Crash! Bang! More bombs. The two Canadians scaled the parapet and sped for their own trench, Clancy glancing to right and left as he ran, looking for his almost prisoner. Just as he reached safety, he saw the fugitive scuttling into the Hun trench at a point further on. He had missed his opportunity.

"Av all th' fool stunts, ye can't beat that!" Clancy was back in the tunnel mouth raving over MacClaverty's yelping about a lost clay. "Niver have truck with a Scotchman, ye lose ivery time," he repeated bitterly, "an' after me havin' captured th' trinches clane back to supports. Bad cess to th' ..."

His grousing was cut short by the arrival of a runner. "They've got him down at the C.O.'s now," he panted. "He's sure some baby, that guy."

"Who is?" demanded Clancy. "What are you shoutin' about?"

"The prisoner - that big guy that the dude officer brought in. Didn't ya see him? Wasn't you on that raid?"

"Th' dude brought in? The dude was wounded - I saw him mesilf." Clancy sat down, weakened by sickening apprehension.

"Sure he was wounded. But he had his gat stuck in that big guy's neck and he made the Heinie carry him on his back. Gosh, he was a big fellow! One of them Bavarians."

Clancy made no reply. How that white-livered freak had pulled such a trick was beyond him - especially as he knew the officer's revolver had been empty. It was impossible, unbelievable. "Arrrh!" he groaned. "'Tis th'luck av th' Irish, wheriver I go."

Major Gillington Pike pounded the broken table that served as his desk and spat into the corner of the "War Office," then glared at the man before him. "Clancy," he flamed, "as a soldier you're a washout.

I cannot understand how men like you can be so cowardly when a-a-when that Lieutenant could bring in a prisoner, after being wounded."

"Twas jist me luck, sir," blurted Clancy. "I kin..."

"Silence!" roared the Major. "Not a word of excuse. I have this report and it says you showed cowardice all the way through." Pike sat straighter and clenched his fist. "Listen! You and that blanked Scotchman are going to stay on post from dark to daylight - at Vernon Crater - and if I hear of any shines, like playing sick. the devil help you!"

"Yis, sir," Clancy saluted and turned to go. "Wait!" The Major seemed to find it hard to speak. "Clancy-you're Irish. It's hard to swallow this report. The Bavarian says they were to be relieved that night, and brigade wants another prisoner. If you get one I'll write your name on this leave warrant I have prepared; if you don't, you are away at a labour battalion, Dismissed."

After the usual evening "hate" the batteries on both sides grew quiet. It was dark but occasionally the moon escaped from the clouds and lighted the weird waste in front of the crater. The post was held by six men and a Corporal, the men working in three reliefs, and was twenty yards in advance of the main trench. It was little more than a sandbagged saucer in that mine-torn wilderness, but valuable on account of the observation it afforded. To the left twin pools of unspeakable slime lurked beside a jumble of timbers that were the remains of a farm house. A morass directly in front was one of of the mud-covered middens that belonged to all the French farms, and bits of brick wall on the right of the post indicated the site of a former stable. When nights were warm the odours were stifling; when it was cold, winds swept the saucer and chilled the unprotected garrison.

"Niver in me life did I have a bit av luck whin in the company av a Scotchman," moaned Clancy as he sat on the fire-step of the post examining his black pipe. It had broken off at the bowl.

"Aye-ye are no fitted tae match wits wi' ither than yer kin." retorted MacClaverty, assuring himself that his clay was intact.

As he did so, something rolled into the darkness of the bomb corner. Clancy noted it but did not speak or turn his head. A star shell soared up from the Hun trenches and burst in sickly glow. There were mild snores from the men behind Clancy, the next relief. A rat scampered along the parapet and MacClaverty struck at the intruder, lunging after him with his bayonet. In that fraction of time the Irishman dived forward and grasped the object the Scot had dropped.

It was like a huge marble and sticky to the touch after he had removed the wrapper. He tasted it cautiously and found it candy of some sort.

"Sic' weather is unco' cauld for sic' a country," muttered MacClaverty. He began to beat and rub his fingers.

Clancy, watching his chance, tried to bite th' candy, found it impossible, and crammed the whole in his mouth. At that moment the Scotchman slid forward the safety catch of his rifle and peered toward the stable ruins. He appeared so intent that Clancy crossed over and stared in the same direction. "Juist watch the brick over there," whispered MacClaverty. "Do ye no see mair than rats in the ditch?"

The Irishman looked long, and tensed. He saw them - two darker blots in the gloom, a pair of Hun prowlers. They were angling toward the Canadian post under cover of an obscene farm ditch that skirted the morass in front, and cut in dose to the twin pools.

Clancy glanced behind him. Corporal and sentries lay in the depths of the saucer, huddled together for warmth. Here was a rare opportunity. If he and the Scotchman could slip out through the wire barricade and get cover back of the timber tangle, they might capture the Germans and get the ten-day leave. He tried to explain his scheme and found that his jaws were fast in the taffy ball. For a second he pawed at the mass, then in rapid sign language, made plain his intentions. MacClaverty nodded. "Aye." he assented, "Juist what I waur gaein' ta propose. We'll gang oot by the lumber; ye tak' a rifle and I'll use this bomb."

He held up the one Mills grenade in the post that was not covered with mud. Clancy nodded vigorously and they crawled noiselessly over the bags and crept under the barbed wire. All the while the Irishman was trying to crunch, emit or swallow the huge gob of candy that held him speechless. His efforts were in vain. The candy had softened enough to hold his teeth solidly but was not brittle enough to break, nor could he chew it. His attention was so taken that MacClaverty gave a snort of impatience and passed him as soon as they were free of the wire. Then they halted and listened. There came a tiny splash, as of a loosened pebble rolling into one of the pools.

Clancy made one more convulsive effort to get rid of the candy and then slid his rifle forward. There must be no bungling. The Scotchman slipped ahead into a shell hole and straightened as there was a scuffling sound as of boots on a plank. As he raised his arm, Clancy saw him clutch at his person - the grenade dropped from his hand and a horrible thrill ran up the Irishman's spine. for he heard the tinkle of a freed bomb lever as it fell on chalk fragments. In six seconds...

For one heartbeat he remained crouched, as if fascinated by the sound of the small iron object that rolled swiftly towards the farm ditch; then he made a mighty leap for the shelter of the timbers. Pinnng! The sharp crash of the explosion deafened him, then flares shot aloft, rifles cracked and excited voices in the post called for the missing sentries.

The flares flickered high and revealed an astonishing spectacle. Clancy was clinging with both hands to a jutting timber that suspended him over the first of the twin pools. He had miscalculated his leap and as the earth crumbled beneath him had caught the saving beam-end. Now he dangled at arm's length, feet barely clearing the awful shoe below and his jaws were locked firmly in good Scotch taffy.

Before the glaring light died, the Irishman saw MacClaverty in his shellhole, peering over the rim. Not ten feet farther on, where a smoking cavity marked the bomb explosion, a gray figure lay twisted and distorted in sudden death.

Phissssst! A flare shot up from the Canadian side. Clancy cringed instinctively and then realized that he was almost hidden from German view. MacClaverty still lay in his shell hole. Five heads were silhouetted on the lips of Vernon Crater all turned in his direction. Smoke still drifted over the pools. Then the Irishman tried frantically to find a foothold. He had glimpsed beyond the Scot, the second Hun feebly raising himself on his elbows. Apparently he had been crawling abreast of his friend and had only been dazed by the exploding bomb. The light died again. Clancy felt his fingers slipping and knew that he could not hold out much longer.

He tried to kick a timber, and did, but the noise he made was drowned by the clatter of a machine gun. Bullets skipped over the Scotchman's refuge. More flares whizzed up from the German trenches. They revealed MacClaverty watching the crawling Hun who was sidling across to the cover of the stable ruins. In order to do so the fellow had to go nearer to the anxious garrison, but their attention was fixed on the kicking frantic Irishman.

Once more Clancy kicked wildly in the direction of the escaping Hun; then his grip gave way, and he dropped waist deep in the filthy pool. Raging like a lion, he tried to spring ashore and still make a capture, but his weight had driven him deep in a tenacious mixture below the slime and he was utterly spent before he reached dry land. A fusillade of bullets snapping and cracking over his head told him that the Hun survivor had reached his mates. A dramatic dive under the wire, a lunge over the bags, and the Irishman was back in his post. The Corporal grasped Clancy. "Why did n't th' other nut come in with ya?" he hissed "What perishin' heroics took you blighters out there?"

Clancy's eyes alone answered as he tore at the gag still in place. The shooting died down just as the Irishman conquered his enemy. He flung the candy from him with all his strength and spat like fighting cats. "Niver-phtt-in all me-phtt-sufferin' life-phtt- did I have sich-phtt-bloody luck," he panted. "Are ye all blind-phtt-deaf and dumb? Ye stuck there like-phtt-frogs on a mudbank-and watched tin days' leave crawl under yer noses. Av all the cussed..." He paused, incoherent.

Puffing and labouring, MacClaverty crawled into the crater.

"An' that-that pig-headed Scotchman niver raised a hand or so much as a warnin', but let that Hun crawl over his back. Arrrh!" Clancy was furious, ignoring his sopping condition.

"Aye." came MacClaverty's slow sarcastic reply. "Why did ye no gie warnin' yerself? Ye waur keckin' ther like a penny jack. Why did ye no speak?"

"Ye clumsy spalpeen!" flung back Clancy. "Ye fumbled th' bomb or we'd had tin days' leave as aisy as spakin'. Yer worse thin an ould woman."

"Mon," said MacClaverty, "ye are a bit distracted. Gin ye want tae ken the trouble-I had, juist droppit ma pipe, an'-"

"An' so ye let go av a Mills bomb with two Heinies at yer elbow-because ye lost a stub clay. By th' sivin pipers yer wan fine..." Clancy choked, coughed and sputtered. "An' why didn't ye tell th' bhoys that Jerry was crawlin' by?" he persisted. "Didn't ye want tin days' leave?"

"Aye," said MacClaverty calmly. "And I hae got it, and mair. I've a hole in ma leg that is ma teeket." For the first time Clancy saw that the Corporal was binding the Scotchman's thigh - a bullet wound that spelled "Blighty." "Ye hair splittin' son of a gun!" he rasped. "Ye would not give alarm because yer own leave was jake. Bad cess to ivery blanked Scotchman in th' army. May I niver see wan again.

"Amen," grunted MacClaverty. "Gin ye waur not sic' a numskull ye would ken I had the chance before and missed it. I wasna gaein' tae miss twice."

"The chance before?" said Clancy. "What do ye mane?"

"Hoot, mon," snapped MacClaverty. "Did ye no' ken I grabbit the big Hun in the ither raid and placed the officer on his back tae save carryin' him over? Then I lost ma pipe, an' the puir fule leeid and tookit the honours himsel'. Gie ma regards to auld Pike."

Sergeant Binks pushed Clancy through the blanketed doorway of the "War Office" and discreetly retired. For a full moment silence reigned. The Irishman and the Major were facing each other without an audience. "Clancy," said Pike at last, “you have come to the end of your tether. Do you know it?" He slammed the broken table with his fist. "I say, do you know it?" he bellowed.

“Tis, yis, sir," said Clancy, hurriedly.

"Then why don't you say so, you yellow-backed four-flusher," roared Pike. Then his voice quieted to a vitriolic calm. "Do you see these papers? This one is the leave warrant I was going to sign if you got a prisoner; this other one is your transfer to the hardest working, poorest-fed labour outfit on the western front. That's the one I'm going to sign, you blasted cold-foot! You hid in that old lumber pile and let a Hun crawl away on his hands and knees. Blast such cowardice...”

A long-drawn whine outside culminated in an explosion that shook the “War Office.” Bricks and debris rained down the stairway. Dust and gas fumes set Clancy coughing. "That wan was near, sir." He ventured.

"Hummm! Getting your wind up, eh?" sneered Pike. “Now, listen...”

They both did, but the peculiar whine of the next shell sent Clancy diving for a corner. Crrraaasssh! A deafening, soul-shaking explosion. The roof of the dugout swayed drunkenly, dropped in the centre and collapsed. Timbers, sandbags. bricks and mud descended in an avalanche.

When the Irishman realized that he was still alive he managed to crawl from under a menacing jumble of wreckage. A low groan assured him that Pike, also, was alive, and by strenuous labours he uncovered the Major and made hasty examination. The old war-dog was badly crushed. Pike groaned again as he felt Clancy pull him to an easier position. “Where's that paper?" he gasped. "Get it, you yellow-tail. I'll sign it if it's the last thing I do."

Clancy trembled anew. If only the Major had been stunned a trifle more! Then hot inspiration set him in quick search. He found the paper he wanted-the leave warrant-and placed it on a plank. Under profane directions he found the pocket that held Pike's fountain pen and placed it in the veteran's shaky hand. "Where-is the-place?" It was the Major's last determined effort that enabled him to scrawl Clancy's name on the dotted line.

Half an hour later the old fire-eater was on his way to hospital, and Clancy was getting his papers O.K.'d at headquarters. The Irishman's leave went through without a hitch and in high elation he rode an ammunition lorry to the nearest railhead. Arriving there he found another of his battalion waiting for the train, and this fellow informed Clancy that he had "come down" from the line in an ambulance that took MacClaverty to a C.C.S. nearby. "Where is this place?" shouted Clancy. "Where kin I find that lousy Scotchman?"

He was feverish with joy. Here was his chance to even the score between them. He would flaunt his leave warrant in the old rascal's face, and jeer. "Five kilos, did ye say? Sure, an thats aisy whin me errand's important. I'll be back in time fer the jitney."

The five kilos proved to be the typical French variety, elastic ones that stretched as one walked on them; and Clancy was dusty and footsore when he arrived at the clearing station. A tired-looking orderly informed him that MacClaverty had departed for the base a scant ten minutes before. "Me fool luck all over agin," said Clancy, despairingly, "but I'll find that ould leather-neck, if I spind half me leave over it. There's more foxes than him."

He sat an hour waiting for a front-bound ambulance, then hoofed back to the railhead, arriving in time to see the leave train puffing leisurely toward Boulogne. Clancy spat and forced an air of cheerfulness. "Niver mind," he said aloud, "I'll have a dacent night's rist, an' I'll take me ten day's leave th' same-countin' from tomorrow."

He found billet in a French cottage, enjoyed a supper of fried potatoes and dark bread, and retired early. In the morning he luxuriated in a long lie in bed. There was plenty of time to catch the train and he strolled there casually, but increased his speed as he saw no lingerers about. Something seemed to click ominous warning that all was not well. He rushed to the window. "What time is th' train due?" he inquired of the grizzled R.T.O.

"Train?" The officer rose impatiently. "Say, haven't I told all you fellows that leave is cancelled?"

"Cancelled!" Clancy repeated the word in a husky whisper and licked dry lips. "Cancelled!" he echoed.

"Certainly. Orders came through last night. You Canadians are going to make a big drive on Vimy, didn't you hear of it?" Then the old stager softened his tone. "You're the chap that was here yesterday, aren't you?" he asked. "Why in blazes didn't you hop it then? - you would have got over all right. Sorry, old timer, but you'll have to go back to your unit."

Clancy struggled for words. He was utterly bewildered, stunned. It could not be. He looked up and down the steel rails that yesterday spelled leave, and groaned. "Tough luck," said the R.T.O., handing the Irishman his haversack, "tough luck, my man.

Like a man in pain Clancy thrust an arm through the strap of his pack and turned to go. "Tis the luck I inherited," he said savagely, bitterly. "If I'd been born a Scotchman, I'd have fooled me ould man intirely."

CHAPTER FIVE

THE GILDED STAFF

CLANCY was back in the trenches he had so nearly escaped. He had spent himself in reviling his luck and was now bitterly resigned to his fate. He huddled against the parapet of the Fifth C.M.R.'s trench and stared at the moving shadows in No Man's Land. Flares went up steadily from the German lines, giving a ghastly sheen to the wet waste in front, and the Irishman shuddered at some of the sights revealed. He was watching, apprehensively, brick ruins that lay some distance in front. Suddenly a German machine gun stuttered excitedly and the "pinnng" of Mills bombs was audible above the clatter. Clancy turned to a darker blot in the corner of the trench bay.

"Git up here, me bhoy," he ordered huskily. "Fritz has spotted th' patrol an' there'll be the divil to pay."

A second Hun "typewriter" joined in the chorus and bullets whined over their heads. For a few moments the "hating" was very active, then came a lull and once more the flares shed their ghostly light. Clancy's mate, who shivered as he watched, sank back on the firestep. It was the first of April, but the Vimy sector held to winter weather.

"Whist-st yer noise," Clancy bent his head in a listening attitude. "There's a groanin' out yonder. What th' divil...?"

Another sentry came rushing into the bay. "Hey, Clancy! Th' patrol's come in - they had a scrap by the bricks - an' one guy's hit bad. Th' officer says who'll volunteer to go out and get him."

"Well, what's th' matter with you goin', me lucky lad? If thim amachoors had sinse they'd niver go near thim bricks. Git back to yer crowd." Clancy's voice was threatening.

"Help! Hullo-help!" Faintly, but distinctly, came the call. From farther along the trench came sounds of argument.

"He–lp! Hi-help!" the cry was insistent. Clancy's mate stumbled to his feet again. "Bli'me, someone should get him," he said nervously. "Old Fritz'll 'ear 'im if someone don't 'urry. Yer a good one Tim. ‘Ave a go at it."

For a moment the Irishman ignored him, then shed his equipment, gas mask and steel hat. "Git up here, blast ye." he snarled. "Have ye sand enough to look over?"

Five minutes later he was on his way through the lane in the wire used by the patrol. It seemed miles out to where the wounded man lay and called for help. Clancy wriggled through slime, through half-frozen mud and water, tore himself on stray strands of barbed wire. Twice he rose up and shouted that he was coming, fearful lest the Germans should hear him. The flares lobbed up steadily.

Spasmodic shooting of the Hun gunner forced Clancy into lower ground and more mire. Finally he reached his man and silenced his entreaties with a savage "Kape still."

Then he hoisted the fellow on his shoulders and commenced to crawl back. His burden made the going very difficult and twice he slithered into loathesome shell holes. The wounded man began to whimper. "Kape hold an' kape quiet," snorted Clancy. "I'm walkin' in; I'll not crawl more in sich a mess."

And despite the sufferer's protests he arose and staggered trenchward. Machine guns still chattered, but by some miracle the Irishman and his burden escaped destruction, and Clancy slid his man over the parapet as though it were a nightly performance.

"Great heavens! You are a brave soldier!" gasped the officer who had called for volunteers. "I'll see that you are rewarded for this work." Approving murmurs arose from the sentries and, as the Irishman went back to his post he hardly realized that he was shaking with cold.

"Bli'me," piped his mate in surprise. "Did yer get 'im?"

"Av course." snapped the Irishman. "What th' divil did ye think I wint for?"

He had just donned his equipment when a runner appeared. "Which one is Clancy?" he panted. "He is to report at battalion headquarters at once."

Clancy stuck out a muddy fin. "So long, Perkins," he said grandly. "Ye are not bad for a Cockney. Hivin bless ye."

He was thrilled, excited. Perhaps, after all, his luck had reversed. And Pike was gone. He hurried down the trench.

"I have a very good report of your work tonight," said the Colonel of the Fifth Canadian Rifles when Clancy reached him. "I am proud that there are such men in my battalion. The scout officer says you deliberately walked in to save the wounded man prolonged suffering. Such conduct shall always be rewarded. I have a message from brigade, saying they need a messenger for their information staff, and though I don't know the nature of this position it is probably - er - cushy."

Clancy grinned broadly. Ye gods! Hadn't he seen the gilded staff riding in high-powered cars mile behind the lines. The few times he had been sent back on errands to their underground domains he had got an eyeful of the splendour and luxury enjoyed by those possessed of the mystic insignia. Special messenger! Information staff! He visioned secret missions to London and Paris. "If ye are offerin' th' same to me," he blurted, "I'll niver fergit ye. I have always had a likin' fer sich work."

"Good!" The Colonel slapped Clancy on the shoulder. "Here's your transfer. Report there in the morning to the officer in charge of special information."

Brigade headquarters were seething with activity when Clancy arrived the next morning. He was shaved and shined to a perfection his platoon commander had never witnessed, and he bore himself with an importance worthy of Sir Douglas Haig. The sentry at the door of the underground splendour might as well have been a rain barrel for all the attention he received from the Irishman. In the passageway, a tunnel with many branches, Clancy encountered a sharp-looking Captain whose glances asked questions.

"I'm lookin' fer th' officer in charge av spicial infermation," said Clancy, saluting. "Here's me paper from the Colonel."

"Special information!" The Captain appeared surprised. He took the chit and read. then coughed slightly. H-mmm, yes. You are to report to Lieutenant Maurice Percival Montague. Second door to your right."

"Liftenant Maurice Percival... Hivin save us!" Clancy gazed after the Captain, then turned. "I'm comin', Percy," he growled.

He scraped his hobnails on the floor, then boldly entered the quarters of special information. It was an insignificant-looking apartment. A candle sputtered on a small table and beside the candle in an orderly row lay three piles of paper slips. They were coloured, yellow, pink and light green. On a bench by the door sat a fat, bald-headed private, who eyed Clancy as if he had purposely disturbed him. "Is the officer about?" 'asked the intruder.

The fat soldier sat up and yawned. "What h'officer?" he wheezed.

"Gineral Foch, Yer Excellency," said Clancy sweetly. "I've a missage fer him."

"Ee hasn't come in yet," said the wheezy one hastily.

"An' whin are ye expectin' him?" demanded Clancy.

"H'any time-h'any time." It was evident that the fat man had decided to become agreeable.

Before more could be said the door opened to admit an officer that the Irishman instinctively knew to be Lieutenant Maurice Percival Montague. He was below the average height and almost lady-like, but his uniform was immaculate, and the seven delicate hairs on the right of his upper lip were in direct line with their seven brothers on the left. In his gloved hand were two pink papers. Clancy jerked his arm in a snappy salute. "I'm from th' Fifth, sir," he said cheerfully. "Here's me papers from the Colonel."

"As you were!" Squeaky as a rusty garden gate was Percival's voice. "Nevah curl your left fingah when you salute, my man."

Clancy coughed, grew red, nearly strangled. That, "my man" was almost too much.

“Try it again," the squeak continued. Clancy complied, though murder was in his heart. "Now, let me see your papahs."

Percival examined them minutely, as if he expected to find they contained secret writing. Then he waved his new aide to the bench. "Wait there for ordahs," he piped.

For half an hour Percival shuffled the coloured slips, and then departed with all the majesty of his five feet, five inches. The fat soldier nudged Clancy. "Git yer mess tin," he grunted. "It's time fer grub."

In another room they drew rations such as Clancy had never dreamed were served to common soldiers. Real potatoes and rich beef were blended in a tasty stew. Bread, jam and cheese followed, served in abundance, all topped with a can of good, hot tea. At the end of the room were two comfortable bunks, deep in clean straw and blankets. "We'll kip in 'ere," said the fat man. "If yer wants a bawth just follow the passage to yer right."

Clancy gasped. A bath! "Pinch me, granpa!" he shouted. "I know I'm asleep. Lind me yer towel before I wake up."

In a few moments he was luxuriating in a makeshift bath filled with plenty of hot, soapy water. There was a warm place in which to dress and clean garments to don. Feeling like a new man, the Irishman went back to duty. Percival was there, quivering with excitement. "Private Clancy," he piped. "heah are important papahs from division. You are to go to battery in supports."

Clancy saluted as he accepted the pink form, and his heart was fluttering. Here at last was real adventure. Very slowly he deciphered a mass of form - code, - prefix - instructions-sent by-sent to - and at last reached the message: "Request number of Presbyterian Faith attached to 4th Field Battery. April 6th, 1917."

The Irishman stopped outside and waited until the fat man appeared with a similar slip. "Do ye mane to tell me that thim is th' straight goods?" Clancy asked fiercely. "Do rale sojers have to waste their time with monkey tricks?"

The stout messenger was startled. "Lor' bless me!" he ejaculated. "We gits good eatin' an' sleepin', don't we, mate? Better go back and git yer armbands. Yet on th' blawsted staff now."

Clancy went back to the stores department and was issued with two blue and white armbands. He slipped them on rather proudly. At last he belonged to the gilded staff. To add to his satisfaction a brigade car slowed and took him on board. It was unoccupied save for the driver who wished to borrow cigarettes. and Clancy lolled in perfect bliss until he reached a cross-roads. He had no difficulty in locating the dugout of the O.C. of the battery he sought. A tired-looking individual sat at the entrance, smoking. "Where's yer old man?" asked Clancy importantly, careful that the fellow should see his armbands.

"Th' O.C.'s in a poker party below. Wouldn't bother him if I was you, Mac."

Clancy, irritated by the fellow's indifference, went down the dugout stairs and brushed aside the gas curtain. Five officers sat around an upturned shell case absorbed in "high poker." A grizzled, bulldog type of officer, a Major, spat angrily. "What th' devil do you want?" he snapped.

"I'm from brigade, sir," said Clancy importantly, "an' I'm sint by th' special infermation officer. He wants to know how many av th' Presbyterian faith ye have in yer battery."

For a moment there was a heavy silence. Only the distant rumble of gunfire reached them. Then the bulldog arose. "You get so-and-so out of here," he grated. "You blasted parrots make me sick. Get out or I'll Presbyterian you." Assenting growls came from the other officers and Clancy hastily backed outside the curtain. His pedigree. printed in any language, read "fight," but for once he decided in favour of discretion. He mounted the stairs at the speed requested. The indolent soldier still sat and smoked.

"Any luck, Mac?" he queried.

"There was not a hint of malice in his tone and Clancy's blood ceased boiling. He had a brain-wave. "They're busy with their poker," he said casually, "an' p'raps ye can furnish me th' information as well.

Do ye know how many Presbyterians there is in this battery?"

"Presbyterians!" The man spat his smoke. "No, Mac, I don't."

"Niver mind, thin," said Clancy. "I'll strike an average. How many men in th' battery?"

"I've no idea, Mac," said the soldier, yawning. "Must be more'n fifty, but I dunno. I just come here to see a guy."

Clancy jumped to his feet. "Why did n't ye say so in the firrst place?" he demanded.

"Ya never asked me, Mac," said the loafer. "Did ya?"

Incoherent with anger Clancy left, and met a short man in a long slicker, a fellow who looked intelligent. "Say," said the Irishman gruffly, "do you belong to this mob?" He swept his arm to include the battery positions.

"Ah-in a way-that is,"stammered the short man.

Clancy lost patience. "Th' divil" he exploded. "Can't ye answer a straight quistion? Do ye or not?"

"Ah - I'm sorry, but-ah, you see..."

Clancy planted himself in the short man's path. "That'll do fer yer 'ahs'." he roared. "Niver did I see such a mess av -" The language Clancy used would ignite wet wood.

'Tush, tush," cried the short man. "I'll tell..."

"Tell me," said Clancy, "how many Presbyterians ye have in this outfit," He was very grim.

With nervous motions the short man unfastened his slicker to produce a note book, and Clancy glimpsed a Sam Browne. An officer! "Ah-there are twenty-nine of the Presbyterian faith in the Fourth Battery.

The Irishman stepped back. He breathed deeply and tugged at his tunic collar. "Beg yer pardon, sir," he managed to say, "but yer an officer an'..."

"I am the padre," said the short man, smiling kindly. "Here is the statement you need. Good afternoon."

"Hivin bless ye!" said Clancy humbly. "Good-day, Sir."

On the way back he tried to board an empty ambulance going his way. "Git outa here," yelled the driver. "I've no room for bloomin' staff monkeys." And the Irishman was still in an unpleasant frame of mind when he reached quarters. Percival was at his table and he seized eagerly Clancy's report. "By Jove," he squeaked. "From the padre himself. You are a wondah." The cook's gong sounded and Clancy made his escape.

He was served a double portion of steak and after his meal lay back to have a good smoke. The door opened and in walked Percival. "I am heah for kit inspection." he announced solemnly.

Clancy's mess tin was condemned, his towel discarded. "Where is your toothbrush?" asked Percival.

"Toothbrush!" blurted Clancy. "I niver owned wan in me life."

"Never owned one!" gasped Percival. "Form 7-L.D. says for every soldier to carry one."

When he had gone Clancy relieved his mind, dwelling long and fervently on parents who bad hampered mankind with such offerings as Lieutenant Montague.

Night had fallen, dark and cold. A fine driving snow cut Clancy's face as he pounded along slippery duckboards that led to the front occupied by the Fourth C.M.R.'s. A heavy leather jerkin covered the splendour of the red-tabbed tunic with which he had been issued, but its warmth was not needed. The Irishman was still heated by the rage which had engulfed him when Percival saw fit to send him forth at dusk on this stormy night - to learn what stock of whale oil the battalion had in reserve. An hour's tramping up a wrong trench had not improved his mental condition. "I'd like to drown that blasted squeakin' canary in th'-stuff," he muttered fiercely, as he stumbled over a broken trench mat. "Divil take th' whole wor-rks."

Then, just ahead, he heard low voices. He quickened his steps. A small party of the Fourth, without equipment, was hurrying to the front, the men grunting and swearing as they slipped on wet, greasy boards. He followed in their rear, glad that the darkness and swirling snow made everything indistinct, for he liked their company.

A voice gave quick command and the party halted. Clancy, followed close, bumped into the man ahead of him and found that he also wore a leather jerkin, a gas mask and an army issue revolver. The line moved on, a few paces at a time, and the Irishman was mystified until he heard in the dark a pleasant gurgling sound. Soon it was his turn and a man-sized issue of rum warmed his interior anew. The officer in charge of the jug put in the stopper. "Carry this for me," he ordered. "We'll leave it at headquarters. By the pipers it's dark."

Clancy hugged the rum jar lovingly and his steps were careful. The trench dipped to go under a covered dugout entrance and in its shelter flashlight beams made repeated stabs at each man as he passed. The Irishman was glad that the jerkin hid his tunic and its staff insignia. The light flashed in his face. "Here's another one." A voice hissed with impatience. "You babies need watchin' every cussed minute. Hold still."

Before Clancy could remonstrate a rough hand smeared his features with a cold, soapy substance "Here's yer bombs," the same voice hissed, and two Mills grenades were thrust into the Irishman's hands.

There was no chance to argue. Those in front had quickened their pace, and someone had passed back word that the officer was wanted. He squeezed by, leaving some gruff order with the hard-boiled Sergeant who had used the flashlight. Clancy knew well what was about to happen. A raid was planned and he had been taken for one of the party, and with his face smeared with black grease would find it difficult to prove his identity.

They turned into the front trench and began to encounter sentries. The Sergeant close behind Clancy stopped to whisper something to the men at one post and as he did so the Irishman crowded up beside a man on a firing-step. Simultaneously another soldier came hurrying up the trench, a fellow who was panting heavily. "I nearly missed you guys." he said hoarsely in the gloom. "Where's th' Sergeant?"

"Right here. Hawkins," came the hiss. "Where th'-were you?"

"I forgot my trench knife and went back for it," came the explanation. "It's so dark I couldn't make time."

"Well, keep goin' now," hissed the Sergeant. "It's funny, though. that I counted them guys and there seemed to be the twelve. Push on, for Pete's sake."

Another second and they had vanished. "Who th'-are you?" breathed a whisper in Clancy's ear. The man beside the Irishman had started to make protest at his intrusion, but had kept silent at sight of the jug until the Sergeant was out of hearing.

"Kin ye beat it?" said Clancy. "I'm sint up from brigade an' wan chap greases me face an' another gives me a jug av rum. Would it be right with ye if I was to leave it here?"

"Would it?" The sentry gripped Clancy's hand.

"Man, this is just the station for such refreshment. I've never seen more'n a teaspoonful for a week."

"Hilp yersilf," said Clancy grandly, "if ye kin manage without a glass. I forgot to bring wan."

The fellow managed, after the Irishman showed him the trick of resting the jar in his elbow, and between drinks explained that he was too good a sentry to be spared for a raiding party. Clancy got very friendly and promised to come often as a visitor, then in a last lucid moment remembered his mission. He placed a detaining hand on the jug as it was about to be elevated for the fortieth time. "How many," he hiccoughed. "gallons of whale oil have yez?"

"Thash a new one," said his admirer. "What's th' answer?"

"I mane it," declared Clancy, fumbling for a pink form. "I have to put it down in figgers."

"Four--five--sixsh, like that?" queried his friend.

Clancy was wavering. "Come some place ligh-hic-a match?" he begged. "Mush put figgers down four five-sixsh-'fore I forget."

Arm in arm, they staggered through the dark to a nearby dugout cover and behind its curtain struck matches. Clancy placed his figures, firm and bold, in the indicated space, then made out the word, Reserve."

"How 'bout reserve, old man?" he mumbled.

"Reserve!" hiccoughed his helper. "Reserve-his-is behind, always behind."

Clancy wrote labouriously and bade his man an affectionate farewell. In some way he manoeuvred to the rear and a kind-hearted A.S.C. driver placed him at brigade. He left a very dirty pink slip on Percival's table and tumbled into his bunk, boots and all.

He was awakened by a shout. "I say-'ullo. What yer been doin'?" His stout messenger partner was trying to awaken him. "Percy's askin' fer yer. Lumme. where did yer git th' black?"

Very stiff was Clancy, very slow in his movements as he arose, and he had not removed all the grease when he stalked into the presence of Percival and a monocled, gold-braided Major. The Irishman saluted.

"Private Clancy," the dapper Lieutenant's squeak was sharp."You are charged with being drunk on duty and ... "

"That will do." Like pistol shots came the words of the man with the monocle. "Whether you were drunk or not is another matter, but the Brigadier wants to know who in Hades had the nerve to state that the Fourth Battalion had four hundred and fifty-six gallons of whale oil behind them. Now answer me you lunkhead. Who put you up to this? That blasted slip got through to Division."

Clancy was sick with apprehension, but he lied bravely. "It was a clerk of theirs told me the figgers, sir," he declared. "I was not drunk."

The Major was white with anger. He glared at the Irishman. "Send this man back to his battalion." he rasped. "He is useless, worse than useless; but wait. Make out the transfer, but don't sign it until you hear from me. I may get time to put him up for court martial." Like a thundercloud the representative of the gilded staff departed. Then a runner called for Percival.

While he was gone Clancy paced the floor. All he wished was to be with his chums again. Then the little Lieutenant came rushing in, his voice squawking in a high treble. "This is important," he announced breathlessly. "Division says there are spies on this front and Intelligence Order 6-H says to watch for a man calling himself 'O'Brien.' Clancy, prepare to go to the Fifth and search for men of that name. I will go to the Second myself. We must be brave in this mattah."

Despite his aversion Clancy tingled. Spy-catching promised excitement. He set out again, picturing the strategy he would employ, and after getting his man he resolved to apply for an honourable transfer back to his company. To his dismay all the communication trenches were blocked with traffic. The great attack on Vimy was to be at five-thirty the next morning. He wormed forward as far as the support trenches and there slept in a bomb shelter until three a.m.

With his leather jerkin concealing his army status he worked forward and at last gained the tunnel that held the men of the Fifth. Once in touch with them he forgot his errand. Men stood shoulder to shoulder, tense, waiting. The air was thick with cigarette smoke, vibrant with expectancy. Suddenly the earth trembled, shook. Candles went out. There came a rush of cold air. A mine had been fired at the head of the tunnel, an opening made directly into the German trench. Every man plunged forward, swearing, pushing, to clamber at last up scaling ladders into shambles, the ruins of the Heinie trench.

There was a flurry of sleety snow and forms were indistinct. Bits of mud spurted beside him. They were under fire. A man fell and Clancy took his rifle and a bandolier.

They reached the second German line, but met slight resistance, and the attack went on. Shells began to fall and slimy debris mushroomed all around them. Black smoke eddied from the new-made cavities. Suddenly the line of advancing men was held up by machine gun fire from a concrete emplacement. Clancy and two others circled the place, dodging from crater to crater, and got to the rear of the little German fort.

There was a moment of savage, hand-to-hand fighting, shots, jabs, thrusts, and the post was captured. One man who had been with Clancy lay dead and not a German survived. A bayonet thrust had split the Irishman's jerkin and the third man of the trio stood, staring. "Do you belong to the perishin' crowd of brass monkeys?" he demanded harshly.

"I do not," said Clancy. "'Tis a tunic I borrowed."

The fellow looked at him dubiously for a second and went on. With an oath the Irishman tore off his jerkin and ripped buttons in his haste to shed the hated tunic. "I hate to do it," he muttered, but he drew the fallen man of the Fifth to the emplacement and took from him his worn, stained jacket. The tunic fitted Clancy, and on the instant he felt that he had been restored to the prestige of a fighting man.

"I say, what are you doing heah?" The squeaking voice sent Clancy into the air as if he had sat on a spiral spring. Peering into the shelter was - Lieutenant Maurice Percival Montague.

He was spattered with filth and seemed completely exhausted. "This is a frightful mess," he moaned. "Do you know where we are?"

"I do," said Clancy grimly. "And ye are th' very man I'm needin'."

In two heart-beats Percival was yanked into the emplacement and disarmed. "Now, thin, me bhoy," Clancy's voice was vitriolic with wrath. "I'll give th' orders. Where's that paper sendin' me back to me battalion?"

"Release me at once," gasped Percival. He was almost in tears. "I'll report..."

"Git that paper-quick!" The threat in Clancy's tones had effect. The paper was produced. "Now sign it, ye miserable misfit." grated his captor.

Percival signed. Clancy's mien would have startled a braver man. "And now." continued his grim voice, "we'll have a proper salute. Don't curl yer left' fingah', me monkey, and make it snappy, one-two."

A trembling arm rose jerkily, like the working of an automatic toy, while Percival's eyes nearly popped from their sockets. "Now git from me sight, and," Clancy paused and pointed a dramatic finger. "if iver ye tell anyone of this I'll tear yer heart out"

Another whimper and Percival was gone.

It was night. Timothy Fergus Clancy huddled against the new-built parapet of the Fifth C.M.R.'s line at the foot of the captured Vimy slope and stared at the moving shadows in No Man's Land. Flares went up steadily from the new position of the Huns, giving a ghastly sheen to the wet waste in front. Beside him shivered Perkins, his under-sized Cockney trench mate, who had survived the Vimy scrap.

"Listen," whispered Perkins. "Blimey, someone is out in front."

Clancy listened. A low moaning came distinctly. "Tis wan av th'

Fourth," he muttered. A guy said they lost a chap from th' patrol."

Again he listened and his muscles tightened as he heard the moaning repeated. Stepping back he shed his steel hat and equipment. Wire had been placed in only the more exposed positions and there was not much to impede a speedy rescue. A sentry rushed into the bay. "Hey, are you there, Clancy?" he whispered loudly. "There's an officer back there who says there's a wounded guy out in a shell-hole and who'll volunteer to get him."

Clancy had frozen at the words. He reached for the equipment he had discarded. "Fly back to yer nist," he hissed fiercely. "Whin I want ye I'll sind fer ye."

The sentry faded from sight. With one quick move Clancy disarmed Perkins. Then he pulled off the little man's steel hat and equipment and boosted the Cockney over the parapet like a sack of potatoes.

"Wot th' bleedin'..." cried Perkins. "Yer perishin' blighter, yer'll 'ave me killed."

Clancy's bayonet touched a tender spot in the little man's rear. "Ye'll go straight out an' git that guy or ye'll niver hear thim Bow Bells ag'in." The Irishman's throaty order expressed a deadly determination. It drove fear into Perkins and he bounded out of range of the prodding steel.

There was an ominous click. Clancy had released the safety catch of his rifle. "Ye can't dodge bullets, Ye pinhead." he rasped. "I'll count three an' thin I'll shoot. Wan-two-"

"Yer 'andin me death." Complete despair ruled Perkin's wail. With a gasp of terror he rushed into the black space beyond whence came the pitiful moans.

The Hun flares rose and fell as before. Footsteps sounded and an officer came into the bay, accompanied by his orderly. "Clancy." he said slowly. "There's a wounded man out there. If you get him I'll see that you get a fitting reward."

Whiss-st ye!" Clancy raised a hand for silence. A low moaning was heard, shuffling, dragging sounds, the whistled pantings of someone who laboured under difficulties. Dark forms appeared on the parapet and into the trench dropped Perkins, dragging after him an inert form that moaned steadily.

"By heavens!" exclaimed the officer. "It's little Perkins. I never thought you could do such work. You're a plucky lad and..."

"It was 'im, Clancy... " Perkins was trying to get breath. An iron grip closed on his shoulder.

"I said, sir," Clancy interrupted. "as how it were a brave thing fer any man to do. 'Tis a bad spot out there, but there was no kapin' Perkins back. It's him fer the reward, sir."

"Certainly, Clancy, and I'll see that he gets it. There is a chance at brigade right now."

"Blimey," said Perkins, rubbing his shoulder. "Do you mean it for me?"

"Yes, Perkins. You must have earned it, haven't you?"

"Well," said Perkins, "It was hard work to go out."

"Noble work, my man. You can come right along with me to battalion headquarters. Goodnight, Clancy. Here come the stretcher-bearers for this wounded chap."

Clancy stepped aside to let the carriers take their burden down the trench. "Good luck to ye, Perkins," he called cheerfully. "Be sure ye have yer toothbrush with ye."

"Toothbrush!" gasped Perkins. "Do yer mean it, strite?"

"Sure, they're nicessary," said Clancy. "Form 606 and S.R.D. and P.D.Q. says so."

The Irishman was cold and wet and lousy and hungry. But as the party disappeared he danced a weird jig on the firestep and spat after a scurrying rat. He had escaped the gilded staff.

CHAPTER SIX

THE HOP-TOAD

AFTER the Vimy show the Dismounted Mudhounds were taken from the line and allowed a breathing spell in order to lick their hurts and have a general inspection. This accomplished they did a few turns on the other side of the ridge, each trip finding them nearer Avion until the front line was in the outskirts of the town. Then came a longer period of rest in the war-battered village of Villers-Au-Bois, and there one July noon hour, three soldiers sat around a table in the estaminet of Madame Rosier, arguing vehemently. Their subject was Lieutenant Louis DeCoste, the officer in command of Fourteen platoon, an undersized but very trim French-Canadian, who was reported to have a family tree prickly with notables.

"I'm tellin' yah," said hard-headed, hard-fisted Corporal Greer, "that th' squirt is outa place. It's a crime to put him in charge of men. Change his duds - an' that guy'd be sellin' papers." After thus relieving his mind Greer sat back and hooked his tunic collar. He was watching through an uncurtained window as if he expected someone.

"You make me sick." The second man at the table, a sallow, cunning-eyed private, spoke the words with biting scorn, but they had not the slightest effect on the watching non-com. "Didn't madame tell you that he's a reg'lar pure-bred? He's a blue blood, with a line clean back to th' Ark, an' one of them family crests, a Fleur-De-Lys, or some such thing, rampant, whatever that means, on a field of azure. Guys with history like that generally have guts an' I bet this kid'll surprise yah." "Shark" Jones had won his title through his specialty of separating his comrades from French currency. Lieutenant DeCoste held like renown among the officers; therefore, it was natural that Shark should defend one of his cult.

"Blast yer blue-bloods! Ginerally spakin' they have th' brains av a canary," broke in a rich brogue. "Ye needn't spring that line on Tim Clancy. That frog, wouldn't be a lance-jack in th' Boy Scouts if he hadn't a drag, an' ye know it. 'Tis a man's luck makes him, same as it's kept a rale man like mesilf in th' rear ranks."

Clancy thumped the table to emphasize his words. His ancestry was stamped in every line of his rugged features. "I'm thinkin', he continued drily, "that I came by th' same whin I was so unfortunate as to enlist with yer likes. Ye may niver know it, but I have a family bush mesilf, bristlin' with rale fighters, an' me crist is four Sergeant-Majors rampant on a field av as-you-were. Kin yez beat that?"

Before there could be a rejoinder the Corporal rose. "Yah should have whispered that mush to Lisette before she give yah th' bum's rush, Tim," he said cheerfully. "Yer always whinin' because yer not a lady-killer." He stepped through the open door with a careless swagger and made an extravagant bow to a pretty, black-haired mademoiselle who was carrying a basket. A moment later and their voices had died in the distance.

The Shark pounded the table. There was a stir in an inner room and fat Madame Rosier waddled into view, gouging sleepy eyes.

"Th' corp'ral has gone to th' garden with Lisette," said the Shark in oily tones. "He asked us to order another fill-up of beer."

Madame raised fat, moist hands in protest. "But ze las' time he parley 'non', it was not." She shook her head.

"That was just a joke of his," said the Shark persuasively. "He'll pay you alright."

"Sure, an' it's th' truth," contributed Clancy, pushing forward his glass. "Ye can trust this gintleman."

After another dubious shake of her head Madame yielded and filled the glasses. Then she glanced at the clock. "Ze Corporal soon return?" she inquired. It was almost closing time.

“Toot sweet," said Clancy between gulps. "He's comin' right back."

Madame disappeared to resume her siesta.

"This stunt," said the Shark, "will not work again." He placed his empty glass by the Corporal's chair and emptied the third beer slowly. "It's up to us to think up a new one."

"Twill kape me mind off that frog officer." Clancy agreed, as they rose and tiptoed from the room.

Some distance from the estaminet was a garden and there they saw Lisette and the corporal pulling beans. "Kin yez beat that?" asked Clancy angrily. "A scum like Greer with a rale lady, and me sittin' in th' background because I lost me chance for stripes last payday."

"Yah should have stayed sober," retorted the Shark. He led the way back of a crumbling wall beyond the garden and they relaxed in the shade of an ancient apple tree. "Because yah lost yer head yer grousin' at th' corp, when yah knows he's a better man with th' wimmen."

"Divil a chance is he th' better man," said Clancy. so loudly that he disturbed a sleeping pig. "'Tis but th' murderin' Irish luck that has followed me like a--a bloody hop toad, skippin' clane over ivery wan ilse. A hop toad I calls it... "

"Ah--hop toad? Ver' strange you speak. I would lak' explain for why. I have follow you - certain - but it ees for geeve orders." As if by magic a dapper figure had rounded the brick wall, a trim little man who stepped as belligerently as a bantam rooster.

Clancy sprang to a quick salute, "Sure an' I was jist spakin' av me luck, sor," he said nervously. "'Tis th' bad luck that has followed me that I name a hop toad."

"Luck?" queried Lieutenant DeCoste. "Hop toad? It ees difficult to understan'."

"'Tis like this, sor," said Clancy eagerly. "If th' rum is short I'm always at th' ind av th' line instead av first, an' if there's a dirty job to be did, 'tis me th' sargint always names. Yez can't beat it."

"Ah, but he has recommen' you are useful in ze platoon."

"I kin hould me ind wid any av thim," said Clancy with easy assurance.

The dapper little man nodded. "Oui, I am sure. I am come for tell you report for advance party in one hour, yes. You will not forget." And he vanished as suddenly as he had appeared.

"Now kin yez beat that?" demanded Clancy, after a moment of open-mouthed astonishment. "That blasted frog sinds me, Tim Clancy, on th' advance party, after me bein' on gas picket last night, him niver askin' a question. Hop toad! 'T is a bleeding elephant that's followin' me."

Sounds of mild uproar came from the direction of the estaminet. Madame's tongue sounded like a machine gun going into action and a grin replaced the scowl on Clancy's red face, giving place in turn to bewilderment. For the berating tongue had suddenly stilled and now there were other noises, like the popping of corks, and much scraping of feet on the red-tiled estaminet floor. With kindred impulse both men left the apple tree and walked by madame's establishment, passing near enough to glance in. They were just in time to see Corporal Greer shaking hands with a stout officer of the French Dragoons, an officer whose breast was a panoply of medals, whose beard was as thin and wiry as hair on a sick dog. Instinctively the onlookers quickened their pace. " 'Tis that uncle av Lisette's that she was spakin' av," said Clancy in an awed voice. "I'm glad I'm gettin' away to th' trenches if she's tellin' him av yer tricks av gettin' beer."

The pair went on with dragging feet and the Irishman thought furiously. He hitched his belt and laid a friendly hand on the Shark's shoulder. "I'm goin' to th' trinches," he said impressively. "I'll not be gettin' another chance to wet me throat. Will ye lind me five francs till pay day?"

"I will not," said the Shark. "Yah got drunk th' last time we wuz goin' in an I had to carry yer rifle."

"Ye are worse than a Jew," grated Clancy. "Ye are -" He choked with exasperation.

"Monsieur Clancy-Teem!" From the rear of the officers' café came Lisette with an empty basket. She had sold her vegetables. "You are not to the field to see me," she cooed. "What is ze matter?"

"Sure an' ye are with that ignorant Corporal ivery time I sit eyes on ye," said Clancy warming to her smile. "If ye'd only give me a chance ye'd find that an Irish man's heart is true. I'm lavin' fer th' trinches, can ye not give me a soft word to take along?"

"Monsieur Clancy is so fonnee," giggled Lisette.

I am sorry you go, Teem. Nex' time you are out we will be friends - I do not lak' ze Corporal."

"Arrah, an' is that so," said Clancy delightedly.

"'Tis like him to push his face where he's not wanted." A whistle sounded a warning for the advance party to make ready. "Sure an' I must be lavin' ye," he said tenderly. "Kape remimberin' me till I come back."

"Wan meenute, Teem," Lisette's soft prettiness became doubly alluring. "If you could bring for me - one souvenir."

"Souvenir!" snorted Clancy. "I'll bring ye th' Kaiser's ears if ye say th' word. What is it?"

"Ze Boche cap, red an' gray, fonnee. I much desire it, Teem."

"Ye shall have an armful," Clancy vowed determinedly. "And a kiss, Lisette, will clinch th' bargain."

She lowered her basket and took a quick look around. The Shark stood idly beneath the"Officer's Only" sign, but no one else was in sight. With quick pertness she planted a kiss on the Irishman's cheek. "For ze bargain," she cried gaily as she snatched up her basket and fled.

"Ye can see that a rale man wins ivery time," said Clancy proudly, looking after her. "an' ye can mintion th' same to th' corp'ral."

"I thought," said Shark slyly, "that you never had any luck?"

"Luck," retorted Clancy, "has nothin' to do with it. Ye are jealous. me lad, av yer superiors, with red blood in their veins."

Fourteen platoon had arrived in the front line. The Avion trenches in the summer of '17 were not famed as health resorts. No Man's Land was an area of gaping cellars and a trip in that sector was, as Clancy termed it, "enough purgatory fer any wan man." Night meant the constant slash of bullets, flickering flares and strange moving shadows between the wires. Day meant a ceaseless vigil, for opportunities offered by the cellars kept both sides wary.

Clancy crouched on the firestep beside the Shark. "Did ye mintion to th' corporal that I have captured th' affections av Lisette?" he queried.

“I did not," was the response. "He was in the estaminet with that wire-whiskered Napoleon and Lisette I had a good run at the Crown an' Anchor board, an' I could see them through th' window."

"Do ye mane it?” Clancy spoke aloud in his anxiety, and retribution was swift.

Sibilant as the hiss of a snak came an inquiry. "Who is it spik’ so? Take hees name."

The new officer had stolen up, cat-footed, accompanied by a burly figure. "It's Privates Jones and Clancy, sir." There was a tinge of satisfaction in the corporal's hoarse whisper.

"So, they don't understand orders, eh?"

There was no response, and the officer went on, moving with extreme caution. It was very obvious that he was decidedly "windy." Clancy's rage was stifling. "Kin yez beat it?" he growled in his throat. "Him an' that two-cent Frinchman creepin' behind yer backs like ghosts. Him hanging around Lisette whin she's tired av th' face av him, an' that frog so scared he's shakin'."

"That frog runt was hangin' around Lisette too,” said the Shark. "She seemed sweeter on him than th' Corp.”

A few minutes later Greer returned with two men."You guys are to go to th' 'ghost hole,” he muttered in Clancy's ear. “Th' frog's goin’ to discipline yah fer talkin' out loud.”

"Where is he?” demanded Clancy. "I hope th' whole German army comes over before it's light." Stepping down he motioned to the Shark and led the way up the trench, snarling answers to challenges until he came to the timbered shaft that led out for thirty yards from their main line. After a scramble over a “lump" of open ground they entered a deep shell crater. Its chalky sides gleamed a ghostly white and indistinct blurs on its lips made signs of caution to the newcomers, then vanished toward the shaft as the Irishman and his mate established themselves.

Phut! A flare soared up and burst in a flood of whiteness. Clancy peeped over the crater rim, scanning the outlines of a nightmare of scummy shell holes and cellars. The flares went up at regular intervals. A fiery-eyed rat ran along the crater banks. Machine guns spat at each other. The artillery droned its hymn of hate. Every hour seemed like eternity. Just before dawn Corporal Greer came shuffling into their post. "You guys gotta stay here all day," he announced. "Th' frog says it's to learn you a lesson."

It was very unusual to leave men for a twenty-four hour shift on such an exposed post. Clancy's blood boiled. "Ye can both go to th' divil," he hissed. "Yet frog monkey hasn't th' guts av a louse, an ye are sore because Lisette has a discernin' eye for a rale man."

"Stow th' chin music," interrupted the Shark, "an' say, Corp, don't fergit our rum an' rations."

"You beer-swipers don't deserve no rations," was the hot response. "It's likely yah'll have to wait till night."

In the "ghost" hole the sun was unpleasantly hot and no breeze cooled the air. The Shark lay at the bottom of the crater, snoring lightly. Clancy attended a bayonet periscope. Suddenly there was a scratching, crawling sound from the direction of the shaft and the Shark sat up. A tousled head appeared and a burly form wriggled ludicrously over the "lump" of open ground. I knowed you guys would be bellyachin' if I didn't bring yah some grub," panted Greer. "That little frog runt said to wait till dark."

Clancy ate ravenously. He knew that the Corporal had risked a sniper's bullet in order to reach them, but they had enlisted together and expected such things of each other.

“Where's th' Frinchman now?" he grunted.

"Down at headquarters," said the Corporal. "There's a raid on tonight, but it's th' company on our right that's puttin' it on, an' me wantin' a chance at Heinie."

"Ye are a cheerful liar," said Clancy. "For why would you risk your precious skin?"

"Lisette wants a souvenir," was the calm answer, “an' I'm th' guy that's goin' to git it fer her. One of them funny round Jerry caps, she wants, an' me throwin' away cartloads of them."

"Tell it to Sweeney," scoffed Clancy. "'Tis me she commissioned fer the job, an' 'twas the Shark that put ye wise."

"You poor thick-head," said Greer witheringly. "I'm th' one she told, and if you'd heard what she said about Irishers you'd-keep out of her sight."

"Ye are a prevaricatin' blackguard," returned Clancy, but doubt was in his eyes. " 'Tis yersilf she named as unwanted."

"Put a sock in it," interrupted the Shark. "Both of yah wants to get wise. Lisette's playing safe, makin' sure she'll get a cap, that's all. She's balmy over that little French ape." Very leisurely he wiped his chin on a tunic sleeve and then reached in his tunic pocket and produced a sheaf of French money. "How's that for an hour at Crown an' Anchor?" he asked.

The Corporal swore and scrambled back the way he had come. Clancy returned to his periscope. The Shark's winnings were always painful to both of them.

All the long afternoon the Irishman could not sleep for thinking of I.isette. Was she fickle or not? Hadn't she premised - at least she had kissed him. And when finally his thoughts swung to the raid scheduled for that night at nine, a brilliant idea came into his possession. He would steal out in the darkness and get near enough to the scene of the raid to secure a "fonnee" cap from possible prisoners.

Punctually at zero hour the barrage opened, ablood-curdling sweep of projectiles, and the darkness was turned into a jumping, spreading blaze of explosives which made the German lines stand out in flickering silhouette. From the trench on the right scrambled the raiders to cross the pock-marked waste with surprising alacrity. Soon bomb - bursts and the clamour of machine guns added to the inferno. The raid was "on".

A few flares lobbed up frantically as if to call on high heaven for aid, and by their light the Irishman, slid from his post and raced for the mêlée. Twice he tripped over wire but he reached the attacked trenches unscathed. With a wild Irish yell he skewered a giant Boche who was swinging a clubbed rifle, and saved the life of a hard pressed raider by a second application of cold steel. The fellow shouted his thanks and for moment their eyes met. “What th' hell?" roared Clancy as he reached to meet a berserk graycoat He had gazed into the rough features of Corporal Greer; there were two unauthorized raiders in the party, with, he realized bitterly, the same objective.

The next few minutes were a turmoil of action. The size of the Hun garrison had been underestimated and the Germans fought desperately. Bayonets, rifle butts, fists, and trench knives were used with sickening savagery. The Irishman charged a group of Huns from the rear, slashing and striking so furiously that his opponents yelled for mercy and threw down their weapons. Their surrender spread contagiously. Cries of "Kamerad! kamerad! " echoed on all sides. An officer, one arm dangling uselessly, sprang on the parapet and shouted an order to return with the prisoners. Clancy scrambled out with the rest and found himself escorting a stiff-necked Prussian Captain. "Divil take yer ugly mug," he growled as he perceived his captive wore one of the inverted coal scuttles favoured by the disciples of the goose step. Then the Irishman gave a whoop of joy that was heard above the din of Hun retaliation. Just ahead, ambling alone, was one of the common or garden variety of "squareheads," and on his close-cropped crown sat one of the usual red and gray pill-box" caps.

With one deft snatch Clancy uncovered the missionary of Kultur, ignoring entirely his squawk of dismay. He slackened his pace to gloat over his prize and the next instant someone came panting beside him. '"What d'yah mean by leavin' yer post an' comin' over here?" rasped a shrill voice.

The Irishman's answer was to thrust forward his souvenir. "Kin yez beat it?" he howled above the clatter of machine guns. "Go chase yer tail."

"Give me th' cap an' I won't report yah to th' frog." The offer was shouted in his ear as both men dove for a shell hole. Fritz was thoroughly aroused and whizzbangs burst in salvos over the front line. Flares were popping along the Hun lines like sparks from a soft wood fire.

"Ye kin report an' be -," Clancy bawled in Greer's ear. "I'm reportin' to Lisette. And who delegated ye to attend this function?"

Ten minutes they were forced to stay in their refuge and for ten minutes the Corporal made tempting offers for the red and gray cap, all spurned by Clancy. Then each man ducked for his respective post of duty.

"Has that undersized Frinch pest been around?" was the Irishman's first question of the Shark.

"Not him," came the surly answer. "They say he's never left his dugout."

"By th' crown av ould Ireland, I knew he had no guts," said Clancy. "I wish no man bad luck but may Fritz drop a 'coal-box' in his front door."

Fourteen platoon was in difficulties. It was raining and they were completely lost. After four hectic days they were on their way to rest billets once more. Their shell-shy and diminutive leader had been too hurried to get away from the shelled area to follow the slippery, twisting communication trench and had essayed to lead straight back overland to the crossroads that served as a guide to all incoming and outgoing troops. It had seemed a clever move, even the Shark had approved of it, but as they went on and on in the dripping dark without blundering on any recognized landmark profane murmurings began to penetrate the night.

"We are miles from nowhere," groaned Clancy, "an' me feet are like lead. Divil take th'-"

The man in front of him fell into a cavity, a halfdug trench. 'It's th' same - ditch we've been at twice before," chorused a dozen embittered voices. "Where's a guide?"

There was no guide, none had been required in order to follow a trench.

“Av all th' blisterin' luck," raved an Irish voice.

“'Tis on me heels all th' time. That bloody hop toad is hauntin' me steps an..”

"Hop toad, eh? you insult ze officer ver' much. Corporal, you will take hees name." The high-pitched voice of Lieutenant DeCoste was quivering with fatigue.

"Sure an' ye are misunderstandin' me intirely," broke in Clancy's rich brogue. "'Tis but me luck I was after mentionin', an' I have ivery respect fer me officer.”

"Good. It ees ze word I do not lak'." The officer was too tired to be aggressive.

Hobnailed boots moved restlessly in the mire. 'We must halt till it ees light," continued the thin. weary voice. "If any one fin' ze track he will call."

"Like so much saltpeter," sneered someone in the dark. There were other growlings, a squelching of wet feet. Every man moved off "on his own."

"Kin yez beat it?" Clancy and the Shark had followed the half-dug trench in the hope of finding some shelter, but the ditch ended abruptly. "Who would n't join th' army?"

"Cut yer chin music," grated the Shark, "an' git out yer intrenchin' tool."

"Since when were you promoted," snapped the Irishman. "And have ye lost yer tin hat and got water on on th' brain?"

"Listen." The Shark was too tired to argue. "Let's pull in the sides of the ditch till we have a bed of earth higher than the water, then we can pin our rubber sheets across the trench and have a roof. I could sleep in a trough."

They worked with a will and soon had a "bed" of soft earth, so narrow that each man had to he straight and on his side minus of all equipment even to his gas mask. Clancy thought with dismay of the stiff, new cap that he had kept clean. Mud would ruin it. He placed his bayonet on his rifle. stuck it upright beside the trench and placed the "pill-box" cap over the butt of the Lee Enfield. Then he wedged down beside his friend, under the rubber sheets, and was asleep at once.

The Irishman dreamed that he had fallen in front of a tank and was trapped beneath the monster. He could not move, try as he might. He awoke - and could not stretch a muscle. The Shark's voice, hoarse with fear and exhaustion, roused him to the gravity of their situation. Rain had undermined the loosened edges of the trench and earth had slid down so softly that they had not been awakened. The rubber sheets were crushed down on their heads. Cramped beneath the weight of earth, they were unable to stir. Clancy groaned. "Are yah awake?" croaked the shark. "For th' luva Pete, do somethin'."

Clancy groaned again. "I can't," he said huskily. "Me neck's broke." He had lain with his head in his steel hat and could not change his position. "Kin yez beat it?" he panted. "We are miles from th' rest."

The answer was a frenzied cry from the Shark. "Great guns Tim, we're going to be drowned. Th' water's risin' an' it's up to me chin."

The Irishman had been conscious of darting pains in his numbed limbs, but now a chill seized him. He knew why his shoulder was so wet and cold. Water had collected rapidly in the dammed space at the trench end. "An' me with the cap for Lisette," he said brokenly. "We are going to be drowned like pups in a sack instead av dyin'dacently in battle."

"An' I've got ninety-seven francs in my pocket," moaned the Shark. Then he raised his call. "Help - somebody - he-lp."

"Ahoy!" Clancy tried, but his voice was muffled by the rubber sheets. "Niver did I have luck with a haythen frog," he said bitterly. Then, like a bolt from the blue, came remembrance of the cap he had stuck on the rifle butt. If they could survive until daybreak it would serve as a distress signal. The thought nerved him like hot wine, and a slackening of the patter on the rubber sheets increased his courage.

The Shark moaned again. "Ninety-seven francs - gone west!"

"Stop yer-bellyachin'," ordered Clancy. "Ye make me creepy. I've a hunch we'll be all right yet."

"Yer hunches are rotten," moaned the Shark. "We're goners."

"'Tis a faint heart ye have," said the Irishman scornfully. "I'll bet we'll be rescued."

"Yah got nothin' to bet." Despite their plight there was scorn in the Shark's voice, and suddenly the Irishman tingled with joy, but he kept his voice cool.

"I have me cap," he retorted, "an' it's worth a hundred francs to th' Corporal. I've as much as yerself."

"Aw-!" The Shark's response was unprintable. Then he moaned again. "I'm a fool for luck." he whimpered. I'll bet yah my roll ag'in yer cap that we don't git out of here. I want to lose."

"Ye are on," said Clancy. "Me beautiful heartwinnin' souvenir ag'in yer lousy Frinch money."

"How long," whined the Shark, "does it take a guy to drown?"

Clancy made no rejoinder. It was only a matter of waiting, and listening intently, he fought against the agony of his imprisoned flesh, the torture of the suffocating folds over his head. One minute dragged into another and the Shark was making low whining sounds like a suffering animal. The Irishman had to grit his teeth to endure.

The first voice he heard was rasping with contempt. "Them two four-flushers have chucked. their equipment and beat it." Then wonder crept into the question that followed. "Why in - did Tim leave his cap on his rifle that way?"

"Hey, ye big stiff," shouted Clancy, spitting rubber. "Pull off this - rubber sheet."

Clawing hands tore off their covering. There were gasps of astonishment, and after strenuous labour both men were practically lifted from their tomb. "In about ten years you guys will know enough to keep clear of sich places," said Greer. "Pound life in yer legs an' let's git goin'. That , - frog's been gone since daylight."

Every fibre protested as Clancy tested his joints. but pain could not alter his intentions. I'll be havin' me money, Shark," he said determinedly. "Ye lost yer bet."

The Shark thrust his hand in his pocket and drew out his roll. "Take it, yah luck hound," he snarled. "Yah knew the cap was there an' I didn't. I hope yah drown."

Greer was surveying the cap on the rifle. "Tim," he said craftily, "I saved yer life. Do I get this lid?"

Clancy's Irish generosity rose like a flood. "Ye did save my life," he admitted, "an' I'll give ye fifty francs instead."

"Keep your money," snapped the Corporal. "If I'd gone with the frog you'd have rotted in that ditch."

Clancy looked at the natty red and gray cap. It had held its shape remarkably well in spite of the soaking of the night. He thought of Lisette, and her welcome, but his Irish traits ruled. "Take it, ye buzzard," he surrendered. "Ye would niver have a chance without it, an' maybe not then."

As Greer examined the cap he gave a low whistle. He thrust it inside his tunic and his walk was that of a conqueror. Clancy, following, tried to solace himself with thoughts of the unlimited indulgence in the products of the Haig brothers and Vin sisters his money would provide. The Shark, trudging in the rear was wordless until they reached the cobbled road leading through Villers-Au-Bois, then his remarks were venomous. "I'll bet th' frog's with Lisette." he grunted. "Him an' that old ribboned guy was thicker than gravy when I left."

His statement seemed to impress Greer. The Corporal shoved his hand inside his tunic and after some tugging drew forth the red and gray "pill-box", now crumpled and limp. '"Tim." he said, quietly. "What'll yah give me fer th' cap?"

Clancy thought rapidly. He could hardly comprehend such a sacrifice, but he knew that Greer was penniless; they were starving, and savoury odours of “eggs and chips" came from the door of a French kitchen. "Fifty francs." he said sharply. "Ye can take it or lave it."

"I will," said Greer, without hesitation. "Count yer money.

With the red and gray cap under his arm Clancy entered the estaminet of Madame Rosier. Secure in the knowledge that he now held the key to Lisette's heart, he had taken time to scrub and shine to perfection, but his first glimpse inside the establishment brought chill apprehension. Corporal Greer was seated disconsolately, alone, at a table, and on the table lay an exact replica of the cap under Clancy's arm. Through the uncurtained window he could see a Crown and Anchor board doing a brisk business, operated by the Shark. There was a buzz of voices in the inner room of the estaminet.

"Where did ye git that?" Clancy pointed dramatically to the cap on the table.

"It was inside the one you've got." Greer's answer was spiritless. Apparently his double-crossing had brought no good results.

"And - she didn't want it?" Clancy licked dry lips as he put the question.

"She didn't. She's got half a dozen of them. Th' frog got them forher. bought them from the Heinies at the prisoners' cage."

"Bought them!"

"Yes, an' that foxy grandpa with th' chin wires is her uncle an' he's worked a transfer for our baby."

"Thank hiven fer that," said Clancy, fiercely. "We'll be rid av th' cratur anyhow. Buys his caps, does he? 'Tis th' only way he would git them." Then his countenance brightened. Greer had lost out, and with the frog out of the way..."

"But th' chimpanzee is goin' to marry her!" The Corporal shot the explosion with deadly calmness. "They're goin' right away - waitin' fer one of them blue staff cars now - this old goat's one of the frog's brass hats n' madame's goin' to pull her freight next - shut shop."

The Irishman sat as if stupefied. He could not grasp such catastrophes. Lisette - her smiles - her "kiss for ze bargain". His heart took an icy flop as he heard her cooing voice answering shrill comments in the next room. Little veins began to bulge on his forehead.

Dazedly he got to his feet, and a quick-born impulse leaped to firm resolve. If it was his last free act on earth he would tell this sneaking, thieving, Jack-on-the-string officer what he thought of him and all his ancestors. He flung his hard-won cap across the room, reached forward and beat a savage tattoo on the table, an imperative summons. There was an immediate parade from the inner room - Lisette, in a chic travelling outfit, the despised "frog," immaculate, fresh-groomed, the wire-whiskered Napoleon, pompous in gold braid. fat madame in a gay apron. Simultaneously a big blue car ground brakes at the door.

"Ahh-it ees my brave garcon - Clancy," shrilled the "frog". "Good luck, my frien'. Do not talk on ze pos."

Lisette's quick eyes saw the cap on the floor. "So fonnee," she pointed giggling. "Dose souvenir are plentee-now."

They hustled to the waiting car, madame kissing them all in turn. Clancy, his mouth open, stared. speechless, impotent, until they were seated. Then he flamed to action. He dashed by madame and reached the running board as the car started. "Listen to me," he yelled, "ye are..."

The chauffeur, evidently anxious to be rid of this shouting, wild-eyed fellow, changed gears hastily and noisily, drowning Clancy's smoking adjectives so that only the last words were audible. "...ye blinkin' greasy hop toad."

The "frog" looked back and waved a merry adieu. His eyes were compassionate. I am compre, Clancy," he shrilled. "It ees rotten luck you have with ze cap an' Lisette. Hop-toad - it ees ze right name."

The car tore from view as his arm settled protectingly around Lisette. Clancy, voiceless again, looked at Greer, at the Shark plying his tricks. "I lost that fifty on the spade," said the Corporal, as if anxious to relieve the strain of the moment. "Let's go out an' get drunk on what yah got left."

The Irishman looked inside and saw fat madame weeping in her apron. He flung his hands outward in a gesture of utter helplessness an he followed Greer. "Kin yez beat it?" he said huskily, shaking his head. "Kin yez beat it? Th' luck av th' Irish."

CHAPTER SEVEN

WHEN KNIGHTS WERE BOLD

THE Dismounted Mudhounds lost Corporal Greer when they marched back to the trenches. He was wounded by a fragment of a stray shell as the Fourteen platoon filed by the ruins of Petit Vimy, and his comrades resented bitterly such a stroke of fortune. "'Tis always thim corporals an' sarg'ints has all the luck," grated Clancy as he plodded in the rear of his section. "Niver will a deservin' man git a Blighty." At the next stop, just at the mouth of the long C. T. that led to Avion, he let loose the dark thought that had flooded his mind. "An' now they'll never promote wan of us for his stripes, but bring some magpie from th' rist av the company."

He was correct in his surmising. The Sergeant-Major ordered another Corporal Greer, who had originated from "Limey Lane," to take command of Clancy and his crew, and, to rub salt in the hurt, he detailed the Irishman to break in a new man who had come up from transports.

Clancy chewed his buttons to keep from saying more than he should and found himself that evening on the firestep of 'D' Company's front, instructing the newcomer regarding things that appeared to move in the dark.

"'Tis th' strain on yer eyes that plays ye trick," he muttered to the watcher. "Whin I first peeped over th' bags up Ypres way, I could see th' intire German army comin' over in mass fermation. Ye'll git used to it by th' time yer Leave comes due."

"Leave!" The newcomer, not much more than a boy, grinned. "Some time yet, ain't it? I'll learn, but them stumps do seem to move. Say, is it any harm to talk up here? I got a letter from my girl an' she's asked a lot of foolish questions an'..."

"Girl! An' ye are hardly dry back av yer ears! Pay 'tintion to yer front. Ye see that old stump to yer lift? Watch it! Ye say it's movin'? Well, look at thim brick heaps to yer right. Now have a squint at yer stump and ye'll see it's in place. What's that-three stumps! Man, ye are worse than I -" Clancy's voice trailed off. There were three stumps where there should be one.

"Stand to!" he yelled. "Watch yer front."

Pinnnng! The bomb he threw spurted redly at the stumps. There were guttural shouts, a cry of pain. Then rose the clatter of rifles in hasty hands; machine guns in their typewriter chorus; bombs burst on every side. Those in the C.M.R. trenches rushed to repelling posts and the combat was swift and deadly. From near the stumps a machine gun spat venomously, with darting, fiery tongues. Pinnnng! Pinnnng! Two Mills grenades burst beside it and the tongues stopped abruptly. A score of gray-clad raiders were scrambling in the Canadian wire.

Clancy fought like a lion. A needle of flame stabbed through the dark and the new man at his elbow sank to earth, agonized hands clutching his throat. A tall Hun loomed on the parapet. Clancy pulled the trigger of his rifle as he swung the barrel upward, but there was no response, the magazine was empty. His bayonet thrust was in time to deflect the German's aim as an automatic blazed. Another terrific lunge brought his attacker into the trench beside him. like a sack of wet grain. Potato-mashers exploded very near and the Irishman scrambled over the parapet and charged the thrower. Again his bayonet decided the issue. He wheeled and slashed at a trio of Huns who had a struggling Canadian prisoner in their midst.

Clancy followed his wild slash with a lightning jab that skewered a second opponent but lost him his Lee Enfield. A leap, a snarling melee, and he had wrested a rifle from the third German and placed him on the casualty list. The almost prisoner recovered his weapon and joined the Irishman in a rush up the trench to where bombs and pistols were going furiously. A last handful of the invaders were fighting like cornered rats. Sandwiched by the arrival of Clancy and his helper at the rear, they "Kameraded" with haste.

The sounds of combat had barely quieted when an officer came rushing up a C.T. and made rapid inquiries. "Grand work, men," he puffed, after getting explanations. "I'll take the prisoners back. Fix up your trench and keep a sharp watch. The enemy may attack again. Someone look after the wounded - where's Corporal Greer?"

"Here, sir."

Clancy turned in amazement. In the heat of battle he had not recognized the man who had so nearly become a guest of the Kaiser. "By th' sivin pipers, Corp," he ejaculated, as they hurried to make repairs, "ye had yer ticket fer Berlin. How did thim porkers git ye so aisy?"

"H'i tripped h'in the trench h'and fell." "Cockney" Greer's reply was surly. "H'any guy might 'ave h'it 'appen 'im."

Clancy's skeptical grimace was hidden in the dark. "An' th' cap. might git here while a scrap is on," he retorted.

The Battalion was relieved the next night. Clancy's haversack was jammed full of souvenirs he had salvaged after the raid, and souvenirs meant money, for they were going to rest billets at Lozinghem, the best area in the Arras sector. At the neighbouring village of Auchel was an aerodrome whose fliers were eager to exchange real francs for trophies of the trenches. Yet the Irishman was not happy. He was still thinking of the youth who had been cut down without a fight on his first trip in, thinking of the lad's girl. This horny-fisted drill-dodger had his sentimental moments.

'Got Mitt Uns' belts, Hun gas masks, shoulder straps and caps of Bavarian blue, a watch and two Lugers were soon sold, then, with eighty-seven francs in his breeches, Clancy strolled to the nearest establishment to toast his luck. The establishment of Madame Doucet sold wine as potent as the magic of a witch, and soon he was at a table sipping a glass of the magical brew.

He sought a corner to escape the merriment of soldiers fresh from the trenches, then cursed his misfortune, for not ten feet from him, in an alcove, he faced Cockney Greer making love to Yvonne, madame's daughter. Yvonne's dark eyes were soft with affection, the glow of her pink cheeks natural, her murmurs of endearment sincere, but Clancy missed these salient features. Instead, some imp of perversity pointed out that Yvonne's neck was not clean, her nails atrocious, her hair neglected.

The Irishman swung his chair to shut out the picture, but he could not help hearing Greer, the masterful lovemaker, extolling the prowess of the Fifth Mounted and casually mentioning a few of his exploits. Vividly he described a heroic charge he had made on an enemy gun, and modestly admitted the slaughtering of a score of "Jerries wot got h'in my way."

Clancy could not stand it longer. He gulped the rest of the wine, spat savagely, and went out. A moment he stood irresolute, then took the main road that led past a field hospital and a Y.M.C.A. hut.

A full moon ruled the sky. He could see a long line of flashes that rimmed the distance, could hear, faintly, the rumble of guns on the Somme. Farther out of the village endless traffic moved towards the

Front. The hospital occupied chateau grounds that were the pride of Lozinghem, and Clancy had just reached the great stone gate at the entrance when a whistle set his nerves tingling. Others echoed the shrill alarm. The Hun was overhead on one of his dread air raids.

Long shafts of light shot skywards and swung about like monstrous feelers. Archies barked like dogs roused in the night. Currooom! Currooom! Two loud booming explosions came clearly. The Germans were bombing Auchel, probably searching for the aerodrome.

All lights had vanished at the first warning whistle, and a curious stillness reigned, so Clancy heard plainly a lone Boche airman who had came zooming over the village like some winged monster of the night. Crrrasssh! A terrific explosion inside the chateau grounds. Crrraaassh! A second explosion, more terrible than the first, which demolished a brick outbuilding as if it were paper, and showered missiles into the cobbled street.

There were shouts of fear from the hospital tents, sharp orders, a scream. Then a hush, as if all waited for the third bomb. None fell. The raider had gone as suddenly as he appeared. Clancy stepped from the gateway in which he had taken shelter - and was nearly tumbled backward by an armload of palpitating loveliness that flung at him from the driveway.

"Save me, please, soldier! Save me!" panted this fluttering fugitive.

"Sure, miss, an' ye are saved already," said Clancy in his most soothing tone. "Th' Hun has gone, bad cess to th' spalpeen. 'Tis like the divils to bomb th' hilpless."

"Gone! Are they really gone? Is it all over?" Very slowly a lovely face lifted from his arms and peered about as if scarcely believing that danger was past. "Oh, I am so glad! Thank you, soldier. I'm afraid I was a bit hysterical."

Clancy saw lips delightfully full and kissable very near his own. He was conscious of the fragrance of hair that brushed his nostrils, of the exquisite, supple body in his arms.

"There - let me go please. I am all right now." The voice held a husky, sweet inflection. "One should never be a coward in this land of gallant men."

"Sure an' Tim Clancy would niver blame any wan fer bein' shaky whin thim divils is droppin' their eggs." Reluctantly, the Irishman released the soft form. The girl still trembled. "Let me take ye wherever ye are goin'," he suggested.

I-I was going to the 'Y'," she answered. "I am one of the V.A.D.'s who came up this week from the base. We are helping at the hospital, and I promised to go tonight and give the boys some music."

"Th' saints be praised!" exclaimed Clancy. "'Tis what we've been wantin', an' if ye'll allow me, I'll see ye there. Me name's Tim Clancy, an' I belong to th' Fifth Mounted."

"Mounted! - But-where are - where is your horse?"

The Irishman snorted. "Sure an' we niver seen horses in this land av mud an' rats. Mountin' parapets is our spicialty."

"Never mind! I think you lads are just like the knights we used to read about - gallant gentlemen who joined the Crusades and fought for right, like you brave boys are doing. This war is your Crusade."

Clancy's pulse raced like mad things. He inflated his chest as he kept step. "You must know of Sir Walter Scott," the sweet voice went on. "Really, I would like to call you Sir Clancy."

"Ye have a bit av blarney, Miss." Clancy was like a flustered school boy. "Sure an' ye must have Irish blood. Ye can call me whativer gives ye pleasure, but I don't remimber th' gineral ye mintion. Have ye seen Gineral Currie?"

The husky-sweet voice trembled briefly. "No - yes, that is, I have seen Sir Arthur. Here we are at last. Oh, they have blankets over the windows. I'm sure we shall have a good time."

The sing-song had ended. It had been a tremendous success and the officer in charge of the "Y" was highly elated. "Boys," he announced, as the applause died away, "Miss Flemming will be here again tomorrow night. We are in great debt to her for coming so near the front to give us a touch of home. I know every one of you will treat her th' best you know how. She will now give us a little talk before she goes to the hospital."

Miss Flemming rose and faced them, while Clancy drank in the beauty of her blue eyes, soft hair, and perfect colouring. "Just a word boys," she said smiling, it seemed, to each one. "I want to tell you how much I enjoy coming here among you men who are the real defenders of the Empire. You are the knights of right and freedom, your heroism will be the history of the future. I am proud to be here with you." She sat down, but a hundred lusty throats yelled and cheered till she stood again. "Now listen," she said gaily. "If you shout like that, we'll have that German back with his bombs. Where's my friend, Sir Clancy? Good-night, all of you."

She was nearly at the door before responsive goodnights rang out. Her hand was in the arm of an Irishman who did not know whether he was awake or dreaming. He could hardly keep from whooping or dancing. He, Tim Clancy, had been favoured among a hutful. And they were at the hospital tents before he had made a sane remark. "Is there nothin' further I kin be doin' fer ye?" he gasped, as he realized the evening was over.

"Not a thing," came the merry response, "unless," she hesitated a trifle, "unless, you can get me a souvenir of some sort. I'd be willing to pay, and I'd-"

"Pay is ut!" Clancy exploded. "Sure an' ye'll niver be allowed to pay fer nothin' up here. Souvenirs-ye'll have thim."

Clancy's dreams that night were wonderful. He charged the Hun army, broke through to Berlin and captured the Crown Prince. While he was searching for Hindenburg, Miss Flemming appeared and amid the plaudits of admiring thousands crowned him as "Knight of the Allies." The applause continued until one loud-voiced fellow shouted in his ear and he woke to find Corporal Greer chanting his nasal reveille: "Snap h'out h'of h'it h'an git yer bergoo."

After parade Clancy debated on the matter of Souvenirs. He racked his brain to imagine just what a lady of Miss Flemming's type would desire, but dare not seek advice for fear of too ambitious assistants. Finally he remembered a little beer shop on the outskirts of Auchel where they exhibited silken dainties advertised as the handiwork of French war sufferers.

There were handkerchiefs of every shade and pattern, patriotic embroidery, pillow cases, shawls and scarves, but his eye was taken by a frilled apron, resplendent in orange and crimson markings, brilliant as sunshine. He asked the price.

"Bonjour," said the old hag in attendance. "Beaucoup monies soldats Anglais."

"Say it, ye old robber," grated Clancy. "Combeang? How much? Spit it out av ye."

Cheap - seventy franc - cheap, cheap!" Madame suddenly developed English. "Cheap-seventy franc, she parroted.

It was useless to parley. Clancy paid and got his parcel.

That evening he boiled inwardly as a medical officer usurped his position of escort to Miss Flemming. The crowd took possession of her when she arrived and the Irishman was hard put to find opportunity to present his offering. It was just about as she was to depart.

"Why - I thank you, Sir Clancy." She had undone the wrappings and dazzling colours seemed to leap to her. She slumped into a chair, incoherent.

"Whativer is th' matter?" asked Clancy desperately. "Tis th' best I could git in Auchel."

"It - it's too funny - it's tragic!" Miss Flemming sought for control, but even the Irishman could see it was hilarity that threatened. 'This-this is the fourth of these aprons I've had presented to me in France," she explained as she regained her poise. "I appreciate, so much, Sir Clancy, your efforts. What I wa-what I suggested, was souvenirs of the trenches - a badge, a belt or a German ribbon."

Clancy choked. "Ye kin kick me fer a blind fool," he said fiercely. "I had so many av thim things I lost count of thim. Wan trip in an' I'll have ye a trunkful." "You are so kind," she repeated. "It will be wonderful to get them. Good-night, everybody." She swept out with the doctor, but an errant breeze brought back peals of unrestrained merriment.

Clancy tore off his tunic and challenged 'D' Company, singly, in pairs, or all together. No one accepted his challenge. "An' what's more," he roared. "if wan av ye tries to butt in ahead av Tim Clancy ye'll sittle later, mind what I'm tellin' ye."

A painful kick in the shins brought Clancy from dreams of Lozinghem to a listening post that branched off Bean Pole trench on the Mericourt Front. It was two a.m., and the night was chill. His mate's teeth were chattering as he told the Irishman that it was his turn to watch and listen for patrols that might pass in the shadows.

Clancy swore whole-heartedly and lurched to the lip of the crater that served as their post. The moon had gone and it was getting darker. A slight wind stirred lank grass about their hiding and a rat scampered by, pausing to stare with ghoulish red eyes. Now and then a flare looped high and revealed the horrors of the land between the lines. Biff! Bang! Crrrassh! Crruuummmph! A salvo of whizz-bangs burst a hundred yards behind, very close to a C.T. Crruuummmph! A soul-sickening crash as a minnewerfer exploded on their right.

A low cry of "Stretcher bearer-stretcher bearer!" came distinctly.

Rat-tat-tat-tat-rat-tat-tat-tat! Clancy ducked in the very nick of time. Machine-gun bullets hissed and crackled over his head, cutting weeds on the crater lip. "Wh-what's that?" whispered the man who huddled at Clancy's feet.

"'Tis that dirty Boche gun ag'in," growled Clancy. "Th' divil is there th' same as iver."

Rat-tat-tat-tat-rat-tat-tat-tat-tat! As if in derision the unseen gunner played his fire on the crater once more. Chunks of clay and debris slid down on the crouching men. There was the sound of someone crawling up the sap that extended from the trench. "Are you there Clancy?" came the guarded query.

"Yis, sir. Kape low. That divil is shootin' th' edges av this hole."

A black figure scrambled into the crater, the scout officer of the C.M.R.'s. The Irishman explained as well he could the direction from which the shooting had come.

The officer disagreed. "It can't be there, Clancy," he argued. "I've searched that place with my glasses in the daytime, and I've crawled around there at night. That blasted gunner is a ghost if he can stay out there while our brigade guns put down their cross fire. There isn't a trace of a pit where he can hide. The C.O. is nearly crazy, for we can't put out a working party on this company front."

"What about that old shack to th' right, thin?" demanded Clancy. "Thim Heinies might be hidin' in th' cellar."

"No chance," was the reply. "I was out there last night with my Sergeant. The cellar is full of rubbish and the ruin is so full of holes that no one could live in it an hour. It's raked with machine-gun fire from both sides. You know, too, that his gun would sound different in a building."

"Ye are right." Clancy shook his head. "If I was to say where, I'd say th' divil was square in front av us, by that garden."

"You would!" exclaimed the officer. "My Sergeant said the same thing. But we can see every foot of that place - a few patches of flowers and ground flat as a table."

"Givin' thim a clear sweep av this whole Front." answered Clancy. He began to unfasten his equipment. A slight mist was rising and the air held the cool of dawn. "There's wan chance," he said slowly. "Lind me yer gat an' make things right with th' Captain. I'll skin out an' git in th' top av that old house. A man kin lay in wan corner and 'niver be noticed. Thin I -."

"But, my dear fellow," remonstrated the officer. "A shell from either side means your funeral, and you may be seen at any time. It's too big a risk."

"Wan shell on top av me bivvy manes th' same thing," retorted Clancy. "Say quick an' I'll be on me way. The Jerry niver fires his gun whin it's gettin' light. Are ye agreed, sir?"

A hand gripped Clancy's and he received a cold automatic. "Good luck to you, you old bear cat," was all the officer said.

As Clancy crawled under the wire barricade in front he heard the men along the trench stamping their feet and pounding their arms as they mustered for stand-to. The rattle of equipment and low mutters of conversation gave him assurance - his mates were near by.

But when he skirted a brick heap and crossed a mess of ruins that was a field of fire for both sides, he felt his flesh creep. Suppose a nervous gunner in either trench wished to warm up his weapon before standing down? There was no escape. The thought nerved him to rise erect and almost run for the shack he sought. It 'bulked eerily in the half-light like a skeleton that had missed burial. He entered by way of a window and found the lower part of the stairs shot away.

Careful of every move, he gripped the casing and found footholds in shattered woodwork that enabled him to scale to the upper floor. Part of it had vanished, leaving a shelf-like portion near the eaves. This was covered with shattered tiles, Clearing a place so that he could lie flat in the corner next to the Hun trench, the Irishman eased himself into as comfortable a position as possible and wished he had waited for his rations.

The east lightened. Desultory rifle shots merged into rapid fire from both trenches. Trench mortars crashed, spasmodically and the heavies made sullen exchanges. Then everything quieted and the sunrise scattered the mist.

The first thing that Clancy noticed was that the roof of the shack was much more shattered than he had thought. Tiles were torn off by sections. To his right was a gap that forbade his rising more than six inches from where he lay. Then his spine tightened as he realized that he could be seen from in front. Three tiles had been shot away leaving openings that made him feel naked to view.

His fingers trembled as he picked up a tile and endeavoured to replace it. It slipped from his grasp and perspiration broke over him as he barely prevented it from crashing to the floor below. With the coolness of desperation, he looked down into the German trench. Five Huns, probably a carrying detail, passed down a C.T. each laden with a petrol tin. Their coal-cuttle hats bobbed queerly as they lowered their heads to pass a low spot. Four stout defenders of the Fatherland were grouped in a bay, conversing.

Clancy alternately sweat and shivered an they kept peering ahead, as if watching for aeroplanes. Presently they disappeared into a dugout entrance. Some yards from where they had been, a lone sentry sat on the fire-step with his eye to a periscope. Now and then - he would relax and glance up and down the trench. Once he removed his helmet revealing the scowling brutish face of a Bavarian, the square, close-cropped head of his kind.

Inch by inch, Clancy pushed backward. Inch by inch he moved tiles in front of the nearest of the dim holes piling them up until they blocked the opening. Then, by lying on his side close in to the end wall of the house, he was fairly hidden and could peer out through a crack under the eaves directly over the suspected garden area. The sun rose higher. Three more sentries were in view and he detected four dugout entrances. He could see, fresh-made repairs to their parapets, a lane in their wire for the use of patrols, their gas alarms, but there was not a trace of the hiding place of the mysterious machine gun that each night spewed death over the party of the C.M.R.'s, shooting so low that the Canadians hardly dare look over the top.

By noon Clancy was aching in every bone and hungry as a shark. He thought of Miss Flemming and resolved for the hundredth time to, take her the wanted souvenirs.

In the middle of the afternoon a five-nine battery began a systematic shoot of a Hun back road, and brisk counter work ensued. Several times rushing shells barely missed Clancy's shelter. He forgot every cramp and ache and lived ages before the fire slackened. The sun was hot and he grew very thirsty. This led him to think of wells, and he saw the shattered stem of a pump near the garden.

Then he saw something that seemed odd, a, path led into the lower plots, a path that came from the Hun trench and followed an opening in the Hun wire. Why this path? As he pondered this problem his wits quickened and he made another discovery. A portion of one of the flower beds had withered considerably, a portion about the size of a door!

The guns awoke at dusk and administered the usual evening hate. Machine guns sputtered and the work of killing was resumed. Clancy swung down from his loft and cat-footed to a shallow ditch near the garden. For an hour he waited and nothing unusual happened. Tiring of inaction, he risked all in a hasty exploration of the withered flower plot. He felt along the grassed edges near the patch, across the front, down the other side. then thrilled from head to heels as his fingers dosed on a large iron ring.

He lifted it. Without a sound a trap door was raised exposing a black opening beneath. For a heartbeat the Irishman paused, debating going for assistance. Then German voices decided the issue. He slid into the darkness beneath, feeling with his feet, lowering the door as he went. His toes touched steps and soon he was on a sort of platform. Bending, he touched a tripod, then the barrel of a machine gun. There was not a sound in the place, but the very silence was oppressive. He could not endure the suspense. He struck a match and its glare showed him belts of ammunition beside the gun, a string of potato-masher bombs, and steps down into a tunneled way.

Cupping his light he went down into the place. It reeked of German odours, the stifling smell of closed-in underground. To the left extended sleeping quarters that held four bunks; niches in the wall held more bombs. To the right was a small chamber that contained a second machine gun and a small table on which lay candies, a water bottle, some cloth caps of queer design. and a wool-covered club. He picked it up, one of the silencers used by patrols. The caps were to pull over the head when on the same mission. The next instant Clancy's heart did a drop kick. Someone opened the trap door!

Flashlight rays shot down the steps. Heavy feet landed on the platform, a guttural voice gave orders. Clancy gripped his silencer and as the light shifted upwards to the gun, slipped by to the sleeping quarters where a gas blanket hung on the entrance. He stood in its folds pressed back to the wall.

There were two Germans on the platform working with the gun. Presently the light went out and cool air rushed in as the trap was opened wide. There came a series of grunts, scraping of hobnailed boots. then the rat-tat-tat-tat of the gun. Two long bursts, then the gunners plumped down on the platform again, the gun was lifted down, the cool air ceased, just as angry snappings above told of answering fire. Clancy could not help admiring the cleverness of the Huns. They could fire quickly and duck into their refuge in a moment.

The light came on again and one of the gunners came down the steps and entered the small chamber. He laid his torch on the table and busied himself with the second gun.

A moment he tinkered with the weapon and then sorted the cloth cap-masks. Stepping back, the fellow stooped and looked under the table, picked up the flashlight and searched the floor. Clancy divined his trouble. The German had missed the silencer.

The gunner above called impatiently and received a tense, guttural answer. Instantly his heavy feet scraped on the lower steps and he bulked into the tunnel. The Irishman freed his arm from the blanket folds and struck as the Hun turned into the chamber. A dull thud told of the force of his blow and his victim dropped without a sound. The first gunner tried to snap off the light a fraction too late. Clancy shot before he could, raise a cry and in the dugout the report of the automatic rang sharply.

The next instant he had plunged over the prostrate man at his feet and seized the electric torch as it rolled toward him. He played the light on the man he had shot and saw he was dead, but the Hun he had felled was still breathing. Placing the torch on the floor he ripped down the gas blanket and split it into long strips that served as ropes. In a trice he had bound his man hand and foot and dragged him to the sleeping port.

Before he could make another move, someone called sharply from the trap door. Clancy scuffled his feet on the plank flooring and made a gruff, unintelligible reply. Thump! Someone crashed down inside and burst into the tunnel. It was an arrogant Bavarian officer his face crimson with rage. "Gott in Himmel!" he raved.

Thud! Clancy's silencer connected accurately with the Hun's skull. None of the machine gun crew wore helmets, as they would be awkward for ducking in and out of the trap door, and their cloth caps were no protection. The officer was pulled in beside the first sleeper and bound likewise.

A string of gutturals descended into the pit, the new voice being anxious and inquiring. Again Clancy essayed a gruff response and once more it bore results, but the fourth comer was more cautious. He beat down and peered into the tunnel from the gun platform. The Irishman knew a slip would be fatal and moved swiftly. He risked all in a blind charge at the newcomer. There was a startled yelp of alarm, scurrying, struggling noises. The German had tried to get out of the pit and Clancy had seized his legs. With a mighty heave he yanked the man downwards.

The trap door slammed shut and simultaneously a barrage of rifle grenades burst outside. The C.M.R.'s were making sure that no gun operated in the garden, and with a shiver the Irishman realized that he was supposed to be over on the left in the old shack. Danger dogged every move he could make. The Hun he jerked down had alighted on the machine gun and the fellow groaned at the impact. Clancy toppled him over the lower steps and thrust him into the tunnel.

"Niver mind yer groanin'," he snarled as he propelled the fellow toward the sleeping part. "Yer lucky to be alive at all."

He used the remaining strands of the blanket to wind his captive into an imitation of an Egyptian mummy, and laid him beside the officer. That gentleman was still unaware of his surroundings and made no objections. “Now, me childer," said Clancy grimly, "I've almost forgotten th' most important part of my errand, th' searchin, av yer pockets. It's souvenirs I'm wantin’.”

He surveyed the gun pit and saw that the trap door was shut tight. Perhaps he would not he disturbed for a few moments. He worked fast. The three privates donated little more than their Gott Mitt Uns belts and shoulder straps, but the officer was a real find. He wore an Iron Cross of high order, had maps and code books in leather covers, a pearl-handled automatic, a watch and a purse stuffed with marks. The Irishman was so excited that he almost overlooked the equipment and clothing that hung in the small chamber where the dead man lay. His investigations there netted him enough to fill one of the two German haversacks he found. He deliberated a moment, then placed both on the floor and divided his booty, two belts in one, two in the other, two trench knives in one, two in the other. It evened out until he had all stowed except the Iron Cross, maps and code books. Buckling up the haversacks, he slung one from each shoulder gripped his silencer, went up the steps and pushed up the trap door.

For the moment all was still, With a long hiss a Verey light shot up in a parabola that revealed every detail of the garden. He saw that there were no sentries watching at the path end but easily made out the machine gun posts he had discerned in the day time. As the flare died he scrambled out of the pit, let the door down, and hurried to his left. His automatic was held ready but he could not afford caution, for at any moment the gunners of either side might loose a few rounds over that deadly flat area in front of the gun pit. His circling route carried him nearly to the old ruin again and he froze immobile as a brick was dislodged by some invisible prowler. Crouched low, he waited while six shadowy figures crept out from the building and passed within feet of him. He waited until they were ten minutes gone. and then hurried on towards the C.M.R. trench. He knew that the Hun would not shoot carelessly while his patrol was abroad and that 'D' Company would be expecting him in.

Hurdling debris, avoiding something from which rats scurried, detouring shell holes, he was perspiring when a sharp voice bade him halt. At the same instant his knees sawed into barbed wire.

"It’s Tim Clancy, ye fool," he snorted, untangling himself. "Where in th' divil is th' hole in this wire?"

"Gosh! He did get back," said the voice. "Bear to your left, Tim. Yer nearly to it."

In the trench Clancy was surrounded by eager questioners. The platoon Sergeant, the scout officer, Greer, a runner, and sentry reliefs, all shot different queries.

"Wan at a time," Clancy shot back. "Is this a tay party?" In graphic words he explained the mystery of the machine gun that shot so low; in another terse sentence his adventure in the pit, then he asked for 3 volunteers to go with him and bring in the prisoners. "I kin be there an' back in five minutes,"he snapped.

"Wan man is all I want."

Every man except Greer offered. Clancy was about to pick his partner when another officer came hurrying up a C.T. It was the same man who had arrived late on the night of the raid, Captain Boyd, nicknamed. "Dolly" by the battalion.

"What's this?" he demanded. "Did you locate the gun, Clancy?"

The Irishman told his story more tersely than before. He was losing time.

"Great stuff!" The Captain slapped him on the shoulder. "You want to get them, eh? Good enough - take Greer with you. Bring the prisoners to the lane at this post."

Clancy spun around and gave the corporal a hoist up the parapet. "Git movin'," he hissed. "Old Fritz'll be investigatin' before we git there."

Through the wire he was forced to guide Greer by a hold on his arm. The N.C.O. seemed dazed with fright, and when they disturbed the rats again, he shrank in horror. "H'i cawn't go h'on," he wheezed, trying to duck into a shell crater. "Go git the jerries h'and H'i will be 'ere when you come back."

The Irishman shoved the barrel of his pistol in the Cockney's back. "Ye'll kape goin' with me or ye'll be mate fer th' rats," he whispered. "Kape yer mug closed and kape trampin'."

But at the last shell hole before the garden he let the Corporal slide into a hole. It would be easier getting the prisoners out alone.

All three were conscious when he flashed the light in the tunnel, and the eyes of the supercilious officer were like those of a wild animal.

"Ye make me laugh, Von Kluck," chaffed Clancy as he slashed the leg bonds of each. "Ye smile so pritty." He kicked them upright. Then he reached up the steps and unhooked a potato-masher. Flashing the light for the last time, he threatened them savagely with the automatic, pointing upward and indicating that they were to follow him. By signs he explained that delay would mean his dropping the bomb among them. Then he tossed the torch behind him and hurried out of the pit.

As he knelt at the entrance waiting for the first prisoner to appear, someone coughed in the German trench. A gruff voice made comment and other voices joined in. The Hun was still in ignorance of events in the garden. A head and shoulders thrust up beside Clancy and he assisted the fellow up beside him, then made him lie down. The second Bavarian appeared and received like treatment, but the Irishman was about to close the trap and hurl the potato-masher before the officer pushed into view. He was handled roughly, the privates were roused and with his trio in front of hint, Clancy hustled to find Greer.

The Corporal was still in the crater when the Irishman located him. Without a word the party moved on, Clancy being too contemptuous for speech.

At the wire he encountered difficulties. A dozen sibilant whispers tried to give directions and during the mix-up every gun in the German trench opened fire. Evidently Fritz had discovered his loss and sought revenge. Clancy was obliged to huddle among his captives in a slimy ditch not twenty feet from safety. For full ten minutes they lay, then the whine of bullets died away and one by one the guns stilled.

Greer got to his feet and crawled till he found the gap, when he called to Clancy. Before the Irishman could herd his prizes into the lane. Captain Boyd had mounted the parapet and assisted the Corporal in turning the captives into the trench.

An hour later Clancy was in his dugout devouring his day's rations. He ate and drank to bursting, then lay back and filled a black pipe. He was at peace with the world for a time. In one haversack under his bunk were enough souvenirs to spell a good time at Lozinghem. A second sack, with duplicate contents would serve as a munificent gift for Miss Flemming. What more could he ask? And as he smoked he pictured the jealousy of his mates as they saw him present his trophy.

"Is Private Clancy there?" a voice asked. It was Captain Dolly Boyd invading the men's quarters. "I hear you have a map and notes you took from the prisoner," said the officer. "Please hand them over. We always give such articles to the intelligence department."

Clancy took the books from his pocket and handed them over without a word.

The Captain lingered. "I don't know whether it's true or not." he added, "but one of the men said you had a haversack of souvenirs."

" Tis true," said Clancy proudly. "An' they'll make yer eyes stick out. Here, have a peep at thim."

From under his bunk he drew one of the haversacks and disclosed it's load of belts, badges, cloth caps and straps, gas masks etc. "Now thim. things is worth money." said Clancy, visioning a quick sale, "an' bein' as wan av our own officers I'll sell to ye right. I'll take..."

"Clancy!" Dolly Boyd could speak sternly when he wished. "You must know it's against regulations to take such articles from prisoners. I must confiscate that lot, and don't let me hear of such a thing happening again."

In helpless, profane amazement Clancy watched his bag of treasure disappear up the dugout stairs. It was unbelievable. The scout officer had known of his booty and had made no comment. "Av all th' lousy skunks that iver contaminated me presence, that bhoy takes th' cake," fumed the Irishman. "Him that's so frightened av iverythin' that he slapes under his cot, th' yellow coot! Do ye suppose..."

The thought was too stunning - impossible. Could it be that Boyd sought the lovely V.A.D.'s affections? Sympathizers crowded about his bunk. One had seen Boyd talking to Miss Flemming, another had seen him at the hospital. Two had known him to be at the "Y" that exciting second night.

Out on rest, Dolly Boyd was a dashing sort of officer, easy to look at, and a glib talker. He had a reputation as a heart-breaker, crisp curly hair, and serene eyes which could have out-stared the devil.

When they marched out to billets again the Irishman had lost his assurance. His conviction that the Captain would sidetrack him had become an obsession. Therefore he dallied over his shaving and cleaning and was last to be ready for the evening. With his haversack in his hand he went to the hospital and asked to see Miss Flemming the V.A.D.

"She is out," he was curtly informed. "She has gone to the "Y", and was accompanied by Captain Boyd."

Clancy could scarce repress a groan. Sick at heart he headed for the road branching to the aerodrome at Auchel. He would sell his souvenirs and get gloriously drunk. Then he halted. Captain Boyd was billeted at the house on the corner. Very grimly he entered and pushed by the stout madame who was sipping coffee. He knew the officer's room, and if any of his souvenirs remained, he would take them along for disposal. They were his rightful possessions.

There was not a trace, however, of the Hun haversack, but peeping from a cupboard was a tall bottle labeled "House of Lords." The Irishman's mouth watered. No better whisky was manufactured. He slipped the bottle under his tunic and came out. Madame still sipped her coffee. Dodging into an alley to have a drink, Clancy saw that he was beside Lozinghem's most elite hostel, a restaurant that bore the well-known legend: "For Officers Only."

Pausing beneath an open window, he heard a husky-sweet voice in startled exclamation: "My, but you are a brave man, a real knight of the trenches!"

"Why, Miss Flemming, that was nothing, I assure you." came the silky tones of Dolly Boyd. "The gun had to be located, you understand, and I couldn't send men where I wouldn't go myself. So, to save time, I leaped the parapet and went alone. I won't describe the scrapping-you don't like to hear of bloodshed - but I'll say this, the prisoners that I rushed back are trembling yet. There were ten of them, and I won't tell you how many I left at the pit."

Clancy stood like a statue, bewildered. Was there no way to save this girl from such a blow-hard? Shaking his head, he went out of the alley without taking a drink, cudgeling his brain for ideas.

Hardly had he gained the sidewalk when two horses came pounding down the roadway, their hoofs striking sparks on the cobbles. A vociferous command and both animals slid to a halt. Clancy stared in surprise at the giant who dismounted, a huge man arrayed in scarlet breeches, blue tunic, and a helmet with a horse-tail plume. In a perfect sputter of language the giant asked questions. Clancy shook his head, and the other rider hurried to the rescue.

"Monsieur, excuse, please, my Captain. He sometimes drink too much wine, but he has monie. He wishes to buy, purchase, some 'souvenir,' you call heem of the trench. It would make fun to do so from some people, but, la - we dragoons have not had opportunity to win them, comprez?"

"An' yer wishin' to buy souvenirs, is ut?" Clancy could hardly believe his good fortune. "Sure an' I'm sellin' thim. Have wan look at this lot, will ye? Wan hundred francs takes thim."

The giant called a boy to hold the horses, then he, Clancy and the orderly entered a small estaminet to examine the offered goods. The collection seemed to please.

"He offer one hundred seventy-five franc." said the interpreter, after a noisy harangue by the big man.

"I'll take ye," snapped Clancy promptly.

His offer had not been understood. Very promptly he buckled the haversack and handed it over. Just as promptly the giant shelled four notes and gave them to the Irishman. They were four fifty-franc notes.

"I've no change." stammered Clancy. "Kin ye wait wan minute?"

The big man spread his hand nonchalantly. Clancy could take his time. The Irishman warmed to such a buyer. With the generosity of his race he pulled the "House of Lords" from its hiding.

"Hilp yersilves," he stated grandly. "I'll be back in wan minute."

"Non, non!" cried the giant, before the Irishman reached the door. The whisky had touched the right spot. He ordered Clancy to forget the change and the bottle was emptied, the Frenchman getting two drinks to the Irishman's one. Then they went out to the horses. The Hun haversack was made fast to the giant's saddle and then the trio walked down the street. The Frenchmen seemed loathe to leave their friend, and Clancy wished to be polite. They were opposite the "Officers Only" when the Irishman began to think at top speed.

“My Captain would buy you one bottle of wine," stammered the orderly, who was having difficulty with his legs, "Wait for one moment."

Clancy accepted the reins of the horses and the invitation. A wild thought had set him on fire. There was a chance to...

Hardly had the Frenchmen entered the place than Clancy had wrenched the Hun haversack from the saddle and heaved it over a wooden gate between the restaurant and the establishment of Madame Doucet. A moment later his friends returned bearing two long bottles of champagne.

"Be pleased to have one token of gratitude," piped the orderly, struggling to mount his horse.

There was a roar from the giant, rapid-fire explosions. His trophies were gone. Clancy was seized. He made hasty explanations to his drink-mad captor. An officer had passed and had taken the bag as a joke and gone into the restaurant with a lady. There was a wild yell as the orderly interpreted, and the next instant the huge Captain of Dragoons went plunging through the doorway.

Clancy left the valet with both horses and rushed to the door. He was just in time to see the irate French giant shake his fist in Boyd's face, cram the souvenirs that lay on the table into the Hun haversack, snap it shut and wheel out. Captain Dolly sat hunched in his chair as if he expected worse things to follow - and they did. The giant dragoon looked back and shouted some wild defiance at the officer who dared play jokes. Boyd essayed a sickly grin, evidently thinking he was out of danger. That weak grin brought fresh disaster.

A waiter had just placed a bowl of soup in front of Miss Flemming. Hissing some mad imprecation, the giant caught up the bowl and deluged Dolly with its contents, then bowed gracefully to the startled V.A.D. A moment later, thunderous hoof beats announced his departure from the village.

Clancy dodged around the corner of the restaurant and unlatched the gate that led to the rear of Madame Doucet's establishment. He found the haversack he had thrown and snatched it up. There was no time to make a getaway down the street, so he calmly entered madame's back porch.

A well-known voice halted him: "H'and then I 'its the blighter h'over the 'ead. 'Don't git so ruddy 'uffy when I awsks yer a question,' I says. Wiv that the 'ole blinkin' crowd, twelve big fat 'Uns, 'ikes back as meek as lambs. Next thing is the Captain wantin' to know wot abaht it. Do I want a medal or leave? 'Leave,' says I. Wot good's a bleedin' medal?' Then..."

"Corp!" At Clancy's low call there was a slight scramble, then silence. " 'Tis Tim, ye fool!" There was no time to lose. "Kin I spake ye a word in private?"

Corporal Greer emerged from a corner bench. "Ye are goin' on leave at tin o'clock," said Clancy impressively. "Listen. Here's me sack av souvenirs fer ye, a prisint to show there's no hard feelin's. I'll stick th' bag in yer blankets while ye are doin' me a little favour. Cut around to this 'Officers Only' an' escort Miss Flemming to th' 'Y'. Don't stop to ask quistions. Beat it, an' make no mintion av souvenirs ayther. But ye can whisper jist what kind of a critter is Dolly Boyd, an' maybe put in a fair word fer Tim Clancy-a fair wan, mind ye. Now, alley toot sweet."

Clancy lost no time. He cut corners to the billet and placed the haversack as promised, then raced for the "Y". He made his objective ahead of a couple who were walking slowly past as he hid in a doorway.

"Miss, I tells yer strite," the high cockney accent was unmistakable, "this Captain Boyd is a germ, e' is. Down in th' dugout when old Jerry is strafin', down in a perishin' 'ole wiv 'is batman. 'Ee's yeller as a canary, miss, h'and Tim Clancy-'im-strike me pink but there's not a blighter in 'D' Company wot' as a bad word abaht him. Like a lion, 'e is, in the trenches. Lawst time in 'im and we went over and pulled in a bally 'Un party wot 'ad a gun planted in a nawsty plice. 'Im-Tim Clancy- 'ee's one of them knights as you wos speakin' abaht-that's 'im."

The 'Y' door opened and shut and Clancy emerged from his hiding. He felt in his upper tunic pocket and assured himself that the ribbon and Iron Cross were there, then took a turn up the street before entering. Greer was by the entrance, waiting. His eyes sought Clancy's, and at the Irishman's nod he left the room as if called.

Never did the CMR's sing more lustily than that night. Miss Flemming, flushed with the evening's excitement, was at her best, and everyone was happy. At the close, Clancy adroitly manoeuvred his way to the piano and asked the favour of seeing her back to her tent.

"Why - it's Sir Clancy!" she exclaimed. "I am honoured. Certainly, you can come with me. I-I'm tired of officers."

She chattered merrily as they went to the hospital. Clancy was tongue-tied till she was about to bid him good-night.

"Wan minute, miss," he pleaded. "I've a bit av a souvenir fer ye. Ye said ye wanted something av th' trinches, an' I've got it."

"Something you won yourself?" she asked breathlessly.

"Not exactly." Clancy was very deliberate. "'Tis a trinket I bought from the cook. He was out pickin' firewood in No Man's Land an' stumbled into a nest av Heinies. He downed thim with a stake he'd picked up and took this medal off th' chist of an officer."

He proffered the Iron Cross, glittering prettily under its ribbon.

"Sir Timothy Fergus Clancy-you-you are one gallant knight. I-I can't pay you - I - she stopped in confusion, and accepted the medal.

Then, before Clancy could gasp, two soft arm went around his neck and a long warm kiss was planted on his leathery cheek. A scurry of feet and he was alone.

Very solemnly he looked up at the moon, and winked.

At the billet he found his platoon making ready for sleep. One enterprising lad had heated water in a dixie he had borrowed from the cooks. "Yah can have a bucket," he called. "It's glood an' hot yet."

A good wash with warm water was a luxury. Clancy flung off his tunic and searched for soap. Then he halted, and a slow grin spread from ear to ear. "Thanks jist th' same, me bhoy," he answered, turning back to his bunk, "but I won't bother. I've wan cheek I won't wash fer a week."

CHAPTER EIGHT

THE FICKLE FEMALE

THE carrying party wound its weary way from the head of Napoo Valley and entered the abysmal murk of a deep communication trench. It was a blasphemous, straggling crew, headed for the front line and burdened with T frames. They stumbled over loose trench walks and tripped on stray strands of wire, and the last man of all was Timothy Fergus Clancy.

He had reasons for manoeuvering to this position. In order to avoid congestion in the front line trench the first carriers to arrive would be sent to the utmost flanks with their loads, while the last of the party would be allowed to deposit theirs at the end of the communication trench. Again, he wished to avoid meeting Major Dash, newly in command of 'D' Company. Cookhouse rumours declared the Major to be imbued with the ardour prevalent at base "bull rings" and enthusiastic about adding to the glory and fighting reputation of the C.M.R.'s.

The previous night this Boche-thirsty individual had issued orders that the men of his company were to be more aggressive. Every shot from the enemy rifle or machine gun, was to be answered by at least two shots, every patrol that the Germans sent out was to be located and attacked; at night the bombers were to harass every known enemy post with rifle grenades. The Sergeant of Fourteen platoon had brought these glad tidings to his dugout directly after stand-to in the morning, and the various comments that circulated about the underground chamber would have curled the Major's hair had he heard them.

Clancy, frying a concoction of bully, biscuits and cheese, had had feelings too bitter for speech. Later, as he lay on his hen-wire bunk, he had heard one of the company runners in whispered conversation with a member of the platoon. "You'll be jake," said the runner, "as soon as the Major knows you're, a married man. The old gink's one himself, got seven kids they say, and he lets the married men off easy every chance and makes the single ones do all the dirty work."

Clancy, raging inwardly, had heard murmured thanks for the information and sibilant resolves to acquaint the Major at once with his marital rank. Then he had lain awake a long time, thinking. The Fifth C.M.R.'s were due for strenuous times. One or two raids were to be pulled off in this Avion sector, that much was certain, and there were persistent rumours of a general attack on Hill 70. What chance, under the exposed conditions, would a single man have of lasting till September and enjoying his hard-won leave? Clancy had reached a decision about the time the Sergeant came to warn him for the evening's carrying party; he would immediately get married.

As the carrying party filed into the front line each man in turn was confronted by the Company Sergeant-Major. He was picking men for some detail, which every member of the party was morally certain would prove something disagreeable, and three miserable victims were already standing beside him.

"You too, Clancy," he growled. "Hand over that T frame to someone, and come here."

Clancy obeyed without a word. He and the Sergeant-Major had an over-ripe acquaintance. "What is it for?" he asked the trio he joined.

"I dunno," grated one, "but I believe it's to bury that Heinie that's out back there."

"Naw," hissed number two. "The Captain's batman told me it was for a sacrifice bunch that's to test out some new-fangled gas masks, and I ask you..."

"You're wrong, both of you," snorted number three. "We're invited special to the Brigadier's birthday party."

"Keep still, will you," grated the Sergeant-Major. "Do you want the Germans to hear us?"

The quartet looked at each other. The regular night strafing was an and it was at least two hundred yards to the Hun lines, but every mud-eater in 'D' Company had his own estimate of the Sergeant-Major's courage.

"Come this way." The four men followed, Clancy again in the rear. "You men are to go out to Newlillers and take a week's bombing course. Get your packs and report to Corporal Dick of Fifteen platoon.

A bombing course! Clancy stifled a groan. Instruction in the use of Mills grenades, how to throw from a narrow trench, how to shorten the fuse for assault work, how to avoid elevation when throwing the shortfused ones. Then-as sure as there was a war on-back to the trenches to take part in a raid. It was the old, old story. Clancy had seen many small parties report to the rear for such and similar instructions, seen them on their way back, all identifications removed, and a "death or glory" sag to their shoulders. Grimly he renewed his decision. He would get married before the week was up.

Newlillers was no treat to the eye, ear or nose. It was the tail-end of a much more imposing village on the road to Mont St. Eloi, but an epidemic of staff officers in the larger town made Clancy feel that he was in a fairly safe territory. He knew his surroundings, remembered them from a brief sojourn there as his battalion came from the Somme the previous autumn, and made at once for a squat house near his billet, a little estaminet, which, like the widow's curse, never ran dry of dubious wines and muddy coffee. He had no intention of looking on the wine when it was rouge, but he did hope to exchange a few pairs of army socks for a plate of eggs and chips.

Madame was a stout placid creature with a bored bovine expression. She was addicted to wooden sabots and she clattered around Clancy like a long lost friend when he informed her that he had visited her establishment the previous year. "Soldats plenty money then," she sighed. "No bon now."

"Sure an' we had no place to spend it on th' Somme," said Clancy. "And now ye can't git out av th' trinches for canteens. But me paymaster is a Jew and I've had no money from home for a long time."

It was but a war-worn chance remark, meant to impress madame, if possible, in the slim hope of obtaining credit.

"Ah," sighed madame. "You are one they call lucky. Me, I am more poor than ever. A sister to keep and now a niece. I am starved soon."

“A niece!" Clancy halved the last egg on his plate and swallowed without effort. "I disremember seein' yer family. Have ye any daughters?"

"The food had warmed him to a talkative point and he now recollected his main purpose in life. And to get a wife in seven days, back of the Vimy front, one must not be too particular.

"No-no," said madame. "I am alone with my husband dead, but his sister comes with me because a shell hits her house at Viller-Au-Bois. Ah, monsieur, it is terrible, and now this niece."

"Is she young?" asked Clancy as casually as possible. "Could she not be helpin' ye' about th' kitchen?"

"But what to do?" asked madame. "There is but the hens and pig and my husband's sister." Madame shook her head. "My niece is nineteen," she sighed.

Clancy lighted his pipe and sat at attention. "Sure an' she'll be fine company fer ye," he said heartily, “anyway she'll soon be marryin' an' leavin' ye."

"Not her," said madame. "Suzanne will not be pleased with men. She is - what you say - particular."

"I'm glad to hear that," exclaimed Clancy. "'Tis th' right spirit and she must be intelligent. Let her pick her man, madame, and she'll git the right wan."

Madame sighed again and gave him another cup of coffee. "You are a Canadian," she said. "Do you have much land?"

Ah-ha! Clancy's heart gave a flop. Madame sounded as if she were interested. This Suzanne was just his chance. She was probably a delicate flower, a convent-bred type, rather dreading the average young French villager. "No," said Clancy. "I'm with the Canadians, but jist on account of me happenin' to be tourin' thim parts when the war broke out. I have me estate in Ireland, madame. Killybegs, Ireland."

"Estate, is it?" gurgled madame. "It would be a grand place?"

"It is, that," said Clancy complacently, lighting his pipe. "When are ye expectin' yer niece?"

"Tomorrow," said madame. I cannot refuse her, homeless one, alone."

"Bless yer kind heart," said Clancy softly. "Ye will be rewarded. Good night to ye. I'll see ye tomorrow."

He was on hand promptly when the estaminet opened at noon the next day, and spent a franc that he had borrowed in order to smooth his way with madame. There was no need of it. Madame clattered about him in kindly fashion and absentmindedly served him an extra glass of beer. Then she coyly indicated an inner room and invited him to enter. He was on his feet in an instant, bowing politely.

"Monsieur Clancy,” said madame. "This is Suzanne.”

Clancy, still bowing, had a total eclipse of his vocal powers. Suzanne, instead of the frail butterfly he had visioned, was a sturdy, full-bosomed, dynamic blonde, as red-headed and sudden and stunning as a train wreck. Her English was as good as madame's. "I expected a Captaine," she said, tossing her chin. "Are you a fighting soldat?"

With difficulty Clancy fought his way back to earth and regained his speech. "I am that," he said huskily. "I belong to th' Fifth C.M.R.’s and any truthful man kin tell ye that they are foremost av th' entire army."

"So," mocked Suzanne, "but where is the medal, the ribbon for valour?"

"Niver would I accept thim," said Clancy, after the briefest of pauses. "Av what use are th' trinkets? I've refused thim a hundred times."

"Oui?" said Suzanne. "It does not seem possible, but you look the brave soldier."

Clancy thrilled, his pulse raced, his heart pounded. This buxom, quick-eyed maiden was becoming friendly. Could he win her in seven days?

He took a seat on a smooth worn sofa and began to relate a few instances on which he had won - and refused - the Victoria Cross. Suzanne, listening attentively, gradually seemed more impressed, and he waxed more eloquent. He liked her breathless way of looking at him. Adoration was warm in her blue eyes.

When the seven days were up Clancy had won his bride-almost. It had been a strenuous case of love making, but he was no amateur. The first impediment had been madame's husband's sister a swarthy, hawkeyed dame who seemed suspicious of all the human race. Her presence had rasped Clancy like sandpaper, and she had taken pains to make her presence evident wherever possible. The very first evening as he and Suzanne had sat in the little room getting acquainted she had entered and sat near them, listening to every word and snuffling with a cold.

Clancy endured it until it was time to go and Suzanne was getting him a bowl of coffee. "Not so much rum in it," said Clancy needlessly. "I'm dizzy now. I've a feelin' that we've been crowded in here. Whin kin I see ye by yerself? T'is a long time since I've had such a trate fer me eyes, and t'is painful to have too strong contrasts at hand."

Suzanne had giggled and giggled until her aunt rose and poured forth a deluge of French, her eyes darting venom. "What's th' trouble with old hawk-eyes?" he asked as she left them.

"Nothing at all matters," said Suzanne airily. "She is afraid you are not always telling the truth. I laugh because it is always so with men."

"Now kin yez beat that?" said Clancy reproachfully. "Me takin' sich care to spake right and truthful, and not believed because I haven't a flower garden av ribbons on me chist."

"But it is difficult to know," said Suzanne, with a tilt of her head. "If it was but one medal I would be sure..."

"Would ye now," said Clancy eagerly. "Thin by th' glory of ould

Ireland I'll have wan."

He had been ready to promise her anything as he gazed at her. She was wearing a fluffy film of dress with frills - as provocative as a glance over the shoulder, and her satiny plumpness made his veins riotous.

Three nights later he had asked her to marry him. It was the first evening they had been able to evade old "hawk-eyes" for an hour at once, and he had made the most of his opportunity. Suzanne made him perspire as she probed him with difficult questions, but he at length convinced her that his representations were correct and accepted him-on conditions. He was to win her a medal for bravery, and when he had the ribbon, she would marry him at once.

In vain he coaxed her to change her mind, and the rest of his precious week went by as if on skids. Then came the inevitable raiding preparations. Though at every hour of the day Clancy's mind was in madame's back parlour, with its waxed flowers in a glass case, and its coloured portrait of Napoleon, he had impressed his bombing instructor, with the result that he was chosen leader of the raiders, and after a fond farewell at the estaminet, during which he kissed madame and exchanged black looks with "hawk-eyes", he left for the front.

No Man's Land at the head of Napoo Valley was the most disgraceful of its kind in the Avion sector. Its powdered, rat-haunted piles of brick were intersected by a foul ditch slimed with greenish water that stank under the July sun, a ditch that extended from the wire of the CMR's to the trench of the enemy. In front of the German line the area was strewn with all the wreckage of a farmyard, spattered with the filth of a shell-tormented midden. A more loathsome spot for men to cross in the dark could hardly be imagined, and for this very reason Major Dash was convinced that it was ideal territory for his raiders. The Hun would not be on his guard at such a point, would never expect a raiding party.

An enemy post had been spotted very near to where the ditch entered the German wire, and various ways of approach were considered. Everything, from the use of a smoke barrage to the launching of a submarine, was suggested without results, and the Major would not hear of anything but a direct advance in the dark, without assistance from the artillery. He arranged, however, for the guns to place a harassing, all-day shoot on the German end of the trench and its environments. The raiders were to prepare for filthy travelling, were to wear any garments they could salvage, and were to be allowed 48 hours off afterward to clean their clothing. "But," said

Dash, "if no prisoners are brought in there will be another raid the very next night."

Clancy crawled forth with fervent emotions, his pistol and many Mills bombs. He had with him a select band of trench pirates but his heart was not in his work. The one silver lining was that he might win a medal for Suzanne.

The raiders crawled and crawled until Clancy was sure they must be near the farm ruins. He halted and they listened a long time. There was not a sound of activity on the Hun front. "Did ye notice," Clancy breathed to the nearest man, "that we have a bit av luck? Th' wind is direct on th' Heinies and th' smells are no worse than they are any time in thim French farmyards."

A long spark streaked into the dark and burst into a whitish glow that hovered for a second or two, throwing eerie shadows over the brick heaps directly in front of them and revealing the contours of the wide ditch on their right. The light died abruptly, and the ensuing darkness was a baffling void. Clancy led on until they were at the bricks, then he waited until all his four men were beside him. A machine gun rattled defiance, the Maxim at the ditch post, and its note rose to a higher, sharper crack-crack-crack as it swept over the group of invaders. It reeded and toned down as it swept away and suddenly ceased. "Careful now and kape together?" hissed Clancy.

They went on, bruising themselves on the brick corners, twisting ankles in the uncertain footing, groping, feeling, and it was Clancy himself who suddenly pitched forward into a barrel-like crater that had seeped full of an unholy mixture. One zealous member of the patrol grasped him at once and dragged him back so swiftly that both his elbows were skinned and Clancy's language, when he could speak, was more livid than coherent. He strangled and spat, and spat and strangled, then deliberately rose to his feet and walked toward the Hun wire, too angry to crawl further and almost blinded by the bath he had taken. The procession went around the bricks in a complete circle, not one of his followers daring to protest, until one hero grasped Clancy just in time to prevent his taking another tumble in the same hole. He had to get down on his knees and examine it before he would believe that he had returned to the same spot. His rage faded then, and the advance Hun-ward was resumed.

The German wire suddenly barred them. They had reached it without alarming the enemy. Again they waited and listened. A dull red flash lit the sky back of Avion, then a long ten seconds afterwards a salvo of whizz-bangs whined over them to burst back of the CMR lines. An uncanny stillness ensued, but the clear rattle of transport on distant paved roads showed how well the night carried sounds. Then, a slight pop as a stream of sparks shot up from some spot near their light and faded in a dazzling floating light. Clancy was facing the Hun machine post and he distinctly saw two figures standing there on duty. He gasped. They looked monstrous, unreal, but as the glow faded he comprehended: The Germans were wearing their gas masks.

"We are in luck, me bhoys," he whispered. "Thim Heinies will never see us with them rigs on."

With the utmost care he reached forward and snipped several strands of Hun wire. No one appeared to be patrolling the trench and no one protested their work. Emboldened, they cut away and cleared a clean passage, then listened some more . There was not a step in the Hun trench, not a cough or murmur. "Let ivery mother's son av yez kape yer ears pinned back," said Clancy. "We're goin' right in an' I don't like this place so peaceful like. Watch yer step."

One by one they filed into the trench, keeping a yard apart, each man with his bombs, a pistol or a "whiffet" held ready. Clancy led, treading like a burglar, and he stopped so quick at the first bay that the man behind bumped into him. A vicious backward poke with his elbow put the fellow into place, just as the sound Clancy had heard was repeated. It was a groan, a long, shuddering, sighing groan, the sound of someone in great agony - and it came from some place very near them.

The groans unnerved Clancy. They were unearthly sounds. His hair bristled under his helmet. Chills chased up his spine. What awaited them? Never had Killybegs seemed so far away or long ago, but suspense was torture. He took another step and another and then his eyes accustomed themselves to the German post. Huddled on the firestep was a diminutive Hun. His gas mask was in his hands, had been jerked off apparently, and his shrapnel helmet lay in the trench where it had fallen. As they looked the man groaned again and became violently sick. Clancy stepped back and clutched his nose. "Phew!" he whispered. "There is something dead in here."

He looked back. Every follower had a firm grip of his nose, and the odours that rode on the night air were beyond description. Then, like a flash, Clancy understood. Their progress down the trench had taken them into the stench-laden wind that came from over the midden and ditch. The shells that had churned them all day had stirred up an aroma exceeding all others.

A moment later Clancy stood, undecided, then he went forward and seized the sick man by the wrist and yanked him to a sitting posture, menacing him with his revolver. The German merely groaned. He stared at Clancy without recognizing an enemy and slumped back on the firestep as soon as his wrist was released. "Wan av yez stay and watch him," said Clancy in an undertone. "Come on, th' rist av ye." The odours were too powerful to admit any delay.

They did not encounter opposition. At the next post was an old flare man, too sick to move. His flare pistol was confiscated and a second man told off to watch him. Clancy and the other raiders stole up to the Maxim post. Its two occupants were still visible, but each man was resting on the parapet, slumped over in an abject posture. Neither of them seemed to hear a thing until Clancy poked his pistol in their backs and grated a fierce threat.

The Germans feebly raised their arms and turned around. Clancy pulled off their gas masks and each man gagged. They were rapidly reaching the advanced stage of sickness. "Come away from here?" ordered Clancy, pointing, and the Huns obeyed with alacrity. It was very obvious that they were only too glad to leave the post.

Clancy halted them by the flare man. Should he attempt to take him as well? Then he saw a stretcher lying on the parados. In an instant he had it down and had rolled the sufferer on it, then prodded his prisoners to action. They bore the old man away, spitting and gasping as they went. "Wan minute," ordered Clancy. "Shoot a flare over th' wire, up th' ditch. It will make th' rist av th' dog-eaters that's kapin' clear av this part think that all is jake up here."

One of the men caught up the flare pistol and tried to use it. He twisted at the trigger, poked, pulled and suddenly the cartridge was exploded. Away soared the streaking sparks - to the rear!

In petrified horror they watched and in the brilliant light saw many coal-scuttle hats coming up a distant communication trench, evidently a relief for the stench-stricken posts, as every man was coming slowly, in his gas mask. "I wished that flare had gone up yer blasted mouth," he finished. "Av all th' tricks I iver seen..." He groaned in unison with the sick man.

But his men proved their worth as raiders. The pair ahead, seeing the approaching carriers, had quickly found a second stretcher and soon had their inert captive through a gap in the wire. The others prodded and hustled the gunners with their burden and in a few seconds the party was clear of the trench. It was too to much to hope, however, to gain back to their own line without trouble.

As they left the slight cover of the brick heaps they heard Hun voices, in guttural argument in the Hun trench, then after a short delay a regular shower of flares went up along the front. There were red rockets, blazing green stars, sizzlin streaks of orange, all giving lustre to the night and arousing the German guns to a perfect frenzy Maxims awoke and grew delirious. From the Canadian side roared retaliation, and hot lead and iron winged over the crouched raiders and their prisoners, until they were awed and deafened to apathy. One of the sick men slept and the raiders calmly seized the opportunity to seek for souvenirs. Clancy watched with disapproval and took care to keep the largest of the huns as his own private property.

Search of his pockets revealed little, however, beyond a few candle ends and a photograph. He thrust in his tunic, resolving to have something to show as a trophy. Then he eyed his captive and had a brain wave. He had managed to salvage enough outer clothing to serve him for the raid, but had only his own shirt. It had seeped in the slime of the crater into which he had dipped. He pointed his pistol and made stern signs. Under muttered protest the gunner obeyed, and under the roaring, crashing, shell-fire removed his shirt. It seemed very new and clean and Clancy donned it cheerfully, giving his prisoner his own defiled garment.

It was over an hour before hostilities slackened and the party got into their own trench. Clancy marshalled the procession direct to Dash's dugout and made a very elaborate report in person, giving account of a hair-raising battle as they were leaving and of a tremendous slaughter of those who had opposed them. His raiders stood by him nobly, verifying every statement, and the Germans themselves were too sick to take interest in proceedings. The Major literally exuded joy. He had heard the tremendous shooting and could imagine the rest. "You have done exceedingly, well," he echoed again and again as he rubbed his hands. "You shall have medals every one of you and you, Clancy, for your share shall have a three-day leave to any of the towns back of the line you choose. I'm proud of you men, and after this we'll put on a raid every time we're in the trenches. We'll go after these Germans until they're terrorized at the name of the CMR's."

There was more in a like strain. The raiders gazed mournfully at each other. Clancy inwardly renewed his resolution to get married to someone, be she madame herself. They mumbled to the Major for his kind words and stole away, slightly heartened by a rum issue.

Back in his own dugout Clancy removed his salvaged clothing and put on his own uniform. He was the centre of an admiring throng, and gravely accepted the homage as his due. With a careless gesture he whipped forth his souvenir photo for examination in the candle light.

"Gosh! is that a Heinie picture? Lookit th' Jane! Them Fritz girls aint so bad lookin'." "I don't like them too fat, but that one ain't bad." This and other exclamations tumbled from the lips of the lookers-on as Clancy gazed. But he made no comments himself. He couldn't. Words would not come to him. He was stricken, paralyzed. The face that smiled up to him was Suzanne in all her plump loveliness. Suzanne, his Suzanne! Why was her photo treasured by a German?

He inspected the picture closely and saw that it was genuine enough, and it had been taken in France, thus proving that she must have sent it to the German. He thought of the fellow as revealed in the dim light of the Major's dugout, a square-headed, heavy-jowled Hun with squinting eyes, who looked as if he should eat out of a trough. Ugh!

Clancy could not answer any of the ribaldry of his mates. He put the photo back in his pocket and went up in the trench to think. There must surely be some mistake - but he had such absolute proof. For an hour he wrestled with the mystery, torturing himself exquisitely, then resolved not to make any judgment on the matter until he was back at Newlillers.

Major Dash had given Clancy permission to wear the ribbon of the Military Medal, as its award was only a question of time and red tape, and his reception at the little estaminet was all that could be wished for had his heart been lighter. Suzanne appeared to him like a bit of porcelain among coarse crockery. She greeted him gushingly, while madame patted his shoulders. Only the hawk-eyed aunt remained aloof and suspicious.

"Now," thrilled Suzanne as they seated themselves. "Tell me all about the ribbon and where the fighting was. Was it at Avion or Lens?"

"Sure an' it was at..." Clancy rolled his eyes. He had barely checked himself in time, and his horrible suspicions were redoubled. Why did Suzanne want to know the exact locality. "It was at Polly Trinch," he finished lamely.

"Polly Trench," echoed Suzanne. "I know not these trenches, stupid. It is the place I wish to know. Tell me, have these Canadians all of Avion?"

"But I couldn't ye tellin' ye if they had," rejoined Clancy. "Ye see it's against orders to tell ye."

"But - to one almos' marry?" pouted Suzanne. "I want so much to know."

Ah! She was too insistent. Clancy was hot and cold by turns. "Were ye acquainted with any av thim Germans afore the war?" he asked casually, trying to joke. "Ye might write an' ask wan av thim."

Crack! Suzanne's moist palm caught Clancy a resounding slap. "It is one insult," she cried.

Clancy rubbed his cheek and forced a smile. "Ye have a swift hand." he said ruefully. "I was but teasin ye."

She was mollified after a time, and then madame saw to it that the wedding arrangements were hurried. They were to be married on the evening of the second day and Clancy could not find a way to avoid it. Moreover, he was not sure that he wanted to. Every debate with himself on the question ended in a draw. The photo was a poison to his peace of mind, but then several of the French had distant connections among the Germans, and anyway he could not forget the blood-curdling plans of Major Dash for future raids. Better be married with complications than single and charging Hun machine guns every trip in the line. He let her vivacious charms sooth his fears and lent assistance to all the arrangements.

Clancy craftily made himself known at a quartermaster's billet in the village and after a succession of treats, at madame's expense, induced the pleasant quarter-bloke to issue him a new tunic and puttees. A new shirt was tossed in for good measure. Clancy changed clothing, shaved, scrubbed. shined and polished. until he was resplendent. Madame was seemingly well pleased with his washing. His shirt and socks were on the line early on the morning of his wedding day.

The Padre who was to marry them was a gentle little man and he beamed on everyone. Suzanne was arrayed in elegant finery and was as sparkling and uncertain as April sunshine. In fact everything about madame's establishment seemed to radiate happiness, except the hawk-eyed aunt. She would have none of the excitement or preparations but remained in her corner, watching.

At length the clock chimed the zero hour and Clancy faced the Padre, Suzanne beside him. It was now or never, but he felt no twinge of conscience, and was rather proud of himself. Not many in the entire Canadian Corps could boast of a similar conquest. Madame, rustling in her Sunday attire, was smiling perpetually, and had around her a group of neighbours, wide-eyed with curiosity. The Padre cleared his throat and began the ceremony-and at that very instant there was a shrill cry from the backyard.

The Padre continued his even tone but Clancy did not hear a word. He had seen the fat quartermaster, who was a special guest, endeavouring to keep in the kitchen the hawk-faced aunt, who was flourishing with wild gestures the shirt that madame had washed. The quarter-bloke strove nobly, facing an awful barrage of vituperation, and the padre put on speed, but at length the woman broke through the defense and fairly hurled herself between Clancy and his lady. "Sale Boche! Sale Boche!" she screamed, finding her voice with a vengeance. "See - a spy - a spy!"

The Padre faltered and lost himself. Madame sprang forward. Necks were craned and a babel of tongues made confusion. The hawk-eyed aunt held the shirt so that all could see, dearly stamped on the collar band, the name of the maker. "Otto Kuhn, Berlin, Germany."

It was damning proof, and Clancy bitterly regretted his slippery tongue. The evening before he had boasted needlessly of receiving his shirt from his home, meaning to impress madame. Suzanne tore the garment from her aunt's hands and thrust it under Clancy's nose. "Is it yours?" she demanded, and her voice was as hard as a Sergeant-Major's. It raised the hair on Clancy's neck.

"It is," he owned, with a desperation of a cornered man. "And is this your picture?" with a dramatic flourish he drew forth the photo he had taken from the German.

Suzanne stared and madame stared and the Padre licked his lips nervously. "That picture is of me," Suzanne admitted slowly, "but where did you find it?"

The silence that followed was filled with foreboding. "Ye should know," said Clancy, mopping perspiration from his face. "I took it from a Heinie that looked like a pig."

"Oh--ooooo!" said Suzanne. Her eyes narrowed like a cat's. Unbelief spread large on her pink and white features. "Brigand! Liar! Sale Boche! I keel you!" She leaped at Clancy, regardless of her finery, fingers curved like claws.

Simultaneously madame paled and screamed and the hawk-eyed lady went at him like a tiger. Clancy swung the palpitating padre into Suzanne's clutches and aimed a counterstroke at the tigerish aunt, a wild swing that missed her entirely, but landed just below madame's bosom. She grunted loudly and sat down so hurriedly that she missed a chair. The next instant Clancy was struggling to reach the door.

Bad luck met him in the form of a military policeman who had entered like a hero and naturally seized the first man he saw in khaki. For once in his career Clancy yielded gracefully to such a minion of the B.E.F. Here at least was temporary refuge. He had a last glimpse of Suzanne and the tiger aunt in a fervid embrace and madame vigorously making the sign of the cross.

Clancy was still at Newlillers, a closely-guarded prisoner, when Hill 70 was captured. For weeks he was regarded as a dangerous character. He was escorted to various inquisitions by an armed guard of at least six men, and his cell, a room at the rear of the police billet, was inspected every day. Suzanne and her aunts were absolutely certain that they had harboured a spy and they were responsible for a daily gathering of the French officials in the village until Clancy hated the sight of them.

All the prisoner's possessions were taken to headquarters and examined by the intelligence staff and his lineage was traced back to Killybegs and the year of small potatoes. The police were proud of having so important a prisoner and treated him with buckshee rations and cigarettes and even brought him mess-tins of beer. At length someone thought of interrogating the Hun prisoner that Clancy had captured. The squint-eyed Teuton sullenly admitted to the forcible exchange of shirts and readily explained taking a photo from a French house in Avion, merely as a souvenir. When an interview with madame proved that the house in question had been Suzanne's home before the war, everything was clear enough for all, and the police reluctantly released their prisoner.

Clancy had not grown any gray hairs during his enforced rest. especially after hearing that Hill 70 had really been a battle, and his feet were not so light as he made his way back to his battalion.

He found his mates at Cite St. Pierre, lined up at the cook wagon, mess tins at the alert and every man grinning. He asked for explanations, and then his own visage expanded in a smile. Major Dash, after a hectic month, had gone!

He had imposed his base-bred ideas of warfare on 'D' Company until the men were on the verge of revolt, had even tried to impose a reign of terror by twisting his moustache like the Kaiser's, and then a salvo of whizz-bangs had unroofed his trench shelter and he had been shipped to Merrie England, a sad case of shell-shock. Clancy was just in time to join in an organized celebration.

The Sergeant detained him a moment, however, to ask for particulars before enrolling him on the strength of the platoon. “What's all this racket I've heard about, Tim?” he asked. "Are you married or single?”

Clancy scratched his head and pondered. He bad never allowed himself to dwell on thoughts of that painful happening in madame’s little parlour. He wondered just how far that Padre had gotten with the ceremony. Would there he any entangling aftermath? "Divil take it, serg'int," he exploded, "I'm blest if I know mesilf. Ye had better play safe. Put me down as a widower. And let me tell ye something, as a man that knows. Niver trust a female."

CHAPTER NINE

THE PROMOTION OF PRIVATE CLANCY

THE Dismounted Mudhounds had a few uneventful tours in the line and then enjoyed divisional rest. In October they entrained for the Salient and there landed one miserable rainy afternoon. Their two trips into the fighting at Passchendaele were filled with all the misery and horror and tragedy that attended each battalion in that autumn of 1917. Clancy went up the long tracks like a man mesmerized. It was hard for him to hope that he would ever come back intact and he was extremely careful not to dislodge a dead man, to carry the rum, or be one of a trio to share a match.

In their attack on the pillbox the first time "in" he did nothing heroic, being stuck in the mud for over an hour through missing his way when avoiding a dead horse. He floundered and cursed in a mire where all that was firm underfoot was a dead man or his equipment and at length crawled up to the ditch his platoon occupied in time to relieve a Hun prisoner of his bottle of coffee - the captured Germans being a relief just in the line.

He plodded back through the darkness the following night, too weary for words, fed-up to the back teeth, drank a cigarette tin of rum and did not wake until noon the next day. Then, after serving as working parties to field batteries and moving guns by man power, the Mudhounds were given a breather at a wet, soggy, evil-smelling billet near Poperinghe. Back there Clancy breathed freer, but every time anyone remarked on his escaping unscathed for so long a time he made haste to "knock on wood."

The second trip in was worse than the first, but once more the Irishman missed all real fighting. It was merely a matter of plunging through the mud, squatting in it all night, shivering through the mist at dawn and trying to find the Germans who were as miserable as they. Then the officer in command of 'D' Company got hit in the head by a sniper, and Clancy was one of a party detailed to take him back to a dressing station. The wounded man was crazed by his hurt. He had to be tied to his stretcher, and it was six hours before they had waded, floundered, plunged, struggled through, the sea of mud to the M.O.'s pillbox. The medical officer took one look at the patient and ordered them to continue with their load, to take the wounded man right back to Ypres.

They did. It took far into the day to do it. They were under shell fire all the way, were bombed from the air, had a thousand narrow escapes, but completed their task, and then slept at the clearing station until 'D' Company, about the strength of a platoon, came back.

The remnant of the battalion was taken away by lorries to a pleasant French village and there recuperated and were reinforced by new men until Clancy felt that he was a relic of the Napoleonic wars. Christmas and New Years meant nothing in particular except a better dinner at Lievin. And there they again commenced to do turns in the trenches.

One evening of their second month strange sounds were heard in No Man's Land - not the twang of barbed wire in careless hands or the scurrying of rats among Bully beef tins, but splashes, gurgling splashes, as if someone were cautiously fording a pond and, to a certain extent, that was what was happening. No Man's Land was mostly water, and Corporal Binns and an assistant were investigating its depths and dangers.

It was the sector to the left of Lievin and Fourteen platoon held the water posts on Tallow Trench. Sergeant Jenks commanding. The Sergeant was an original of the Fifth, a grizzled connoisseur of eggs and chips who knew every estaminet from Ypres to the Somme, and he was bitterly resenting the fact that he had ever been such a dash-jingled, gull-minded idiot as to put his name on the dotted line in a recruiting station in far off Canada. "If this war keeps on another six months," he growled to a dim figure slouched beside him on the firestep, "The civies'll have to come and take a shipload of bughouse Sara Brownees out of this country. Every blasted brass hat is cuckoo right now, and it's spreading to the front. Did you hear the orders the Cap. sent up, orders right from brigade?"

The slouching figure was Clancy and he rolled slightly in order to scratch under one arm. "No," he grunted. "I didn't hear? What's up?"

"He wants us to get across to the slag heap and take a prisoner." The Sergeant delivered his news with the air of a victim of undeserved prosecution and seemed to expect a protest. There was no comment.

"Did you hear what I said? he demanded. "He wants this post,

Number Six, to make up a small party to swim or float across that pond or canal or whatever you may call it and attack the Heinie posts, which we don't know where they're at, and bring back a prisoner. Did you ever in all your life hear of such plain, unlimited brass hat devilishness? Brigade wants to know whose holding the slag heap posts, as if it made any difference whether they're Wurtemburgers. Brandenburgers, or Limburgers.

The Sergeant got up to kick at a rat that was investigating the bay. He spat savagely, then turned back to his seat. "If anything was to happen to the Corp what would I do!" he demanded morosely. "I've too much responsibilities as it is. And to ask Number Six, of all posts to put on a raid." He spat again. "Ten of us, herded up in a dirty cellar, out on this forsaken corner surrounded by swamp, on half rations, two more nights afore relief, and we're asked to cross a dirty water hole fifty yards over and filled with wire stakes and old timbers, and catch us a Fritz and bring him back. You can't beat that." He shook his head and watched a distant flare sizzle up and over as it burst into light.

Clancy roused himself and scratched his armpit again. He was off duty for the hour, but had preferred to sit on the firestep sooner than try to rest in the smoke-filled cellar where the off-duty men were boiling tea over a makeshift stove. "It's a crazy scheme," he agreed whole-heartedly, "and I'll be remindin' ye that it's not my turn on wan av these fool stunts. I did me trick th' last time we were up Cow Trinch."

The Sergeant was slow to answer, but reluctantly assented. "I remember that, Tim," he said cautiously, "but you wouldn't see me stuck would you? You're away the best man on this post and you know it."

“I am that," asserted Tim. "an' barrin' none, but I'm jist takin' me turn for all that. Ye kin twist out av this fix th' best ye know how."

"But how can we get across to that blasted slag heap?" asked the Sergeant querulously after watching another Verey light rise and fall. "The water's too deep to wade and it's full of wire anyhow, and if we had a raft it couldn't carry more'n three or four, and how'd we bring the prisoner back?"

"Ye had better catch him first, I'm thinkin'," said Clancy. "Ye could bring him back after."

There were sounds of footsteps in front, the squelch of waterlogged boots, then dark forms loomed beyond the parapet and entered through a lane in the wire. Corporal Binns and his assistant had returned.

"Did you find out anything?" growled the Sergeant.

"Not a thing," said Binns. "We waded as far as we could, but there's wire everywhere, except over to the right, and it's too deep to wade there." The Corporal stepped heavily into the trench. He was holding one hand stiffly in front of him and it was conspicuous by a white bandage. I ripped my hand on the wire," he stated mournfully. I hope she don't go bad."

"For the luva Pete!" roared the Sergeant. He sprang up and bent over the injured hand. "What the blazes..."

"Don't touch it ,"snarled the corporal. "It hurts like the devil."

Nevertheless the Sergeant insisted on an immediate inspection, which was carried out by means of a match lighted under a rubber sheet. The hand was rather badly scratched, not deeply, but painfully, and had been liberally treated with iodine. The hurt would not take the corporal out of the trenches, but it meant that he could be used only for minor duties. "Now what will I do?" wailed the Sergeant. "You've gone and got yourself hurt when I need you the most. What'll I do?"

No one answered him. Sympathy was not abroad in Tallow Trench.

"Well, we got to try something," continued the Sergeant; "You know what the Cap'll say if we don't."

"What's the matter with leadin' the way yersilf?" asked Clancy. "Th Corp could look after this post."

Tim's interior was warmed with unholy joy. For two long years of trench warfare he had seen Sergeant Jenks' dodge detail after detail that would have taken him into actual contact with the enemy. The non-com was a shrewd, smooth-tongued manager and luck had always seemed to favour him. Now for once, he was apparently stumped. Tim rejoiced.

"But how do you know where Fritz is after you get over?" queried the corporal. "We listened and we couldn't hear a thing, and after this big rain you can see that the slag heap point is cut off from the trench just the same as we are here."

"We'll just have to hunt around till we find one of his posts," said the Sergeant heroically. "That is, if any of us is left alive by the time we get over. We'll get over in that cellar to the right before it's daylight and from there we can get a good look at all the ground around that heap. What do you say, Clancy?"

"There's just one thing I kin tell ye fer a fact," said Clancy solemnly. "Fritz is where ye find him."

Sergeant Jenks and Tim Clancy lay in the cellar that was far to the right of Number Six post. They were in a position they could not leave until it was night again and were anxiously awaiting the dawn. The slimy stonework and debris chilled them and the rising sun would bring welcome warmth. Suddenly there was a sound of feet on the gravel, a distant "tang" as someone caught a loose end of wire, and then a figure approached, calling to them in husky undertone. "Come here," hissed the Sergeant, "and keep quiet. What do you want?"

It was a runner from company headquarters. "Message for Sergeant Jenks," he whispered. "Captain said to be sure you got it." He handed a yellow slip to the non-com, and turned quickly.

"Hi, you, go careful," hissed the Sergeant after him. He turned to Clancy. "That's how we're treated," he muttered. "That chap would have come out to us, giving this place away, if it was broad daylight, and now he'll be crossing the planks when they can see him."

Clancy bit off a chew of tobacco and remained silent. He despised the continual whining of the Sergeant. A match spluttered and shed a flare of light over the yellow slip. The Sergeant was huddled over it at the bottom of the cellar, taking grotesque caution that no gleam of light escaped. He bent low over the message and read to himself. There was a long silence. Apparently he could not quite comprehend the written words. "Well, what th' divil is it?" asked Clancy at last, exasperated by the silence.

"It's hard to believe," said the Sergeant. "Sorry I kept you waiting, Clancy. But it caught we sudden-like. You're promoted, man, promoted. You're lance-corporal, right on orders."

It was Clancy's turn to sit in silence, absolute, rigid silence. Never in all his hectic army career had he been so dumbfounded. From his first army pay day he had been an incorrigible transgressor of army regulations. There had not been anything serious, but a list that covered his crime sheet had deprived him many chances for "cushy" jobs and kept him short of funds. How had the Captain overlooked his sins?

"I suppose you had it coming to you," remarked the Sergeant, still shaking his head. "For you've been twice put down for the Military Medal, and you're the best man in the platoon - if you'd stay sober."

"What's that to you?" said Clancy sharply. He rose to his knees, he wanted to stand upright. At long last his worth had been recognized and his chest swelled until his tunic was strained. He felt a warm regard for his rather austere company commander and resolved that he should prove he was worthy of the honour given him. "Sure an' ye know I could have been a Serg'int-Major by now if I'd wanted to be wan." Then he rose quickly. “I'll be sendin' a man out to take me place," he said grandly. " 'Tis no need av two N.C.O.'s on a job like this."

"Wait a minute," said the Sergeant. "This is just where you want to stay - for you'll be in charge here yourself. You just got promoted in time."

Dark sinister suspicion flitted across Clancy's mind. "Do yez mane...? " he blurted.

"I do," said the Sergeant. "It's just the job for you. You'll take the party over the pond."

Clancy glared down at the Sergeant and shed every trace of deference to rank. "Ye are nothin' but a schemin', cold-footed bomb-proofer," he flamed. "If it was but yersilf that counted, I'd make ye go if I had to drag ye across by main force, but there's me Captain to consider. I'll go, seein' as he's needin' a prisoner and knowin' ye'd niver git within reach av wan yerself." He subsided and sank back to his seat. The Sergeant made no answer. One by one the distant batteries quieted. Machine gunners ripped off a last few rounds before taking down their guns. The sun rose, glinting on dew-wet wire, touching the top of the slag heap with a crown of sparkles. Then it was day again and Clancy snuggled close in his observation nest, peering through a passage he had made in the weeds and piled brick.

He viewed a desolation that appalled. Three days of continued downpour had flooded the swampy terrain and had made a virtual "island" of the slag heap territory, as well as isolating the end of Tallow Trench and making post Number Six a second "island", only to be reached at night by a risky overland crossing of lengthwise planks which were under full range of a never resting Maxim. The pond-like expanse of water that constituted No Man’s Land had no current until it reached a distant wrecked culvert, and the stagnant surface was most uninviting to behold. Half-way to the German side the piled wreckage of a building rose some distance above the water. Twisted and splintered beams and braces stuck out as if defying anyone to approach them, and in the center a floor-like expanse of timbers sloped a foot above the water level. Clancy eyed the wreckage keenly. A twisted signboard was in view keeping aloft its white-painted warning. “Weg von der Strasse!" Clancy had seen many of them in captured territory. "Kape off the streets, is ut?” he muttered. "Kape out av th' water would be more to th' point."

He looked over at the slag heap, a sombre, misshapen monster. There was not a trace of entrenchment near the water edge and farther back, against the heap, debris and sandbags were so scattered about that it was impossible to detect a strong point. He wriggled higher up the cellar bank to get a better view, then slid back and began to take of his equipment. "I'm goin to swim out to that mess av timbers," he announced calmly.

"Swim out! Why, for Pete's sake?" asked the Sergeant, a certain admiration in his tones. "The Heinies'll pop you off before you're wet,"

"They won't see me," said Clancy. "Crawl over here and have a peek. Look," he pointed a very grimy finger. "I kin belly down to th' water without thim seein' me, if I kape low, because that mess av planks is in line. See thim planks in th' middle, like a floor? They're loose, I kin tell from here."

"But how can you get them here?" asked the Sergeant, wonderment still in his tones.

"I'm going to pull out three or four at a time and swim back with thim." said Clancy, unwrapping puttees.

The Sergeant rose up and peered long at the wreckage. "The only thing I don't like about it," he said slowly, "is that you can't see his shore either."

"An' who cares?" snorted Clancy. "Thim Heinies is in their holes right now, havin' their slape."

"You goin' to strip right clean?" More awe in the Sergeant's tones.

"I am", said Clancy, "an' ye kin signal to th' boys that I'm goin' out, so's they won't pull any more foolishness than usual."

The Sergeant crossed the cellar, rose up and under cover of the weeds made fantastic pointings and fearful facial contortions intended to convey his meanings. One round, vacant-appearing visage looked at him blankly, but Corporal Binns appeared and seemed duly impressed. "They're so dumb they need a keeper," said the Sergeant morosely, then sympathy tinged his voice. "You may make it all right, Clancy," he said kindly, "but things happen queer in this war, and if them's any messages or anything..."

"Pull in yer neck," snapped Clancy. "All you got to do is to kape yer bean workin'. You watch an' if anythin' happens signal to me."

"All right, I will," said the Sergeant hastily." "Keep low, for Pete's sake. You're so white..."

"An' what colour did ye think I'd be?" growled Clancy as he wormed over the cellar bank, moving carefully among the sharp fragments and exhibiting a vast expanse of goose flesh.

There was no reply. The Sergeant had sunk low and was hugging his shelter.

The slag heap and its surroundings were strangely quiet. Not a rifle spoke, no machine gunner became hysterical, there were no sounds of pick or spade or bailing buckets. Clancy entered the water, keeping low, and soon swam with steady strokes. It was but a short distance to the wreck and in a moment he had heaved himself up on the floor area. Lying flat he began to tug at a loose plank, but even as he tugged his blood ran cold. The wreckage had tipped strangely!

Clancy looked around and danger tensed him. A close-cropped head thrust into view above the timbers and was followed by naked, well muscled shoulders. An enemy swimmer had come to give him combat!

The weight of the intruder bobbed the raft-like wreckage and Clancy sprang straight at him. The German grinned, flashing a set of strong white teeth, but the Irishman was not to be deceived. He dived in, eager to get the advantage of sudden attack and their bodies locked with an impact that sent them reeling to one corner.

The battle that followed outclassed anything ever seen in the roped arenas back of the lines. The German was bulky and heavy-muscled, but Clancy was supple and tricky. Three times they went down, rolled over, separated, got up, and charged each other again. Once the advantage seemed with Clancy, but a tremendous knee-drive broke his hold. Then the German got his grizzly-like grip and bent his opponent backward until he was almost vanquished, but Clancy dropped suddenly and twisted as he dropped, crashing his foe to the timbers with a shock that dislodged the wreckage from its foundations. It moved several yards to the right, toward the deeper, wider part of the pond.

The swaying, dipping movements of their arena made the gladiators hesitate a moment before resuming hostilities, but they soon attacked with renewed energy. They sparred a second, for an opening, then the German caught at Clancy's neck - and missed his hold. Clancy ducked in close and attempted a hip throw, but the German's podgy body slipped in his grasp and he had to surge desperately to avoid another dangerous neck grip.

Straining every sinew, their breath conking in whistling intakes, they fought for position and all at once. Bashed manoeuvres so swift that the eye could scarcely follow, a darting of arms and legs, a terrific grunting lock of bodies, a grinding, splintering protest from their flooring - and the entire structure parted into loose floating sections.

Clancy came to the surface at once, blowing and spitting. He caught a plank, and, on it, struck out for the home shore, puffing like a harbour tug. As he stepped on the bank he looked around and saw the German on the farther side, scuttling for cover.

"Hi, Clancy." It was the Sergeant calling, calling loudly. "Don't come in here. Duck for the trench. You'll give this place away."

Clancy tossed his plank on the bank and almost strolled to the cellar, stepping down very deliberately. He was so angry that he cared not what happened. "Ye poor scut," he grated '"Thinkin' av yer own dirty hide. Why did ye not come out and give me a hand?"

"Me!" gasped the Sergeant. '"What could I do?"

"Ye could have come out th' same as I did," said Clancy eyeing critically several large blue spots that decorated his person. " 'Tis the first time I caught a Heinie and couldn't bring him in."

"Caught him," faltered the Sergeant. "Why - I thought he had caught you."

"Ye are a liar as well," said Clancy, using his shirt as a towel. I had that square-head where I wanted him, an' if th' floor hadn't gone down he'd been here now. Did ye see what was happenin' or were ye too frightened to look over?"

"You keep a more civil tongue, or I'll report you to the Captain," said the Sergeant weakly. "I've been as close to the Heinies as you have. I was up at Ypres when we were so close we both used the same wire and..."

"Stow yer chatter," said Clancy. I've heard that one at th' horse lines." Then as he thrust his head through his shirt, he looked over the bank and grinned. "Luck's comin' to me fer wance." he chortled. 'Thim planks is driftin' this way. They'll be ashore whin it's dark."

The usual night strafing was on. Winking red Bashes rimmed the horizons left and right of Tallow Trench. German heavies were shelling the ruins near Lieven. Every now and then would come a great rushing noise, followed by the roar of explosion, and a flash of fiery crimson split the darkness.

These heavy crashes and the rolling din of guns served to smother all the sounds that came from the canal bank where three men toiled to manufacture a light plank cruiser. Lance-Corporal Clancy was in charge of operations and was assisting in binding salvaged planks together with old telephone wire, using stout cross pieces as stays. An hour's strenuous labour and they had completed their craft. Clancy led back into the trench. "Who's comin'?" he demanded. "I want two av yez."

Not a man offered. The occupants of Post Six were old dogs of war and held to old-timer mottoes. "Very well, me beauties," said Clancy. "Ye'll draw fer it."

He sliced a pair of two-by-four rifle rags, making seven strips, and two of them were an inch shorter than the others. "Now draw," he ordered, exposing one end of the strips. "Th' ones that gits the short rags comes with me."

The drawing was made, and Clancy groaned again. He had got the two most useless members of the garrison. Tubby Dawes, a very stout, very lazy, very dirty individual, and Sam Fish, a scrawny thin-voiced cook from headquarters, who was doing a trip in the line as atonement for some misdemeanour. It would be difficult indeed to choose a worse pair for such a venture, but Clancy had an ancestry that stood him up to any situation.

"Niver in me life," he orated, "since I was fool enough to leave Killybegs in Donegal Bay have I laid eyes on yer likes, but ye are goin' with me, an' as a non-commissioned officer I'll see that ye do yer duty. Lave yer tin hats here. Ye'd be bumping yer blocks together an' makin' more noise than wan av thim Portygee gas alarms."

The raft bobbed and swerved as Tubby was placed on board but the sun-dried planks were very buoyant and shortly they had poled themselves well towards their objective. "Now listen," hissed Clancy. "Ye are to jump th' first Heinie we meet. Don't give him time to yell. We kin take him by surprise, an' if we meet a man-sized Fritz, with a nasty face, lave him to me. 'Tis the chap I had by rights on th' timbers an' I'll deal with him mysilf."

Clancy tingled all over with each push nearer Hunland. Here he was, a full-fledged non-com, leading soldiers, in charge of a raid. From now on he would show his Captain the supreme fighting qualities of his race, show him who was endowed with a talent for leadership. Wouldn't it be sweet to supplant the Sergeant? Then he looked anxiously toward the dark outline of the slag heap. The continued silence bore ominous portent.

Tubby sneezed and rocked the raft. Clancy swore luridly and caught balance with his pole, then hurriedly deposited it beside him and caught up his rifle. An instant later they struck ground. upsetting Sam Fish. He splashed loudly in shallow water. "Hush ye!" hissed Clancy.

"Did ye hear anything?"

They listened, but only the roar of gunfire came to them. "Come on," said Clancy grimly, "an' use yer brains - if ye want to git back."

The slag heap loomed gigantic before them and distant. Verey lights only served to make the darkness more intense. "This way," said Clancy, and he headed to the right. He would be too crafty to advance directly against the enemy posts.

Foot by foot they advanced, halting twice to listen, and then they blundered into a sort of a trench. It was too shallow to afford cover to a man upright and was flooded a foot deep. Every step was a splash and at intervals the parapet had been blown in, making it necessary for them to clamber over the wreckage, yet neither of Clancy's followers complained. They were right at his heels, panting and blowing from their exertions and high tension. Then Tubby slipped and almost mounted Sam Fish in his efforts to avoid falling. Clancy quieted them with a terrible threat, and then called a halt. "There's something wrong," he declared. "Fritz is up to some av his dirt. We should have mixed with him before this."

"Let's go back," suggested Tubby wheezingly. "We don't know where this trench leads to."

"It's awful bad walkin'," piped Sam Fish. "I'm soaked to th' skin."

"Ye'll be changin' yer colour then," grated Clancy. "I'll ask let yet opinions whin I'm needin' thim. Kape shut."

He led on until they reached a branching trench, wider than the first and also flooded. In places there were boots, bottles, old equipment, bits of blankets, all rotting in water. They went up the wide trench, the water squishing in their boots. Nothing interfered with their progress, however, and Clancy, his eye on the slag heap all the while, knew that they had almost circled it. Then Sam Fish stumbled and fell into a bucket. Investigation showed that they were at a point where the Germans had recently bailed the trench, and just ahead they encountered a wooden trench floor. To their nostrils came the unmistakable odour of German occupation, yet no one challenged them, they heard no voices or footsteps.

"Git ready, I'm strikin' a light." whispered Clancy.

His raiders whined instant protest, but the match flared, cupped in Clancy's hands, and they saw they were beside crude trench shelters, lately occupied. Greatcoats, blankets and ground sheets were mingled on the shelf-like sleeping places. Where were the Huns?

Clancy led on around the slag heap. He was almost back to their starting place. The moon struggled through a mass of clouds and gave a sickly light. They crouched and stared about them. There were faint flickers of red reflection on the water. In the distance the Verey lights rose and fell in endless play. Clancy snorted. "I'm..."

He stilled instantly. They had heard distinctly the quick scramble of someone near the slag heap. "Watch yersilves," hissed Clancy. "They're tryin' to surround us."

There came a loud splash in the trench, as if the Germans were abandoning all caution, and Sam Fish lost his nerve completely. Eluding Clancy's detaining hand, he made a mad plunge for the raft. Clancy's bellow for his return was disregarded, but an instant later the echoes were reawakened by Sam's howls.

"Where," he moaned, "is the raft gone?"

Clancy raced to the scene. The raft gone! "Where did yez lave it?" he said fiercely. "Didn't ye hitch it upon the bank?"

"Tubby was last," whined Sam. "I didn' leave it."

"I didn't do nothin'," said Tubby indignantly. "You can't blame me."

"And so you two beauties left th' raft to float away, an' th' squareheads is creepin' around us," growled Clancy, his rage boiling within him until he could almost commit murder. "How th' hell are we goin' to take th' prisoner across?"

Tubby stared at him, moon-faced in the gloom. "What prisoner?" he asked blankly.

Clancy strangled, then led away, both men following like lost puppies. They crawled all around the slag heap in a desperate game of blind man's bluff. They waited, they listened, they circled, they doubled back again. Then Clancy declared for drastic action. "T'wdl be daylight if we kape this game goin'," he snorted. "I'm headin' for them Fritzies. Ye kin do as ye like."

Clancy made a straight advance on the trench that had shown signs of occupation. Sam Fish tripped over a wire and whimpered as he sprawled in the mud. Clancy ducked low, expecting a burst of machine gun fire, but none came. Tubby Dawes blundered on. He had missed his mates in the darkness and was travelling in "high" in his attempt to catch up with someone. Suddenly there was a "plop" of a heavy body falling in soft muck, a dismal groan, partly smothered, and then a howl of fright. As the howl died away there was a splashing in the German trench, a scuttling sound as someone went over the trench side, and then Tubby's voice calling plaintively for help. "I'm fell in," he gurgled. "Come and get me. I'm here."

Clancy's remarks danced blue in the murk. He plunged straight for the trench and jumped down into its watery depths. Tubby was getting slowly erect, shedding mud and filth as he rose. "I fell in," he said. 'Why didn't you tell me where I was?"

"Where's th' Heinies?" grated Clancy. The night was getting his goat. Every rule of warfare had been split apart, nothing was going according to Hoyle. He felt that he was having a huge nightmare. "I wish they'd grabbed ye, ye wooden-headed fool. Why did ye go ahead?"

"I thought I was behind you," spluttered Tubby, still spitting mud, "and when I tried to wait I slipped. Nobody said nothing to me."

"So help me, St. Patrick," exploded Clancy after a whistling intake of breath. I - I - you two guys ain't real..." Words failed him.

He sprang upon the parapet and headed straight for the bank where they had landed. He would disrobe and swim to the other side, leaving these two misfits to shift for themselves. Slipping, sliding, puffing like a fat woman, Tubby wailed in the rear, and Sam Fish, panting nervously, kept dose behind. Then Clancy stopped. There was the sound of a pole working against soggy timbers.

Some person or persons were poling a raft directly to the spot where they stood.

The incoming craft loomed before them, manipulated by a very small figure. Tubby lunged out to meet it, moving like a giant bullfrog leaving his bank, and his weight tipped the raft like a shingle, sending the with the pole headlong into the arms of Sam Fish. Sam yelled wildly and clasped his captive in a frantic embrace. "Catch him, catch him," he howled. "It's a Fritz!"

The German, apparently as frightened as Sam, made a desperate effort to escape, but the ex-cook clung like a burr and they went to the coal-grimed sand together, rolling over and over, half in and half out of the water. Clancy's rough hands pried them apart, and he placed the undersized Hun on his feet . "Explain yersilf," he ordered sternly. "Where did ye come from?"

The German emitted a perfect deluge of gutturals, accompanied by much arm-waving and pointing. He gurgled and bubbled and coughed gutturals at such a rate that was forced to check him.

"What does he say?" queried Tubby from his crouch on the raft. "I can't make it out."

Before Clancy could make a fitting retort or use force to express his emotions, there came a dramatic interruption. Feet crunched on gravel and out of the dark came another stream of tremulous Teutonics. It was answered by the small man in Clancy's grip, and then a stout figure materialized in the mist and came to them. It was another Hun, unarmed, his hands over his head, and he was chanting, "Kamerad! Kamerad!"

Immediately Clancy's captive caught the fever. He reached for the clouds. "Kamerad! Kamerad!" he parroted.

"Git on the raft," grated Clancy, after a long look to see that there were no others. "Some of us is crazy. This war is all mixed up."

But their combined weight was too great for the raft. It could not carry them. Tubby had hooked his fingers under the cross pieces and dung to the deck, a fixture. Sam Fish was locked to him. It was a moment for decision and Clancy took the easiest way out. He pushed the fat Hun ashore. "I'll send fer ye later," he snapped. "Stand there till I come fer ye."

He had only been asked to bring one prisoner, and he had one, and what was more miraculous he had his two helpers intact. He had succeeded in his first mission.

It was only a few moments before they ground on the further bank. The Sergeant strolled out to meet them, walking erect on the shore that was so often swept by bullets from the machine guns at the base of the slag heap.

"Didn't we have luck?" he chortled. "That rain was a blessing. Who'd ever think it would a drove them Heinies over here?"

"Rain!" echoed Clancy. "Heinies?"

"Wake up, Clancy," said the Sergeant. “Don't you know what happened? The Heinies all surrendered. That guy you wrestled with was swimming over to give himself up. The rain flooded them out of their dugout and the other Heinies never got up to them with rations or anything. They were fed up, and when you chaps landed they sneaked your raft and come over and give themselves up, two raft loads of them, all but one fat guy they couldn't bring either time. I'll have to send someone over for him. Did you see him?"

"I did," said Clancy. He was suddenly feverish and licked his lips. Words would not come.

“Gosh," rattled the Sergeant, "the Captain's tickled pink. I sent one batch along to him and he sent back his compliments and extra rum. Six prisoners, no, seven, when we get that other chap, ain't picked up every night.”

Clancy began to revive somewhat. Anyhow, what was the difference if the Sergeant did share the credit. "An' what did he say about me?" he asked. "Didn't he think I had nerve?"

"Gosh, Clancy," said the Sergeant hastily. "I clean forgot to tell him you went out at all. You see - er - ahem - I really took them prisoners myself. I was laying out in front, so's to keep watch for you, when I heard them."

“Niver mind, niver mind it," said Clancy bitterly. "Ye'll strain yer imagination." He was growing hotter every moment and he felt that he would soon be delirious. "Tell me," he blurted, "Why in th' name of Hiven ye didn't signal me about it. We might have killed somebody."

“Well, you see, Clancy." said the Sergeant placatingly. “I - er - thought it was such a good chance to jet Tubby and Sim Fish broke in. The trainin' would do them good."

Clancy strangled, struggled to hold himself, and just in time to avert annihilation - the Sergeant extended his water bottle. Clancy took a long pull at its contents, then wiped his mouth with the back of his hand. "And now, Clancy," said the Sergeant as he backed towards his dugout again, "it's safe as a church over there. Take one an with you and get that fat man."

"I - will- not!” All Clancy's hatred spat forth in each word.

"Then you refuse an order?"

Clancy knew that the Sergeant had probably imbibed enough rum, to give a sort of insistence, before witnesses, but he was not to be cornered. "I'm not refusin' an order," he blurted with cold sharpness. "I'm resigning me commission, an' ye'll, have to go yourself. I'm through. Ye kin kape yer stripes. I've resigned."

"But." Before the Sergeant could speak further them was the sound of much splashing on the bank. The sentries, Clancy, and the Sergeant stood up on the firestep to peer into the breaking light. They beheld a wondrous figure. A stout German, clad only in high boots and underwear, was coming to the wire, making desperate efforts to tug a wet and scanty shirt over a large "bay window." The fat German had swum across.

"Welcome, Hindenburg," called a sentry softly. "This way in."

The others laughed, all but Clancy. Him they avoided and gave the right of way as he stamped into the cellar and flung down by his own blankets.

Sergeant Jenks came softly into the cellar. He did not want to awake the sleeper and he had almost forgotten to make out the list the Captain wanted, the number of thigh boots or waders stocked in the cellar at Post Six.

The request for information had come to him as he lay in the other cellar awaiting dawn - and only the cunning of such a campaigner as Sergeant Jenks has transformed it, for the moment, into a notice of promotion for Private Clancy.

CHAPTER TEN

CLANCY'S COMBINE

WHEN the Dismounted Mudhounds went back to rest billets Clancy felt that the universe had voted solidly against him. He developed a case of mumps and was sent to the Imperial Hospital at St. Pol. There he stayed several weeks, using his Irish craft to get double rations of cocoa and bread, and trying to get evenings in the big town. Rumours drifted about, at times overwhelming all else, of a Hun breakthrough, but Clancy would have none of it. He was still in that frame of mind when he was discharged.

Three days later he swore mightily as he pivoted on his heels and gazed in succession north, south, east, and west. He had possessed vague instructions as to where to find his battalion and had started well on the first leg of his journey, but during a traffic jam in a war-torn village had dismounted from a lorry that was bearing him Vimy-wards to quench his thirst in an estaminet. There, to his amazement, sat a friend of his youth, wearing the regalia of the "pick and shovels" who repaired the roads in the back areas.

Clancy had many questions to ask and answer, and madame kept the glasses filled. It was with much difficulty that the Irishman finally got to his feet and assisted his friend to do likewise. He had hazy recollections of a lorry waiting just outside, and sure enough, there was one blocked close to the curb. Clancy had crawled aboard - and fallen asleep. When he awoke he had a bad head and little else. His equipment had vanished as well as the lorry, and he was lying in an open field.

He did not know it, but he was stranded on the Somme area, and there the Big Push was a grim reality. Clancy's nightmare wanderings in its path had driven home the fact that truth and rations were necessities hardest to come by in that region. Wild rumours kept him going a zig-zag course, and it was his conviction that "Der Tag" had come. One travel-worn portion of His Majesty's forces was rushing to meet the Hun, the other portion was seeking a place to draw its breath and reorganize. But which was which?

He looked to the east. Silhouetted against the skyline was a soldier leading horses. Man and beasts slouched along as if on the verge of exhaustion. To the north a party of machine gunners staggered under loads of ammunition. He turned westward. Down another trail came a family of refugees, following a wagon drawn by a skeleton horse. To the south travelling at another angle, moved a battery of light field guns. Clancy groaned and shut his eyes. "It's th' end av iverythin'," he said solemnly. "Th' army's gone cuckoo."

He listened. A low growling thunder reached his ears. He turned, and the rumble seemed to come from every side. A lone soldier trudged toward him. Clancy sat on a deserted plough and awaited the fellow. "Which way are you bound, mate?" he called, as soon as the man was within hearing.

"To a blinkin' bird 'ouse if they keeps up this gime," came the answer. "Where's this place they calls Ozzyme-beany?"

"Ye can search me," returned Clancy. "Where are we now?"

"One bloke says as how its called 'Pickle-ears,' or the like. I calls it perishing wilderness. 'Ave ye anything to eat?"

"Not an earthly," groaned Clancy, "not since mornin'."

"It's orfull," agreed the weary one. "I'd grin at 'ard tack. I would."

Clancy left him abruptly. His stomach called for supplies, and his intimate acquaintances in the Mudhounds had compared its needs to those of a hungry elephant. Down a sunken road came four languid mules, urged on by a profane driver who sat on the forward section of a G.S. wagon. In answer to Clancy's query of direction he jerked a stubby thumb rearward. "I passed a place with a name like 'Tra-la-lillers'," he said cherrily. "There's a canteen upset op back and get yourself a can of sardines."

"How far is ut?" demanded Clancy. "An' which way is thim Huns?"

The driver looked back and removed his cap. "Oo knows," he said in a very hushed voice.

Clancy investigated a series of gardens, the remnants of a large farm. He circled a pond and wondered if it contained fish.

Luck favoured him. A lorry rumbled up the road he had chosen and was slowed by a big gun that blocked the way. Clancy scrambled on board. He crawled in at the back and found the truck to be laden with bales of blankets, and slid forward into a depression. As he did so his hands brushed an unseen face, and an instant later he was fighting for his life. Relentless fingers tore at his throat, and he was heaved against the side of the lorry.

Gathering energy, he surged back and tried for a strangle hold of his own. A bundle of blankets tumbled between the combatants, and Clancy lost his grip. The lorry lurched violently, and his assailant sprawled away from him. Clancy's frantic clutch in the dark gripped a very bony, hairy knee. For a fraction he was as embarrassed as a Clancy should be, and then he voiced his rage. "What do ye mane, ye reptile?" he yelled. "Are ye a kiltie or a divilish Hun?"

"Whist yer tongue, mon," came the reply in burry Scotch. "Why dinna ye speak furrst? I thocht ye were after ma money."

"Money!" snorted the Irishman. "Whativer would I be wantin'with money in this lousy wilderness? What I'm wantin' is a square meal. Have ye any rations?"

"I have not," said the voice in the dark, "and I'm fair stafvin' mysel'. Have ye seen any of the Gordons?"

“Ivery branch of th' army has criss-crossed this country today," returned Clancy. "They're delirious."

“Ay, the Germans hae broken through. They'll push in the whole front if they canna find the Gordons."

"Gordons me grandmother!" retorted Clancy. "'Tis th' Canadians they're needin’."

" Whist yer fool talk," came the hot return. “What's the name of the mob ye deserted?"

"I belong to th' Fifth Mounted rifles," blared Clancy, "an' no Scotchman chips me with desertion. Stick up your fins, ye-'petticoat'."

"Get on yer horse, ye Mountie!" roared "petticoats." He came at Clancy in massed formation.

In the darkness each man missed wild swings. They fell into a desperate clinch. The jolting of the truck sent them down on the bales and the maledictions that issued were hair-raising. The lorry lost speed and halted. Then the rays of a flashlight shot back from the driver's seat and disclosed Clancy and a dour-faced Scot furiously entangled. The driver was a burly man, and he wielded a large wrench. "Git outa this lorry," he commanded, "or I'll split yer fool head. G'wan, I mean it."

Clancy and his opponent dropped from the rear of the truck and it moved off immediately. The Irishman swung around, prepared to carry on the argument but found the Scot picking up a bale of blankets. "What th'-?" ejaculated Clancy. "How did them fall out?"

"I pushed them out, ye muttonhead," came the answer. "We'll be needin a bed."

"Correct," said Clancy, "but I've got to eat first. By th' sivin pipers, we're dose to a town. It may be this Tra-la-lillers I'm seekin'."

"Carry half these blankets," said the Scot calmly, "and ye can travel with Lock MacTavish of the Furrst Gordons."

"Kape yer yap civil an' Tim Clancy's yer friend," came the quick response.

After this exchange they plodded in silence. The town was devoid of men. Only rats scuttled to cover as their hob-nailed boots clattered on the street they followed. Few buildings remained. Vile odours reached them from a cellar and Clancy shuddered as he saw the end of a battered trench. "There's been fightin' here," he growled. 'We might find an'ould tin av bully."

The words died on his lips. MacTavish had suddenly gripped his arm and crouched. Clancy ducked with him and listened, then picked up a cobble-stone. There came a rustling sound from the disused trench, then the "squelch" of boots in sticky mud. Someone was stealing away under cover. Armed with his cobblestone, the Irishman dashed forward. "Kape th' ind av th' trench," he yelled. "I'll git him with this bomb."

"Hellup - I am friends. Safe me!" startling and piteous came the cry as a head appeared.

"Kape yer hands up," ordered Clancy, "an' crawl out av that trinch."

There emerged an odd looking figure, a little man in oversized khaki, wearing a woollen trench cap like a French toque.

"What's yer name an' regiment?" demanded Clancy, as he felt for weapons in the baggy garments of his captive.

"Sammy Rakovesky," the accent correspond with the cognomen, "and I belong to the Ninth Pioneers. Also I am starved already, and for a week it was cold mulligans, nothing else."

"Ye lie like a dago!" yelled Clancy, dragging the little man's gas mask to the fore. "Here's four tins av salmon, MacTavish, an' the Sheeny says he's starvin'. We'll ate at once."

"Hellup!" squawked Rakovesky. "It's mine. I am robbed, is it? And me a soldier like you was. What have you?"

Then ensued dogged argument. Rakovesky produced his pay book and by the light of a match proved himself genuine, then requested the rights of a soldier. He was willing to share his canned salmon, provided his friends chipped in equally, and his chief wish was to find a stove on which to warm their meal. "Always it was cold mulligan." he complained. "until I may die."

"That's no trick in this country," said Clancy. "Where did you salvage th' gold fish?"

"Back there it was," He pointed vaguely in the dusk. "This town is long in houses, and people is in some. A shell hits a lorry and there is stuff for canteens. I gets goldfish, nothing else is there already."

"If there is frogs in thim houses, there is grub," said Clancy. "Let's take a look and meet here. Lind me a match, Raky."

One end of a ruined house was still intact. Clancy descended the cellar steps and found a stove, three chairs, and a table. It was a damp, spidery place, evidently long deserted, but the trio could use it without fear of interruption. MacTavish deposited his blankets at once.

"If ye all agree to stick, "he said calmly, "lets's shake hands for a square dealing."

"Correct ye are," said Clancy heartily. "We'll make it a combine. Each man'll bring in his share an' we'll have wan grand blowout. Who'll stay and salvage wood?"

"I will," said Rakovesky eagerly. "I have a candle to see by." He produced a dozen bits from his respirator.

Clancy had remarkable luck. He found a kitchen from which light oozed and therein sat an old hag, guarding a bale of household treasures. It was evident that she was expecting transportation. Part of her possessions were a basket of French bread, and several slabs of bacon. The old woman's beady eyes glittered as she saw Clancy and she began a chatter that was ear-piercing. Then she sprang up and looked out.

The Irishman could hear the rattle of a motor truck and he had the quickest brain wave of his hectic career. He rushed outside and into the roadway and by dint of much shouting halted the lorry. "Ye are to take th' old girl with ye," he said loudly to the driver. "Th' Colonel left orders to stop th' first lorry an' put her in. I'll give her a hand."

"But," protested the driver. "I'm supposed to be..."

"Ye are supposed to do what th' Colonel says," snapped Clancy. "It won't put ye out of yer way."

He saw that the fellow was dubious as to how to act, and took advantage of his hesitation. Whipping back to the kitchen he found the old hag coming with an arm load of her possessions. "Toot sweet, old gal," he chortled, "an' th' sweeter t'will be fer me."

She hustled with a vim, and the Irishman followed in her wake with the basket of food. The old woman climbed in at the back of the lorry as the driver let in his clutch, loudly wishing that Clancy would choke to death if he were lying. The Irishman shoved in the basket he was carrying, but it was a simple matter to help himself to a couple of loaves, a stab of bacon and a paper parcel. Another moment, and the truck had vanished.

He found Rakovesky curled up like a dog on the blankets. "What th' divil are ye doin' there?" he roared. "Git out an' salvage some wood. I've the makin' of a rale feast here. Git out in that gardesi nixt th' trinch an' see if ye kin find a cabbage."

Raky obeyed after many whining protests and Clancy busied himself gathering splintered furniture and door frames from the wreckage above the cellar. In a short time the little pioneer returned, but he was not carrying cabbages. Instead, he was laden with a sack that contained chocolate, canned peaches, biscuit, sardines, and a square brown-paper parcel. "Where did yez git thim?" Clancy could scarce believe his eyes.

"Oy," whined Raky, "they was by the busted canteens. I picks them up to save mine life."

"But why did ye not mintion thim before?" demanded the Irishman.

Rakovesky squirmed. "I was not sure that some eats you could find," he said weakly. "It was not fair to give all mineself."

"To think that wan kike could be so rotten!" ejaculated Clancy.

There were steps overhead and MacTavish appeared, looking rather disappointed. "I couldna' find a morsel," he said gruffly. Then he saw the array of food on the table. "Whaur did ye find it?" he asked respectfully.

Clancy explained, "Ye can't expect much better av the tribe, anyhow" He concluded, "We've got all we need fer a regular feed, but water. There's not a tank in the village."

"Aye! but I found a pump," said MacTavish, proud that he could make some contribution. "I've brought a kettle o' water wi' me."

The Irishman ripped open the parcel he had stolen from the old lady's basket. It contained coffee. "Kin yez beat it?" he shouted happily. "Set the table, Raky. an' git th' kettle boilin'. Wan minute, I'll make sure this flue is workin', an' I'll hang wan of thim blankets over th' door. We're not wantin' visitors."

As Clancy fixed the blanket in place he was surprised to see a gleam of light from a house farther up the road. It had not been there before, and he decided to investigate. As he went up to it he heard voices on the road, and he located two very profane workers tinkering with the engine of an aerodrome tender. Detouring them, he approached the house from the rear and peered in through a slit in the burlap that curtained the window. As he gazed he gripped the sill to keep from shouting. He was too astounded to think clearly, his jaw fell open, and he stared pop-eyed into the darkness about him, then looked again. It was true - a man must believe his own eyes. There in the room, dancing in the arms of a dapper officer, was the prettiest girl he had ever seen.

A long time he stared, then sank back. What could a girl be doing in this desolation, when danger threatened at every turn? Clancy was proud of his record as a lady's man. He peered through the opening again and his heart began to throw hand-springs. The girl's form was perfection. Blue eyes flashed from darklashes, and her mouth was a red rosebud, a red that fascinated the Irishman. Her splendid crop of curls was a midnight blackness. As he watched, Clancy noticed that the girl was humming the time for her steps, that their dancing was rather mechanical. "She's fed up with that simp." he whispered fiercely to himself. I wish I had th' chance to spake..."

His wish was granted with startling suddenness. The officer seated himself and began to roll a cigarette, and the girl walked to the door and looked out. With remarkable presence of mind, Clancy mewed like a cat. A rather husky contralto voice called, "Pussy, pussy. Come here, pussy."

Clancy mewed again, and the girl came around the corner. As she halted in alarm, he spoke low and fast. "Excuse me, miss, but I wanted yer attention, an' I know ye'll never hold deceit against a poor Irishman. I jist happened to look in, an' I'm wonderin' if ye know the chances ye are takin' in such a country."

The girl had drawn back hastily, but now she came nearer and peered at him. "It is good to meet a real friend out here," she murmured in perfect English, "and if I had a chance I might tell you my situation." Then she edged closer and a soft hand squeezed Clancy's. "I'm nearly starved," she said plaintively. "Have you any bread or cheese you could spare?"

Clancy's heart swelled within him. Here was a golden opportunity. "Niver be it said that Tim Clancy failed a lady," he said grandly. "Come with me to a banquet th' Combine is prepaxin' on this same roadside."

The girl was silent for a few heart-beats, and then she leaned towards him impulsively and whispered. "That officer will get suspicious if I stay here longer. Whistle twice when your meal is ready and I'll give him the slip, and maybe you can help me escape him afterwards. Molly Fitzgerald will never forget your kindness."

"Molly! I knew yer name would be a sweet wan," whispered Clancy. "Ye kin dipind on me an'"

The door opened and the officer stepped out. Clancy dodged from view and sped to the cellar. "Are you ready yet?" he panted. "Give a hand to clean up the table."

"Whist yer noise, man," said MacTavish peevishly. "Ye have kept awa' while we got the stove to work proper. Don't step close to that board, I've my monev dryin' there. This Sheeny spilt water on my tunic wi' his clumsy ways."

"He makes talk of a lousy ten-franc paper," whined Rakovesky, "which is no good only by Arras."

Beneath the stove Clancy saw a board on which lay the note mentioned. It was an exact replica of one in his pocket which he had tried to pass on numerous occasions. "Niver mind money," he said scornfully, "I've a rale surprise for ye. There's a lady comin' to eat with us that's as pritty as th' Irish, an' she's not had a bite this day."

"A bargain's a bargain," rasped MacTavish. 'We've chipped for three and no more. If ye bring in skirts in sic a country ye can feed them yersel'."

"Stop yer yappin'- or yar wife will be a widow," ordered Clancy. "I'm goin' fer th' Jane. Make the coffee."

Hardly had he given the signal than Molly appeared. "Where's th' loot?" he whispered, tingling with joy as the girl took his arm for guidance.

Strange noises issued from the cellar as they approached and Clancy hurried down the stairway. MacTavish was armed with a long stick and was poking in the corners while Rakovesky watched him anxiously and kept the table between them. "This belated scum says a rat stole my money," roared the Scotchman. "I had it on the board and its gone. "I'll..." His voice trailed off as he saw Molly at the Irishman's elbow. "'-an..."

"Miss Molly Fitzgerald, meet Jock MacTavish."

"Of the Furrst Gordons, Miss," interrupted the Scot making a wonderful bow.

"How thrilling!" gasped Molly, "I've always adored the kilted men."

"But he is in such a fuss over a lousy ten francs by Arras," broke in a tremulous voice. "This cellar is no luck yet..."

"Stow it, ye shrimp," bellowed Clancy. "Miss Molly. this is Rakovesky, th' mascot av our combine. Th' poor critter can't help his birth, ye understand."

"Rakovesky - how romantic!" gushed Molly, "He may be a duke or a count."

"He might," snorted Clancy, "an' th' Kaiser might be an Irishman, but he's not. Sit right down, miss, an' fergit yer manners. Me friends niver had any."

His warning was not heeded. Four tins of steaming coffee flanked fried bacon, pink salmon, French bread, sardines. MacTavish ate like a wolf, crunching his food. Rakovesky, true to his faith, stuck to the salmon and bread. Clancy could not keep pace due to his amazement at the feats of Molly. She gobbled bread as if the slices were wafers, she swallowed huge portions of salmon, and seemed always reaching for bacon.

The banquet developed into a speed contest, but Clancy remembered the biscuits, chocolate and canned peaches that reposed in a bag in the corner and were to be served as dessert. He slackened his efforts and eyed Rakovesky. "Are ye needin' a shovel, ye..." His voice died to a whisper. The other three tensed, food suspended.

Rakovesky was the first to move. The pupils of his eyes dilated, and tiny beads of perspiration stood out on his forehead but he managed to scramble from his seat. He dropped his knife and it fell with a clatter. Then only the tense breathing of the quartet disturbed the stillness. From somewhere, seemingly back of MacTavish, a ghastly moaning sound came, ending in a weird sigh.

The candle sputtered on the table, and no one spoke. Every moment was drawn in suspense. Then the moan came again, clearly, from Rakovesky's corner, and as the sigh ended a faint, sepulchral voice whispered: “Dead men - everywhere - dead men - dead."

With one wild leap Rakovesky cleared the stove and bolted up the stairs. The patter of his feet died away in the distance. Clancy felt cold shivers race up his spine. "There's something - it came again, long-drawn, shuddering. "Dead men - everywhere - dead - dead."

Clancy licked his dry lips. "Let's move," he said huskily. "There's something wrong."

MacTavish stood up, and became rigid as the sounds were repeated. "I've lost ma money," he wheezed, "but I'm leavin' th' place."

A fourth time came the awful sounds, more weird than ever. Molly rose, swayed, and fainted into the Scotchman's arms, but Clancy assisted to carry her above. Then they made a chair of their arms and bore her a safe distance. The Irishman thrilled to the touch of feminine apparel, and jealousy took charge. "Ye can go back an' get th' bag av treats, Jock," he said roughly. "Molly will be all right in a minute." He felt her hands fluttering.

MacTavish halted a moment, but the light still burned in the cellar. "I'll go," he rasped, "but ye come if ye hear me call. I've na likin' for th' place mysel'."

Molly sat up. "Where am I?" she gasped. "Oh - did that thing sound again?"

"There now, ye are with brave men," soothed Clancy. "Jock an' I will see -"

He was interrupted by a terrible yell from the cellar.

"Go quick." cried Molly. "Go help Jock."

Clancy rushed to aid his friend, rather dazed at the command in Molly's tone. Her recovery had been remarkable. MacTavish met him at the cellar top. "We are a pack of fools," he roared angrily. "Our treats are gone, stolen by a man wearin' a Sam Browne, a thievin' officer. I couldna' catch him - an ma money lost too. If ye could leave gurrls..."

Clancy's brain was dizzy as he heard the irate Scot describe the dapper thief he had seen vanish into the night with the remnants of their rations as well as the bag of treats. It was all a mystery. One thing was certain - he would not go back to the haunted room below. He raced back to Molly, stopped distracted. She had vanished into the night!

Down through the village came a lorry, and Clancy realized that it was the first one in a long time. The area was being abandoned and Jock gave mutual consent that they board the truck. For an hour they rattled over cobbled roads, halting at last by a large shed, where light flickered from a crowded doorway. He and MacTavish descended stiffly. They were cold, and a fine drizzle was failing, "What's goin' on in there?" he asked a man.

"The aerodrome concert party, the 'Sky Scrapers' is putting on a show," said the fellow. "Th' place is packed."

"Let's go in, Jock," said Clancy. "A little entertaining will rist our minds."

They pushed, shoved, elbowed and squeezed until they were inside the building, and found standing place on a large packing case at the rear. The stage was well lighted, and the announcer came on as a clever dancer finished a performance. "The next on the program," he called clearly, "will be Corporal Riley, our famous female impersonator. I introduce Miss Molly Fitzgerald."

Clancy grew dizzy. He shut his eyes wearily and opened them again. On the stage tripped a light-footed maiden whose figure was perfection, whose eyes were blue; the red of her lips was fascinating. Swinging to lilting music from a battered piano, she broke into a song, a throaty contralto: "When Irish eyes are smiling. all the world... "

Clancy groaned aloud, so that the crowd turned to look at him, and before the song had ended he was perspiring freely. MacTavish had set his mouth like granite. "The next," called the announcer, "will be our ventriloquist, Lieutenant Ballinger."

From the wings came the dapper officer who had danced with Molly. Seating himself, with a stuffed representation of a Jerry prisoner on his knee, he gave a humorous performance. At the finish a voice seemed to come from the box on which he sat, and he jumped up in alarm. "Dead men - dead men - everywhere - dead - dead." The moan could be heard distinctly.

Clancy, his features a fiery red, ground his teeth. The announcer came forth again. "Listen, men!" he shouted. "There is a truck outside for all Canadians in this area. All are needed in the line at once. Pile out quietly, Canada, and then the show will continue."

The Irishman was wild with rage. His thirst for vengeance would be thwarted. Then a peculiar voice reached him. "Push more yet one way," it said. "I am already in, but to see is bad. Such a luck it was tonight!"

Rakovesky, wet and muddy, wedged in near Clancy's feet. The Hebrew pulled a red handkerchief from his tunic pocket and wiped his nose vigorously. Like a flash a brilliant idea seized Clancy. He thrust a hand in his own pocket and sneaked forth his Arras note. With an adroit movement he dropped it into Rakovesky's open pocket.

As the little man replaced his "wiper," his fingers touched the paper money. He jerked it forth. "Oh, such a luck!" his high-pitched voice rose above all murmurs. "That cellar was no good."

He got no further. MacTavish had looked down, and he dived for his man and his money.

By superhuman effort Clancy gained the outside. His biting fury had subsided. "What th' divil is loose in there, mate?" asked a soldier. "What busted?"

"'Twas th' smash av th' combine," replied Clancy, curtly. "It's done intirely."

"Combine? What sort o' bloomin' thing is that?"

"A contraption av three parts. that was worked from th' outside," came the answer.

CHAPTER ELEVEN

THE COAL DUST TWINS

AFTER his return to the Dismounted Mudhounds Clancy found that life at the front had changed. The battalion moved back, after a trip of record length in the line, and had a splendid rest period. Then began a series of easy tours in comparatively quiet sectors, and it was not until August that the Mudhounds got a real taste of fighting. And when they did, it was a taste they had often dreamed of, but had never realized. Old Fritz was on the run. Every fresh attack meant another hearty kick in the pants for him, and the Irishman nearly went wild.

"Tis a turn av th' game," he said happily, as Fourteen platoon hitched on equipment and prepared to go back in the line near Arras, to partake of another grand assault. Then his leathery countenance hardened as he looked about him. Nearly two-thirds of the men were new arrivals, mostly drafts just come up from the bast. "I'll be better pullin' me neck in," he remarked sadly. "If th' Kaiser could see this outfit he'd be yellin', "As ye were' an' there'd be no tellin' what would happen. "

It was whispered that the Mudhounds were to take Monchy and press on towards Orange Hill, and every man was exceedingly nervous as they moved into the trenches, every man except Clancy. He had clicked for a carrying party, and this at a time when new men were so abundant was very trying to his temper. Then the skies grew leaky and the Irishman became dangerous. They were in a narrow, winding communication trench full of treacherous holes and as he paused to pick his step the man behind him crashed into him. Blummmp! "Divil take ye," snarled Clancy. "Watch yersilf or ye'll wake up in a hospital. Use yer eyes, ye half-wit!"

"Oi, such a business," wailed the offender. "If I stops it bumps, if I go it bumps, and it is rain all the time. I should die if something happens."

"Kin yez beat it!" snorted Clancy. "A kike for our siction. Well, me pork-hater, if ye bump me again, Heaven hilp ye."

"Oi, yes,- no - the Sergeant gives it to walk careful," moaned the newcomer, keeping close to Clancy in spite of his threats. "It's the jug, he says, if I am to keep my life. Oi, what a war!"

The Irishman stopped short and received another rude jolt, but instead of retaliating he hissed a sibilant query, "Have ye got a rum jug?"

"Yes - no," came the response. "it was so the Sergeant says."

Clancy stood a moment, almost dazed by such good fortune, then he swung about. "Kape close to me," he cautioned. "Ye are in luck, Abraham."

“No - yes," came the protest. "My name was Levi. Levi Cohen."

"Can yer chatter," was the swift retort. "I have some thinkin' to do."

Clancy spoke the truth. He had to think and to think quickly. One hundred yards more and they would be at company headquarters, and before they got there he must find means to cache a burden he bore almost reverently. It was a jug lettered "S.R.D." In some inexplicable way the new man behind him had also been entrusted with rum sufficient for the company, and two issues must never arrive.

Clancy knew the trench, and near their destination a length of duck board bridged a mud hole. As he crossed it he bent low and set his precious booty in the miry softness beside the boards. He kept on in his place in the file and though he had only a sack of bread to represent his load he escaped checking and then heard Cohen venting noisy relief at being rid of his burden. He caught the new man as they left headquarters. "Come with me, me lucky lad," he chortled. "an' we'll sample the jug I carried."

"Oi, yes - no," wheezed Cohen, "And it gives you one too? What a wart It was my first times I was here yet, and I should get lost if I am by myself. Where was... ?"

"Listen," hissed Clancy, "Spake less and ye'll know more. I'm for listening post, jist th' two hours, and ye are to come with me. Tis quiet out there, and we can have a drop without bein' bothered. Wait fer me."

He was gone before Cohen could object, and for once the Irishman was thankful that the rain had made the night such a velvety black. He recovered the jug and thrust it in a sandbag, then got his partner and led to the lane in the wire used by those detailed for the outpost. "We jist lay out there and kape our ears open," he explained as they stopped by a sentry stationed at the entrance to the wire lane. "Th' wire is for signals. Jist tug it now and then so's this guy knows everything is jake."

"Yes. but maybe some Heinies should be out there by us," Cohen protested, straining his eyes to peer in the darkness.

All along the front the Verey lights rose and fell like bubbles from a million pipes. Guns roared their hate and winking flashes of shell fire on either flank did not abate. A stretcher party came along the trench, making difficult progress in the dark. "Who have ye there?" Clancy asked.

"One of them new blokes nimed Perkins," came a weary answer in Cockney accent. "Forgot to duck his napper at the machine gun post. Would n't that give yer camel's 'ump?"

“Oi - oi," "Cohen shuddered as he pressed close to Clancy. "I was sleep by Perkins and he is already dead. What a war!"

"Git up here and kape yer fin on th' wire," ordered the Irishman. "Follow me an' ye'll find this war could be worse."

Levi clambered over the parapet land grasped the guiding wire that led them to a deep crater well across No Man's Land. From such a vantage point they could hear enemy patrols and signal their presence. It was a risky position, but Clancy, certain that no marauders would venture forth in such disagreeable darkness, felt the post to be a haven of enjoyment. After whispered instructions to Cohen be carefully extracted the stopper of the jug. His mess tin served as a mug and he indulged in several very liberal rations before he passed refreshment to Cohen. "No more already," Levi choked and sputtered. "too much is bad to swallow, but already it feels warm..."

He ceased speaking. A flare had looped high from the German lines, the first in their vicinity, and by its light Cohen could see what a nightmare of scummy holes surrounded them. "It was worse to see," he gasped, his teeth chattering. "Was you heard something, maybe?"

Clancy listened. Despite the steady mutter of the guns he thought he could detect the squelching of boots in sticky mud. He hastily swallowed another “ ration." "Git wan av thim bombs in yer mitt," he ordered, "an' kape listenin'."

Another flare shot up and before its glow faded a beady-eyed rat stole through the weeds that rimmed their crater. Cohen sprang back and cried out in fear. Clancy menaced him with his rifle. "Ye poor fool," he grated, "if ye yap like that again I'll plug ye. Do ye want Fritz to come over?"

Cohen subsided, shivering at the bottom of the crater. Clancy had another drink. He disdained the cowering man and conceived the idea of giving him a thorough scare. "Git yer rifle," he snapped. "Have another drink, and then we'll crawl out a bit farther and listen."

Cohen gurgled his nip and had another. They left the signal wire and climbed out, walking upright. Zip! Another flare. Its light made fantastic moving shadows over the eerie waste. Both men glanced ahead. A huddled figure lay there, exposing blackened flesh and teeth bared like ivories. Darkness. "We'll go back an' have another drink," said Clancy.

There came a dull "plop" from the Hun lines and a fiery object described an arc high above them, descending into the trenches of the Rifles. A deafening crash told of its arrival. "Blast thim Minnies," said Clancy, "I'd like to git me hands on th' guy that shoots thim."

Before they could move, a second and third Minnewerfer looped over them. "Fer tin cents I'd go an' look fer th' divil that's shootin' thim," said Clancy grimly. He took several paces before Cohen caught him. "No - yes, but it would be murder for myself," pleaded the new man. "And the signal wire should be pulled."

"Hell's bells," spluttered Clancy, "ye should have tugged the wire before we left. Ye'll niver learn this war."

But No Man's Land had twisted itself in the darkness. Clancy could not find their crater. He found a score as deep, and Cohen fell into several, but the one with the wire and rum jug avoided them. "Ye got me mixed with yer blasted chatter," said the Irishman angrily, "kape still till I try wance more. Thim lights..."

He got no further. Hulking forms materialized as if by magic. Guttural commands grated on their ears and rough hands seized them before they could make a move in defence. A plaintive wail from Cohen was checked abruptly by a blow from a rifle butt. Two burly missionaries of Kultur grasped Clancy by the elbows and propelled him over the rough ground at amazing speed. Before he could utter protest or attempt resistance, the earth seemingly dropped from beneath him as his captors heaved him into a dark abyss fronting a dugout entrance. Cohen fell on top of him. Bayonets prodded them erect and both were hustled through an evil-smelling gas blanket and down slippery steps into an underground chamber.

Candle light dazzled them. Clancy made out a stout arrogant German Major with an Iron Cross dangling over his paunch and three satellites hovering in the background. Cohen loomed beside him, a monument of mud and misery, but as his features appeared in the candle glow, Clancy gasped. Had the rum distorted his vision? Could he trust his eyesight? Levi Cohen's features were firm and bony, and his nose predominated, but not to an alarming degree. Exactly the same could be said of Clancy's profile. And Cohen was the same build as the Irishman. Were their countenances the same brick-red it would be difficult to tell them apart, but Cohen's bore a pawn-shop pallor. Clancy shook himself. Here was a man who but for an accident of geography was his actual twin. "Hell's bells!" he muttered

"Kin yez beat it? Why," he demanded fiercely, "do ye look like me?"

"Oi, no - yes," moaned Levi, "but it was not my fault, and the looks will leave us. We are already dead and prisoners. What a war!"

"Silence!" roared the German Major, speaking in English. "Pigs! Fools! I will the speaking do. Where is your post tonight?"

"Oi, it was by der rum," said Cohen, pitifully anxious to please. "We was hold the wire and hear things."

"Silence!" Again the roar of command.

A messenger had come down the steps and after saluting spoke rapidly. "Push these swine into one comer," said the Major, "I will attend to them after." He repeated his order in German, and the prisoners were hustled into a comer.

Clancy sobered at once. He knew that the dugout must be in front of the Hun wire, it was plainly a disused one, and the Major was probably making it his temporary quarters as he directed a number of patrols. There was a rude map on a table and he was pointing and tracing lines for the messenger. The dull report of a Minnewerfer gun came more distinctly than when they had lain in the crater.

Two other squareheads entered and gave, reports, and apparently received new orders as they departed hurriedly. Then came an earthquake. Clancy had heard the usual "plop" of the Minnie gun and had cocked his ear for the crump of the explosion in the Canadian lines. Instead, he was hurled against Cohen by the force of an awful explosion at the mouth of the dugout. The Germans were bowled over like ninepins, and air from the blast puffed out the lights. Fragments dropped from the ceiling as earth and debris slid into the chamber. Simultaneously all sounds of the night died away. His groping hands felt Levi. "Wait wan sicond, then strike a match," he hissed. " 'Tis our chance."

Gauging his way by the gasping exclamations in the dark, Clancy watched the match flare, and when it came struck down a figure that was rising beside him. As the German went to the floor, a Luger barked sharply and a bullet thudded into the wall. Clancy dodged and his knee struck the table. Picking it up he hurled it in the direction of the man with the pistol. There was a crashing of wood, three rapid shots, a hoarse yell of agony from some one. A man fell near Clancy and the Irishman dropped beside him, wrenched a Mills bomb from his pocket, tore out the pin and tossed it gently in the direction of the shooter. Pinn - ng! A vivid sheet of flame, an ear-splitting crash. Cohen's voice came, shrill with fear. "I was dead if you do it again."

"Strike a fight," shouted Clancy, keeping low, "and git a move om" He choked with the fumes of explosives.

A match spluttered. By its feeble rays he saw the Major prostrate near the blown-in stairway, saw that the other Germans were finished with war. "Light th' candle," he snapped, pointing to an end. "We've got to wurrk, me lad, if we don't smother in this rat hole."

The Major groaned and rolled over. In an instant Clancy was beside him and had secured his Luger. The German sat up. He had only been stunned by the concussion. Clancy saw a shovel near the entrance. "Git hold av this tool, Von Muck." he ordered grimly. "Yer girth control is not what it should be, and I'll hilp ye to reduce . Dig out them steps, and kape yer shovel hot. Move!"

The Major glared but saw the futility of argument and began to shovel. "Hand me that bayonet." Clancy pointed to one that hung in equipment on a peg, and Cohen obeyed. The Irishman made a jab at the German's rear. There was a howl of pain and anger and the Major wheeled to confront his own pistol. Clancy's finger pressed the trigger and his jaw was determined. "Git goin' faster," he grated. "Hop to it. Scoop it out or I'll peel yer backbone."

The German worked, desperately. Every time his shovel lagged, a prod in the rudder doubled his speed. Cohen held the candle and Clancy held the pistol. Step by step the way was cleared, and each man felt the need of fresh air before a last upward thrust brought relief. Earth slid down, a cart-load of it, leaving a yawning opening. Clancy gripped the German's arm. "Wan peep out av ye an' yer wife's a widow," he threatened. "Cohen, take this other guy's gat and kill him whin I do, if he says a wu-urd."

The Major was too exhausted, too thoroughly cowed, to say a word or attempt escape, and the trench garrison of that sector had evidently felt sure that the Minenwerfer that had fallen short had killed every inmate of the dugout. There was no one near, and no one challenged their going. But the night was as dark as ever and Clancy did not know which way to travel. The jungle between the wires was as unreadable as before. He halted, perplexed, then had a brilliant idea.

"Cohen," he whispered, "walk around me, slowlike."

He sniffed and sniffed until the odour of stale perspiration came on the wind. "Stop there," he called softly. "I have th' direction. I could smell ye strong on me right as we came out, so ye should be on we left and we're right. Come along."

His scheme worked. A little later they were challenged by C.M.R. sentries and soon were over the parapet, boosting the corpulent and weary Major before them. In the headquarters dugout Clancy told his story, providing thrills as he saw fit, and magnanimously gave Cohen credit for slight assistance. "Take th' prisoner to brigade," said the delighted commanding officer. "It's not often we catch a Major. Clancy, you and your-er-he's not your brother, is he, or relatim?'.

"If he was," said Clancy savagely, "I would have killed him mesilf whin I was born."

"I'm sorry," said the officer, "that is, I hope I haven't hurt your feelings. Anyway, you and your helper can have a couple days rest back of the lines. Here are passes to Gendelles."

A military policeman halted then in Gendelles and read their tickets, then showed them to a billet. It was an out-building, but the straw was clean, and hens about the barn meant eggs. “There’s a good show at the movie hall tonight,” said the M.P. “Go early if you want a seat.”

"Show!" said Cohen. "Why should I want it? I am starved all the time. When do we eat?"

"Any time ye feel like it," said Clancy. He was feeling gay. "Didn't ye bring the unexpended portion av yer day's rations? Ivery soldier should carry thim. Now ye'll have to salvage a bit."

"Salvage, is it?" said Cohen. "Is it take things I should?" Then his eyes glistened. On a beam in their shed sat a tin of bully. In a moment he was stolidly eating, as though it were an occupation instead of a meal.

Clancy watched him a moment in disgust, then flung his gear in a corner. "Niver mind yer manners," he said drily. "This is a hog-fillin' station anyways." He tilted his cap rakishly and stepped into the yard. "I'm fer a drink," he announced. "'Tis th' land av fair maidens and free wine - I don't think."

"Oi, yes - no." said Cohen, "but what should I do now?"

"Have yer beauty sleep," came the acrid answer. "Kape watch av th' equipment. These frogs would steal warts off a toad."

Before the evening was over. Clancy had forgotten the war. The show he attended had been staged by a divisional concert party and was all that any care-free buccaneer of the trenches could demand. "Robinson Crusoe" was the name of the play, and Friday, as played by a bony artilleryman, clad in an ancient feather boa, was worth any price, but all stars faded when Miss Twice, a fair "island maid", was introduced. The manager appeared and announced that their regular female impersonator was ill and that this mademoiselle had kindly consented to take his place. His announcement was unnecessary as far as Clancy was concerned. Any Irishman with half an eye could see that the lady in the flimsy crepe de Chine was the real goods and, seated in the front row, he was anaesthetized by the glad look she gave him. He was determined to make her acquaintance after the show but got stranded in a thicket of heads and elbows. As a man in a dream he went to his billet and kicked off his boots before he was aware of an aching tooth. Cohen was in his blankets. "I was had some eats," he said sleepily, "but some francs was no good by this place."

"Rist yet jaw," snapped Clancy. "It's after yet bedtime."

In vain he tried to sleep. Visions came of a cute blonde, soft as cushions, with eyes that set you dizzy. He knew she had admired him, had read it in her glances. He must find her. Then an unearthly cry pierced the night. Cohen raced to the door, raving. The partitions of the building were not substantial. A calf had reached through and licked Levi's pale visage. "Shut yer trap," ordered Clancy. "Th' baste is sick already."

But he could not compose himself to lie down again. He put on his boots and went out. There was a turn in the street, just beyond their billet, and mistaking his way he found himself in a sort of alley, a cul-de-sac, and at the end a blind wall with huge double doors. Feeling over it be found a cord. Clancy had had experiences with various "speak-easies" in France, and he craved enough strong drink to soothe his aching molar. He pulled the cord and the door he was pushing against opened so suddenly and noiselessly that he almost fell inside. Then he stood - dumbfounded.

He was in the kitchen of a house, and in the next room stood Miss Twice, a captivating coquette, bidding adieu to a caller. In spite of the unquestionable ardour of her visitor she was keeping him at bay by the hauteur of her pose. Clancy felt his pulse race. His fists clenched. He would like to hurry the caller, but it would be exceedingly poor judgment to attempt it for the caller was an officer, resplendent in red-tabbed insignia. After a last attempt to embrace Miss Twice the gallant brass hat took a sullen departure.

The moment he was gone, Miss Twice came to the kitchen as if she had sensed Clancy's entrance "Ah, but monsieur, I do not know you, eh?" she said cooingly. "It ees ze Canada soldat."

Her low-keyed murmur made his head swim. "Miss Twice," he said fervently, " 'Tis more luck than th' Irish kin expect that I should find ye so aisy, and now that I have I'll be a gentleman. 'Tis a late hour and if I may be so bold I'd like th' pleasure av callin' on ye tomorrow. Me name is Timothy Fergus Clancy."

"Oui, Monsieur Clancy, eet will be one pleasure. Ze Captain will come when I say 'no', but for you I say yes .

"Th' blackguard!" fumed Clancy. "'Tis th'way av thim brass hats. Say th' wu-urd and I'll see he doesn't bother ye more."

"Ah-but he ees beeg officer an' ze family tree ees heavy with the general, he say."

"Is that so!" said Clancy fiercely. "I'm a man av distinguished family mesilf. Family tree! 'Tis a scrub bush he's under, I'm thinkin'."

Miss Twice giggled. "You are so fonny," she said. Then she tapped her dainty mouth to suppress a yawn. "It ees so late" she sighed. "Tomorrow night you come, ch?"

"Thank ye, and I will," said Clancy huskily. "Would ye mind a kiss as sign av rale friendship?"

Her eyes gave him answer, and so he took her in his arms and bestowed a real Irish kiss on her pretty lips. Then she pushed him away. "You are ze gentleman I am sure," she cooed. "Next night you come."

Clancy went back to his billet on wings. Not until he shaved the next morning and saw his swollen jaw did he remember his toothache. After shining his brass and cleaning his shoes he strolled down the street. By a squat farmhouse he saw Cohen seated in the sun, apparently at peace with the world. A French girl came from a shed. She proved the attendant of a rather bony cow. Her hair was wound in a loose knot at the back of her head and the key of her dress was a large safety-pin at the back. Clancy spat disgustedly. "Kin yez beat it!" he muttered to himself. "How kin there be sich cratures in th' wu-urld? 'Twill bea relief to git me eyes on a rale lady this even."

He passed the noon hour at an estaminet but found the hours hanging heavy at that. Passing shop windows gave him the idea of purchasing a gift for Miss Twice. He entered a shop - then stopped as if struck, and swore violently. His money was gone!

The officer who gave them passes had arranged that they each drew twenty francs, and he had lost every cent. His mind went back over every detail of the previous night and could not solve the mystery. Then he thought of Cohen. Every kike had money. He would borrow.

He went to the squat farmhouse again, went around to the back and saw Cohen inside. He was seated at a table, and the fact that his belt was loosed and hanging from his hooks proclaimed that he had had a satisfactory session. Before him were remnants, and remnants only, of bacon, mashed potatoes and fried eggs, plum jam and cheese, French bread and honey. An empty vin-rouge bottle stood sentry over the bare dishes. "Oi, such a town," grunted Cohen as Clancy entered. "I was full at one time, and there is more."

"Ye are a hog," said Clancy. "Lind me twenty francs."

"Twenty francs!" echoed Cohen blankly. "No - no - yes - I was not loose so much money at once."

"Ye'll git it back," said Clancy truculently. "I'll give ye extra five for th' use av it. Come across, I nade it immediate."

“Oi, no," Cohen fumbled in his pocket. "You would not die by me and not pay," he whined. "Its was worth ten francs for the loan."

"Ten it is," exploded Clancy. He was in no mood to argue.

Very carefully Cohen wet his fingers and counted out twenty francs. Clancy pocketed them without a word and shot into the street. He looked around the comer, and there was the brass hat of the previous night talking excitedly to an old French woman in front of the home of Miss Twice. Assuming a nonchalant air he sauntered by, saluting as he passed. When he looked back the staff officer had gone.

Clancy hurried to the old hag who stood by the gate. "Is th' young lady about, Madame?" he asked pleasantly.

A perfect deluge of broken English and French met him. He heard "Brigand", "Sale Boche", "Robber" and other like terms not so refined, and by dint of patient effort discovered her young lady boarder of two days and nights had gone without settling her account, and had also taken with her more than she brought. Clancy was astounded. He licked his lips and tried to smile, then remembered their brief embrace. Pickpocket! "Hell's bells!" he snorted, "Kin yez beat it! 'Tis no country for to fight over, nor a place for an honest man. Miss Twice-ye niver missed anything!"

Late that night he went back to his billet. Cohen was snoring in full content, but awoke at Clancy's bellow for a candle. "Some one was take it," said Levi drowsily. "Salvage is the word I should say. “Oi, but I should live here."

His smug satisfaction stirred Clancy mightily. "Ye monkey-faced hog," he shouted. "Ye should stay in a pen-if th' other pigs would stand for it."

"Monkey face is it?" said Cohen with some show of spirit, "Lisette the girl who gives eats - says are we brothers, and I say we couldn't be."

"Are ye sayin' I look like yersilf?" There was a dangerous iciness in Clancy's question as he left his bed.

"No-no," blurted Cohen. "I would never want to say so. You look like yourself."

Clancy swore in a blood-curdling fashion and put out the light. In the morning they went up the line. The Germans were being driven back, and they found their company at Orange Hill.

A rumour came to them after dark that on the morrow they would be marched back to the rear and that another brigade would carry on. "'Tis always me luck," growled Clancy. "I'm back here with that kike whin th' fightin's on an' now I'm to go back without seein' any."

Some of the new men sympathized with him. One bold lad suggested that the section to which Clancy belonged get "lost" in the dark and go on with the attackers in the morning. In a moment all had agreed to it except Cohen.

"What a war!" he wailed. "It was fights when there is no need. I wish I was by my shop."

"I wish ye were too," said Clancy fervently. "An' nixt time ye are home, take a bath." Then he saw that Cohen did not comprehend the intentions of the section, and he remained quiet on the subject. Cohen, if he did not get wise, should see some real fighting for once in his life.

He forgot him at daylight, when the party went over with an ardour that spelled their ruin, for in their race to out-do each other the company to which they attached themselves over-ran their objective. Soon it was a case of fall back or be surrounded. They were in a small village, and as shells began to rain in the streets, Clancy saw a runner dive wildly for a cellar. The sprinter was Cohen.

Clancy ducked to the same cover. He knew that the unlucky Cohen had lost his way, and his conscience twinged him. The storm of shrapnel finally ceased, but before they could move there came the tramp of many boots, and guttural voices. The Germans were in the village. "Down with ye," hissed Clancy. "'Tis caught we are. with yer wild, crazy runnin' in th' wrong direction. Have ye a match?"

They found the cellar divided into four sections. One contained partially-decayed vegetables, one was a coal bin. and a third was stocked with bottled goods. In the fourth they found refuge, as it only contained cobwebs. Heavy steps sounded overhead as someone made a quick search of the house. The searcher came down the cellar steps and used a flashlight. Its rays found the coal apartment and then rested on the array of bottles. There was a guttural exclamation, and a stout German came down the steps and helped himself to a pair of longnecks. He went back upstairs without more than a casual glance at the other spaces, the musty smell of the rotting vegetables apparently satisfying him.

After he had gone, they heard the enemy come through the yards and take posts in different quarters. Shortly there was much machine-gun fire, and Clancy knew that the Boches were using the village as their front for the day. He was painfully hungry and became exasperated when Cohen suggested that they surrender themselves. "Ye poor fish," he grated. "Do ye wish to be fried into boot grease? They would do it with yer kind. One of our lads escaped and wuz tellin' us how they pick out the well-fed ones fer lard."

Cohen began to tremble. He seemed on the verge of collapse as it grew dark, and then men came into the house, the Germans, evidently making a more thorough search of the surroundings. Once more the rays of a flashlight came into the cellar and again a thick German tongue grunted with satisfaction. Three ardent goose-steppers hurried down and each got himself a load of bottles. They went up again and Clancy heard them seat themselves in the kitchen to enjoy leisurely their find. "'Tis our chance", he whispered to Cohen. "Well creep up th' stips and go out th' front way. Th' house will be th' same as all these French places."

Clancy made Cohen strip his equipment and did likewise himself. They left their steel hats on the floor. "Kape goin' once ye start," warned the Irishman, "but make no noise. Use yer butt and bayonet, fer if ye shoot ye'll have a hornet's nist over us. Here, colour yer dial so they won't see ye so aisy."

With the words Clancy gathered a handful of coal dust from the next bin and rubbed Cohen's features. Levi opened his mouth to utter protest and was cruelly smothered.

"Wan peep an' ye'll EAT it," hissed Clancy. pointing overhead. Cohen stilled, the whites of his eyes being all that was visible in the faint light that came down the steps.

The Germans had left the cellar door open and Clancy was able to gain the hall without making a sound. In the dim shadows he was not detected by the trio around the kitchen table, and the next instant Cohen had followed him. Then a heavy step sounded just outside and someone raised the latch of the front door. Clancy started back and bumped into his comrade. "Oi," squealed Cohen. "It's my foots." They had stepped on each other.

Chairs rasped back and there was a rush from the kitchen as the door opened and three more soldiers came in the front way. Caught between two fires, Clancy did not attempt to fight, but he made a desperate effort to escape by the back door. In the melee the Germans made no use of weapons and captors and captive piled on the floor in a football tangle. The Irishman was rudely booted to an upright position and flung into the kitchen. The leader, partly drunk, leered mockingly. "Das schwein wass hiding", he said in guttural English. "Die Germans wass goming."

"Is that so?" snorted Clancy. "Ye are a long time on th' way."

"So, schwein!" An angry scowl crossed the German's face and he deliberately struck Clancy with his open hand. "You wass not to speak."

The Irishman tensed like a baited tiger, then remembered that Cohen had vanished. Where had he gone? Curbing his red-hot desire to tear at the German's throat, he stood without making reply and paid no heed to further jibes. Then someone came running to the back door and made some excited announcement. Four of the six soldiers left at once and the big leader turned to Clancy with fresh gloating. "Another schwein Englander wass a prisoner," he stated. "And it wass the officer, ja. The Germans wass goming. Hoch der Kaiser."

An officer? Clancy was puzzled. The other German reached for a bottle and drunkenly poured a drink into a mug. He poured a second for the big man and they drank a toast. "Der Tag." said the smaller man. "Der Tag," shouted his mate.

At that instant Clancy glanced toward the hall. He had fancied something moved - and he saw himself! From the shadows his own reflection came back startlingly, and he moved a hand to make sure he was not dreaming. The big German looked - and leaped. The Irishman seized his chance. The other soldier still tilted his mug, and Clancy's trusty right caught him flush on the button. As the fellow crashed down, the big leader smashed headlong into a full-length mirror that had mysteriously appeared, and at the same instant a rifle clattered to the floor farther along the passageway.

"I was surrender quick," shrilled a familiar voice. "It was me only.

The German stumbled back. He had seen a black-faced soldier in the hall, before the glass broke, he had one captive in the kitchen - and here was a third of exactly the same appearance. Then he looked again. A fourth peered at him from opposite where Cohen stood.

Dazedly he turned, and a kitchen chair splintered on his head as Clancy struck with vindictive fury. It was not the work of a second to secure his rifle and lead Cohen outside. "It was to the upstairs I went," panted Levi in answer to a jeered question. "I was hide there and a mirror found and I brings it down to show..."

"Stow it," snapped Clancy. "Listen, if ye quit again without tryin' I'll put a bomb in your pocket with the pin out. Git me?"

“Oi, I was not means to...”

"Shut up!"

They hurried across the yard keeping close to the buildings. After a quick survey of the next street Clancy led the way. Facing them was a long row of buildings and on the other side lay the open field and their own lines. They had only to get by the row of houses to reach comparative safety. But lights winked at them from several cellars and he saw indistinct figures pacing by each opening. Their only hope lay in going direct to some house and making through it. "Whin I give th' word," he muttered impressively to the shivering Cohen, "ye are to run as fast as ye kin. Yer life depinds on it. And follow me."

Cohen nodded miserably, his eyes eerie in his blackened visage.

Clancy tightened his belt and looked around. "Go," he barked, as he put his head down and sprinted. Feet thudded after him and he could hear Cohen's gasps for breath. They were within yards of the house he had selected, a larger one than the rest. before they were noticed. Someone yelled a challenge, then a group of men came running in pursuit. "In here," panted Clancy, driving at a back door.

To his amazement a figure detached itself from the gloom, and a German sentry ordered him to halt. Clancy's reply was a shot, and the man dropped heavily, his helmet clattering on the tiled walk. The Irishman took the door like a mad bull, bursting it open. A light gleamed from a passage and he slid down it, then doors opened on both sides and he was engulfed - by German soldiers.

He used the butt on the first man, and in the narrow way had the advantage. The soldier collapsed and Clancy fired once, twice, three times, as fast as he could work the bolt. Gray-coated men plunged to cover as their comrades sank in death. And at the instant came a wild cheer from the room on the right, and a German was hurled back into the passage by a terrific blow from a clubbed rifle. "Canadians this way," came a shout, and Clancy saw a Captain of the battalion that had attacked, his tunic in tatters, batter his way into the hall. The Captain had evidently been the prisoner the German had boasted about and was now making an effort to escape. Clancy rushed to join him as the back door crushed inwards. Other Germans came in at the front. The Irishman could not shoot as the officer moved so quickly, and he resorted to butt and cold steel. One German, his neck spurting blood, managed to get the Captain around the knees. Clancy kicked him loose as he bayoneted a third squarehead. Then an explosion rocked the kitchen. Someone had tossed a bomb among the in-rushing men. Groans and calls mingled with a shrill shout. "I was here, Clancy. It was my bomb. Save me by the stairs."

"This way," yelled Clancy, "we're goin'." He had downed three men in succession, and the Captain, now armed with a loaded rifle, had cleared the entrance.

There was a scramble in the kitchen among the wounded men, then Cohen shot through the hall and continued outside. Three shots rang out, but he kept on, and the Captain followed. Clancy fired as he left the doorway and saw the Germans scatter. A party of them were doubling to intercept their escape, but as the officer pumped three more bullets among them they fled wildly to cover. Shouts in the darkness ahead guided them, and soon they were in a sunken road among a company of the Ninth Brigade.

Clancy was almost finished. A soldier told him rations were up and he headed for a distant cellar where they were being served. There a cook offered him a dixie of hot tea, and Clancy wolfed bread and bacon drip, cheese and jam. When he could eat no more he went back to the sunken road. A group were talking in a gunner's dugout that was being used as a company headquarters. He peered in. A Major was shaking hands with Cohen, others were grouped around patting his back, giving vent to their admiration. "He's worth a regiment himself," he heard the rescued captive state. "I never saw such fighting since Ypres. He must have killed a dozen Heinies. Who has the whisky?"

Clancy stood as if glued to the spot, then he ground his teeth. "Kin yez beat it?" he grated. "Av all th' crawlin' varmints I iver met, that kike beats them all. I'll git square with him if it takes me to me dyin' day."

As he plodded on, his foot began to throb. When he and Cohen collided in the house, they had trampled on each other and Levi's boots were not slippers. Sitting on a bank Clancy made investigation. His instep was severely bruised and was swelling. Along the front flares rose sparingly. There was little gunfire except in distant areas. Back of the Canadian front he could hear lorries and traffic pouring up for the morrow's offensive. "'Twill be hell again," said Clancy to himself, "and some kike will git th' credit. Divil take th* war, I'm goin' out with this foot. 'Tis a Blighty I've got."

He made his way to the rear, caught an ambulance and was hustled to a dressing station. A harassed doctor made a brief examination and then tied a ticket to Clancy's tunic and motioned him out of the way. "All right in a day, my lad," he said.

Clancy swore under his breath. Was he foiled? He tried to read what the Medical Officer had written, but the strange terms baffled him. "I'll add a letter here and there," he said grimly, "An' tack on a couple av wu-urds av me own. While they're makin' thim out I'll have a bit av rist."

With a pencil stub he made the alterations, then he went outside. He was at a cross-roads, and traffic passed unceasingly. While he watched, a French ambulance stopped as the driver avoided a tractor. Clancy had a brain wave. He darted to the French car and crawled into it. There was room for him. An hour later he was unloaded into a French hospital.

An orderly who spoke broken English examined his ticket, shrugged his failure to understand it, and put Clancy to bed in an isolated room. The hospital was installed in a brick building that had been a factory of some sort, and several of these smaller apartments were next to the kitchen quarters. The Irishman sniffed and smiled. "Me luck's come back," he muttered to himself.

He was scarcely between the sheets before a French doctor came in, a small dark man with a beard as thin and wiry as a billet broom. After a long look at Clancy's ticket he went away talking excitedly with an attendant.

Then came a chic French damsel who questioned him in her own language. Clancy decided that she was asking about medicine and said "No", very positively. There followed embarrassing moments. Apparently she had wished to know whether he could wash himself or not, and now persisted in washing him all over. The doctor popped back like a jack-in-the-box as she finished, whispered to the nurse, and tapped his head very significantly. The door of the room was closed as they went out, and Clancy heard a key turned. "Kin yez beat it!" he ejaculated. Then the subtle comfort of a bath and clean bed overpowered him. He fell asleep, and when he awoke the sun was shining.

Through his window he could see into the hospital yard, and as he looked he saw his muddied and ragged uniform ascending as incense from an incinerator there. His few personal belongings, minus his razor and service knife, were on a table by his cot. He drew back the sheets. "Kin yez beat it?" he asked the shut door. "Niver a look at me foot, and me here th' night." As if in answer the key grated, and in came the little doctor, accompanied by a stout attendant who watched Clancy closely. The doctor bowed and bubbled broken French. " 'Tis me foot," interrupted Clancy, thrusting the injured member into view "are ye cuckoo in this joint?"

"Ah, nevair ze worry," said the doctor, bowing again. "It will be all well wit' monsieur. Ze head-it aches? Non? It ees good. In a few days - weeks monsieur will feel better, ees it not? Rest comfortable an'eet will be good. Your breakfas' is serve."

Another burly attendant brought in a tray. Eggs, toast, a soup, and some fruit. "Ye feed well here," said Clancy, sitting up, "but what about my foot?" He felt that he must argue the point, for the swelling bad gone down overnight and it required critical attention to see the damage.

"Ze food will be all right," said the doctor soothingly. "If there is something monsieur would like?"

"Not now," said Clancy decidedly. He wished to be left alone while he tried to solve his position. Did these frogs think he was cuckoo?

The attendants remained while he ate, eyeing him with determination and refusing all his attempts at conversation. When he finished, they took the dishes and departed, locking the door. Dinner was served in the same fashion. Then they brought him tobacco for his pipe, but the chic damsel never returned, and all his requests regarding medical attention were politely ignored. Before evening Clancy knew his only hope lay in planning an escape. For some reason he was regarded as mildly insane and was virtually a prisoner.

On the afternoon of the second day he was growing desperate. His window was heavily barred and his guardians were never lax. Their stolid watchfulness irritated him beyond measure, and they had ignored his pleas for treatment. Then he heard a high-pitched voice in the corridor. "The name is Clancy and if it is brothers, it makes no difference. It means money to see him."

"Cohen!" shouted Clancy. "Come this way if ye love yer soul." There was real welcome in his words. Never had he expected so to rejoice over the appearance of a kike.

After much torrid speech outside the door Levi was admitted. Clancy scarcely knew him. Cohen wore a clean new uniform, new boots, and a new cap. "For the luva Mary," sputtered the Irishman. "How did ye git thim?"

Cohen strutted. "It was all a joke," he said proudly. "The Fifth was all mixed up. The Captain was think I was not myself with the coal dust, and give me your name. Clothes he gives, boots, cap, and -" with a flourish he produced a leave warrant, "ten days to London. It would be a bad joke to say anything, so I keep still and - here I am, but it is twenty francs you borrow and I am for money."

Clancy strangled as he tried to speak. It was unbelievable. This kike had been mistaken for him, had been issued new khaki, had been given a leave warrant bearing his own name. and had actually accepted all without making known his identity. The coal dust application had hidden the difference. The Irishman fought for words, then his brain raced at feverish speed. Here was golden glorious opportunity, if...

Cohen sniffed. "Oi, I was hungry yet," he said plaintively. "No breakfast it gets while I am all night looking to see this place for my twenty francs. The driver tells me crooked - and the eats, was they plenty yet?"

"Levi,' said Clancy with oily pleasantness, "if ye'll stay a bit ye can have a feed av chicken, with jelly an' all the fixin's. I'm havin' th' same till I'm tired av it."

"Was you telling me crooked?" queried Cohen, his mouth watering. "I am sick yet for emptiness."

"Ye could eat till ye busted, if ye was in my place," said Clancy craftily. "They bring me more than ye kin hold ivery time."

"Oi, what a war!" said Cohen. "Tell me something to do for to eat."

Clancy placed a warning finger to his lips. He heard the attendants outside but noticed that they had not locked the door. "Slip out av yer duds and crawl in me place here," he whispered. "I'll make out I'm yersilf. an' they'll never twig. Ye can eat tiff yer sick, if ye want."

"If it was not crooked," sighed Cohen.

"How kin it be crooked? ' Ye eat while I'm here, thin put on yer rig again."

"It will do," said Levi, "the chicken smell too loud."

As he shed his uniform, he very carefully transferred a bulky purse and his leave warrant to a place under the pillow. Clancy made no comment but donned the discarded clothes, minus the undergarments, which he tucked under the mattress. The exchange was scarcely completed before the door opened. Cohen stared expectantly, wetting his lips, but it was the wire-whiskered doctor who entered. Clancy's barrage of complaints had evidently borne fruit. The attendant, at an order, reached and tugged the clothes from Cohen's feet. The result was staggering. The only water that had reached those feet for several weeks had filtered through leaky boots.

The little doctor gave a shrill cry of alarm and seized his nose, then he sputtered like a machine gun and men came running. One carried a bucket of steaming water, another had bars of soap, a third an armload of sponges and towels.

"No, no, no!" howled Cohen. "It was never me - it was Levi. It gives me sick and to die with water. Hel-lup!"

Clancy tapped his brow and made a significant motion. The Frenchman went to work with a vim, and at the rapid-fire orders uncovered more of Cohen that needed washing. Levi fought desperately in sheer terror, and for a time it was a real struggle. Clancy appeared to lend a helping hand but managed to secure the leave warrant from under the pillow. Then he stepped back and shook his head mournfully. He had regained his own personal effects from the table and was ready for departure. "'Tis only a bath ye are havin'," he consoled his rival. "Kape thinkin' av th' chicken that's comin'- sometime. I'll have one to yer health whin I reach Blighty."

"Come-backs," screamed Levi. "It is stealing he is done. It was not him and he is me. Catch him! Oi!"

"I wish ye a soldier's farewell," said Clancy from the door. I..."

There was a hair-raising cry. The doctor had grown fearful of Cohen's antics and had given him a hypodermic.

On the leave boat that glided to the dock at Folkestone men crowded eagerly to be near the landing. Clancy, resplendent in his new uniform looked on in lazy comfort. What need to push and rush? He had ten good days ahead of him. A well-meaning Padre, happy as the others over seeing England again, paused by the Irishman.

"We're all boys together on a holiday," he said cheerfully. "Every man's a brother. Isn't it a glorious thing to be all like one big family?"

"It may be," said Clancy, as he spat over the rail, "but twins is a hell av a relation."

CHAPTER TWELVE

CLANCY'S DEPRAVITY

CLANCY disconsolately opened a tin of bully. He had been travelling since break of day, moving at the request of self-important officers who were herding all the stragglers to their battalions in the forward area, and the sun was now high in the sky. He had not eaten since morning, when his breakfast had been a tin of cocoa and a few biscuits, given him by a Y.M.C.A. man who had stonily refused further favours. Clancy had expressed fervent hope that a shell hit the canteen and knock it loose from it's triangle. Then he had plodded on and had found the bully near a discarded pack.

He was going back to the Mudhounds with mixed feelings. For one thing, he would be proud to receive the congratulations of the Sergeant and a few old-timers on the way he had earned his leave, on the other hand he was having a difficult time to console himself regarding the army belief that a soldier's third trip to France was usually an unlucky one.

"Th' front is th' only place for a rale soldier," he had remarked to a friend at Boulogne. "An' th' men that's kicked Fritz ivery time should have th' chance to tickle his tail whin he's runnin' fer home an' th' Kaiser."

The friend, a hard-bitten artilleryman, had stared at the Irishman. "You don't mean you're going back just to have a last crack at the Heinie, do you?" he had blurted. "Hell man! You can get killed now just as easy as any time. Any man that goes chasin' into barbed wire an' shell holes when he don't have to is either crazy or shell-shocked or both."

And now, as Clancy sat on a biscuit-tin and ate his bully, he agreed with the sentiment. Behind him was Bourlon Wood and at every line of vision were signs of activity. Marching men, lorries, limbers, ambulances, batteries and transport of all kinds were on the move. Here and there were small parties sleeping by the roadside, sleeping as they had slumped to earth, steel hats tumbled off, arms outspread, rifles slung at their feet. Overhead were swarms of aeroplanes, glinting in the sun as they wheeled like great falcons. He saw a file of prisoners go by, their pot helmets and gas masks bobbing queerly as they went over the uneven ground.

Some men of Clancy's own battalion went by. They were sweat-streaked, dust-covered, tired-looking, but they plodded on as if they were going away from the war instead of going straight towards it. Clancy wiped his knife on his puttees and hailed the soldiers. "Where's th' Fifth?" he queried. "Up ahead," said the leader. At a place called Saint All, I think. It's right at the canal near Cambrai, they say."

"Whin are they comin' back?"

"They're not comin'," came the eager answer. "They're goin', th' whole darned push. Th' Eighth brigade's goin' right into Cambrai tomorrow. They've got Heinie on th' run now."

Clancy kicked the bully tin out of his way and stood up. He fell in at the rear of the little party. "I'll go on," he muttered to himself. "'Tis th' only place for me whin th' Mudhounds has so many av these new men that's list heard av th' war, an' 'tis th' luck av th' Irish to be born fighters anyways. I'll have to look at th' bunch."

He did. When the sun went down that evening he was established in an enlarged shell hole at St. Olle. His covering was two German greatcoats and he rested on blankets. Beside him were a rifle and equipment. He had salvaged all in a few moments, had gotten himself a huge supper from the company cook, had dodged the eye of the Sergeant, and had chosen his crater in order to ensure himself a night of undisturbed rest. It was about three in the morning when his illusion was shattered.

"Hi, Clancy you old mudhound! Snap out of it!" The husky voice of Sergeant Binns held an eager note. "Come on, old man, you're needed."

"What th' divil is wrong with ye?" growled Clancy. "I'm not on th' stringth av yer mob yit. Go git some av thim umpty-umps ye've been nursin'. What do yez want anyways?"

The Sergeant was a horny-handed, old mud-eater who had ascended from the rear rank, and the Irishman tolerated him more than any other of his ilk.

"Orders is come," said Binns, "for the Fifth to send a patrol across th' canal to bomb out a post on th' other side. 'D' Company's clicked for it and th' Captain told me to pick my gang. There'll be ten of us."

"How do yez git over?" Clancy was donning his equipment.

"We swim," said Binns," and that's why I come for you.

Clancy spat savagely and swore, and the Sergeant grinned. Twenty minutes later they were gasping with cold as they lunged across the canal, each man supporting a bucket of bombs. They crept like ghosts to where German sentries had been observed and made perfect throws into the position. The sharp "pinnng" of explosions cut the night alarmingly, but there was no response. No wounded man cried out and no potato-mashers came hurtling in retaliation. All was still. Binns and Clancy looked at each other and then walked boldly to the post. It was deserted. Only a German ground sheet and a few stick bombs lay there. The garrison had flown and it meant that the Hun was leaving Cambrai.

The rest of 'D' Company was not long in crossing by the bridge and two hours later Clancy was wearily picking his way through streets that were flanked by burning buildings. The fleeting enemy had set the city on fire in order to retard pursuit and confuse pursuers. Clancy was lost, save for the fact that he had with him a little man called "Chips," a fellow who never had enough fried potatoes.

"Now where," said Clancy, peering through smoke wreaths," is th' rist av that hell-raisin' outfit? Niver did I see sich a bunch fer gettin' lost. Where do ye think we are at, Chips?"

"I don't know," said Chips, without animation. "I know I'm hungry though, an' we didn't have a decent supper. Do you suppose there's any spuds around?"

"Spuds, is ut!" said Clancy scornfully. "What do I care about thim now? I've niver had me night's sleep yet, and I'm not yit on th' stringth av th' mob. I'm goin' to find a dacint bed in a house that's not burnin' and have me rist. Ye kin do what ye like."

"But, gosh, how do you know where we are?" protested Chips with almost feminine shrillness. "We must have walked miles since we seen anybody."

"What difference does it make?" demanded Clancy. "Ye are for spuds an' I'm fer a bed. Th' Heinies are out av town so... I'm goin' in here."

As he talked Clancy had seen a big brick house that was clear of the fired zone, and he entered by the front door. He faced a gloomy passage. The blinds were drawn at the windows and it was very dark, but he knew by the odour that the place had been occupied by Germans - and at the same time he was suddenly and painfully aware of a hard object pressed against his spine.

"Surrender," came a guttural threat. "Be quick."

Clancy dropped his rifle and put his hands up. There seemed nothing else he could do when the enemy had a revolver planted at his back. An electric torch flashed and he faced a big, sullen-looking German.

Then came curt orders and the soldier pulled Clancy forward by grasping his tunic front. A door closed behind him and an officer pushed by, a haughty, monocled Major, exuding Berlin swank. It was he who had put the Luger to Clancy's back. A second soldier followed him in and they made a hasty search of the Irishman's clothing, then pushed him aside as they bundled maps and papers from a table.

Another moment and they were in the streets, and there Clancy saw Chips cringing under the attentions of two burly goose steppers. The captives were hustled together and then the party hurried down the street.

At the suburbs they saw a car and several wagons making way through a tangle of wreckage. The officer gave orders to his men and ran to get passage in the car. Clancy and Chips were urged to a double and they caught at the rear of a transport cart and scrambled on board, their guards following. Shortly they were en route for Berlin, and Clancy found his speech again. He had often visioned capture, at times had feared it, and had always resolved that he would never be taken while he had his strength and was armed and here he had been captured and herded away inside of five minutes, as if it were a regular morning event for his enemies. "Chips," he said hoarsely. "'Tis me third time over, an' ye kin see th' luck av it." Then his voice hardened, "and ye kin put this in yer pipe. Whin I git half av wan chance I'm goin' to make a break for it. Niver will they cart Tim Clancy to th' Kaiser without knowin' they've got a live Irishman."

"Tim," pleaded Chips. "For th' love of Mike don't try anything. jist look at the guys all round us." He pointed at a long procession of marching men, pallid-faced youths and tired-looking men, in baggy trousers tucked into long boots, with "pill-box" caps on their heads. All along the road were plodders, and parties resting, transport of every description, the German army and its backwash was in full retreat.

"Fourteen, platoon could beat a rigiment av them," grunted Clancy, then he relapsed into silence and studied the situation.

It was certainly galling to be plucked up like an over-confident chicken by these fugitive Heinies who had been put to utter rout, but what could he do about it? There were Germans to the right of them, Germans to left of them, Germans behind and in front of them, all travelling the one way, all too fed up to bother about taking a Canadian prisoner. He knew, despite his declarations, that he would be committing plain suicide if he were to make a bolt from his guards. Then the monotony of their ride was suddenly broken. First a wheel came off their decrepit, rope-tired cart and they were pitched out so roughly that one of the guards twisted an ankle. He could not walk and he seemed glad, he pulled Clancy and Chips to one side and there they awaited another cart. It had just come and they were getting on board, after ditching several bags of plunder to make room, when a British airman came over, flying low, and dropped bombs on the long-drawn mile of stragglers. The German driver whipped his war-worn horses and tried to get free of the huddled traffic. He did succeed in getting on a side road that led from the scene of carnage, but he could not find a way to turn and at last, after a long barrage of grumbled comment from the two soldiers, kept on and took a road that would, apparently, swing back to the original route of retreat.

They went on and on and presently the soldiers began to growl anew. The road they were on was veering in the right direction but they were entirely alone. A few timid-looking peasants were about their farms, and they watched with interest the unusual passengers in the cart. Chips, who had kept a nervous watch about him and overhead since the appearance of the bomber, began to look at Clancy. "When do you suppose we'll eat?" he asked at last.

"Whin we find some grub," returned Clancy grimly. "Kin ye not see that's what troublin' these two burrds at th' prisint?"

Chips gave a long sigh. "Gosh," he said. "I was never so hungry before. This cart jars my stomach lower every mile."

They came to a more prosperous-looking farm and the bigger soldier barked a harsh command. The driver at once halted his horses and the guard dismounted. His mate with the sore ankle picked up his rifle and kept a scowling watch on the prisoners. The German went into the house and shortly they saw him re-appear at the door. He shouted some orders and the driver clucked at his steeds. They pulled the cart into the farmyard and were allowed to graze at the dead grass and weeds. Chips sat up and looked interested. "What's goin' to happen here?" he asked.

"Ye niver can tell," said Clancy solemnly. "Fer one thing, we'll see these Heinies fill their bellies, an' maybe ye'll git a spud fer yersilf. Fer a sicond thing, I'm takin' any rale chance at gettin' away. Are yez with me or are yez not?"

"Gosh," said Chips. "I can't run on a weak stomach, and you can't run faster'n a bullet anyway. What are you plannin' to do?"

"I asked ye," said Clancy, "are yez with me or not?"

Chips paled and coughed. He knew his man. "Yes," he said. "What did you say it that way for?"

The German soldier glared at them, but made no effort to check their conversation. Then his comrade came out and helped him down and the prisoners were hustled into the farmhouse. The old woman of the farm had placed on the table slices of dark bread, fried potatoes and eggs, as well as steaming cups of coffee. Both Germans ate noisily and greedily, and Chips suffered as he watched them. "Gosh, won't they give us anything?" he whined.

"Ask thim," said Clancy. He was having a difficult time to conceal his own hunger.

Chips made a request for food. "We're hungry," he said loudly. "Can't we have something to eat?"

The Germans scowled. They had their rifles beside their chairs, and had the table moved in front of the door. Then the old French dame calmly deposited another plate of fried potatoes on the table, and cut more bread. She also sat two extra cups of coffee in place, Clancy looked at her, and then deliberately shifted his chair to a position behind the food. One of the Germans opened his mouth to snarl, and seized his rifle, but hesitated as Clancy ignored him and helped himself to the bread. Chips slid in on the farther side and scooped half the spuds to his plate. There was a real snarl from the other German, but the old lady shouted something and pointed. She had put more potatoes in the pot, there was plenty for all. Clancy and Chips ate till they could not hold more.

They settled back to smoke, and then Clancy grunted with pleasure. The old woman had resurrected a long bottle from her cupboard and she came forward with glasses. At that moment there was a knocking at the door. It was the driver, cold and hungry. The sight of the bottle evidently warmed the soldiers' hearts. They motioned the prisoners from the table and allowed the driver to sit down and gorge himself. Meanwhile the bottle was slowly emptied. It was seemingly of excellent content, and the Germans smacked their lips and made guttural comments as they drank. Clancy licked his lips and watched every drop disappear, then he groaned. "Kin yez beat such hogs?" he said.

The Germans looked at him and leered, then snapped a finger at him. The old lady, however, busied herself at the cupboard and came forth with a second bottle. The German who had snapped his fingers now thumbed his nose at Clancy and calmly poured a glass of liquid for the driver, who drank it with loud relish. The second bottle went the way of the first and in less time, then a third appeared. The Germans were now very generous with their driver and he got more than his share. Finally the Hun with the sprained ankle reached for Clancy's cup and poured him a man-sized drink. Clancy reached for it eagerly. and at the instant heard a very low but distinct hiss. Chips started to rise and knocked against the Irishman's elbow, upsetting every drop of the liquor.

"What th' divil is wrong with ye?" shouted Clancy, gazing at the spilled refreshment.

Chips did not answer, but looked sullen. The German who had been so generous reached to fill Clancy's mug again, then changed his mind and emptied the bottle into his own throat. Then he sagged forward on the table. Very slowly Clancy got up. He had suddenly become aware of the fact that something very potent had been in those bottles. The driver was dead to the world and the other German was as stiff in his chair as if he were paralyzed. "Now, do you see why I jiggled your arm?" asked Chips. "Didn't you hear the old lady hiss at you?"

Clancy looked at the smiling old French woman. "Bless yer kind heart," he said. "I'll remimber ye in my prayers."

He looked at the inert figures, then at the old French couple. "Chips," he said,"when these dog-eaters wake there'll be hell to pay if they're here."

"Yes," said Chips, "but I hate to kill them. I'll shoot them in the legs, but I won't do anything else."

Clancy stared at the little chap with his almost feminine features and dainty hands and feet. "Ye blood-thirsty haythen savage," he blurted. "I'd niver trust ye with anything. Who said we'd kill thim? We'll load them on that wagon and sind them on."

It was laborious work, but they teamed the ancient horses close to the door and the three "drunk" men were put in the cart. Then the old Frenchman drove out on the road and headed the pair towards Berlin. They jogged a distance and then settled to a steady walk that would take them far over the horizon before dark, and Clancy had wits enough to request some empty bottles and place them at the Germans' sides. When discovered the finders would not be puzzled.

The old woman could not speak English, and she was very anxious to have the Canadians leave her. "She did us a rale turn," said Clancy, "and she's nervous about what w9uld happen to her if any av thim Heinies would happen along. Let's go."

Chips agreed. He was too full to travel rapidly, but he followed contentedly across the ploughed fields and pastures and they were far toward a wood before Clancy, looking back saw German infantry marching by the French house they had left. He dropped. to earth at once and Chips followed suit. Then they crawled, and the mud was soft and soon they were wet and soggy. When finally they reached the wood they were in no mood for pleasantries, and both stared, speechless, through the trees. There lay a canal, a canal that was not bridged anywhere within a mile of them.

"Kin yez beat it?" Clancy found his tongue at last. "Th' bridges will be in th' villages. an'..."

"I'm not goin' into that water," said Chips dismally. "It's awful dirty and I bet it's colder'n..."

Clancy suddenly gripped him by the arm and swung him around, pointing. A platoon from the marching unit had entered the fields and were following a path or trail which led very near the wood. Chips groaned, and looked, looked and groaned, and then he hurried to the canal. Clancy, shivering, waded out till the water was well over his knees. "Hi - say, wait for me." Chips, shaking and trembling, stepped in like a thin-blooded maiden lady, then plunged to catch Clancy, sobbing his fear. "Wa - wait for me." he gasped.

Clancy however struck out boldly, just out of reach, and Chips, plunging, kicking, splashing, fought the water with the energy of the desperate. A moment, and Clancy rose from the water and walked up an the bank. Chips found earth at the same time and followed his friend, still gasping and shaking. "Go-gosh, th that was aw---awful," he chattered. "Wh-why didn't you wa-wait for me?"

"I would niver be over yet," said Clancy. "if I waited for yer like. Are ye comin' or stayin'?"

The Irishman had headed into a sort of sunken road and he had began to jog in order to get warm. Chips followed, but he had great difficulty in keeping up. Clancy gradually increased his pace until his little companion called on him to slacken. "I - can't- go another step," panted Chips, as Clancy slowed up a fast walk.

Clancy paid slight heed. He had hurried in order to get warm after their immersion, but now his attention was taken by the sight of several farm buildings clustered ahead. Half a mile farther on, the sunken read would lead them into a farmyard. "I'm - almost dead," gasped Chips, still in the rear, but gaining. “Wait - wait for me, Tim."

Clancy never looked around, but he climbed the bank of the road and looked across the field. Coming straight towards them was a straggling trio of German soldiers!

The Irishman tumbled headlong into the road, sprinted up it then turned abruptly and sprinted back. Chips, amazed, scrambled up the bank and had his look. When he hit the road again he almost passed Clancy. Each of the soldiers carried a bayonet in his hand!

Where the road swerved and made a corner the runners paused. They were too exhausted to go further. Clancy, struggling to get his breath, climbed the bank warily and peeped over. The soldiers had disappeared. Chips, watching him anxiously, swarmed up the bank himself, "Gosh," he whispered huskily. "Where are they?"

Then he looked the other way and with a wild swoop dislodged Clancy and slid to the road. A party of Huns, in full marching order were coming along the bank of the canal. When they passed the end of the sunken road they could not help seeing the two fugitives.

"Where?" gasped Chips. "What'll we..."

Clancy thought rapidly. They were certain to be discovered if they stayed. Why not try to reach the houses and trust to a peasant helping them hide? It was one chance in a thousand, but to remain where they were was hopeless. He faced around and hit into high speed. Chips, after a gurgling cry, ran a close second. They made good time until they were two-thirds of the way to their goal and then Clancy stumbled and fell. Chips sprawled over him, and narrowly escaped a tremendous fist.

"If they heard ye," Clancy hissed through his teeth, “I'll..."

He did not finish his promise, but risked precious time in looking over the bank again. It was a lucky move. The three Germans had appeared again, and the situation was solved. They had been in a cabbage patch. Each had severed a head with his bayonet and now they were bearing their booty back to the farmhouse, probably the chief dish for their supper. But they had swerved over and were dangerously near the sunken road.

Clancy gave one long look, and his leathery countenance evinced despair. To remain in sight seemed to court disaster. It was possible that the marching party had passed the other end of the road. He turned and ran back the way they had come.

Chips trailed him, but the little fellow's breath came in whistling gasps. He tried to call out in his agony. They reached the bend again, peered around it, and Clancy mounted the bank. The marching men had passed. He looked at them a long time and then slid back to cover. "Niver," he grated, "did I git in sich a mess before. 'Tis with havin' a Jonah with me."

Chips made no reply. He had dropped full length on the earth and was intent only on filling his lungs. Clancy waited until he was somewhat revived and then he ventured to watch the distant farmhouse. He saw the Germans go in at the rear door. It would be folly to go nearer the buildings. He looked back toward the canal. The plodding party was far in the distance, but others might come along the same route. Only one course remained. They must cross between the two danger points.

He stepped down and explained to Chips. "Ye do as I say or I'll hand ye over to th' first Heinie I see," he blustered, "an' if iver ye climb over me with thim boots again I'll..."

Chips arose and followed. They hovered low awhile and then ran for the cabbage patch. In between the plants they crawled on hands and knees and so reached a hedge that led to a second garden. Chips caught his tunic on a bush and had difficulty in getting free. When he did so, Clancy was far ahead and making good time. The little man sprinted, straightened full height and ran. Bow-wow-wow! Bow-wow-wow! A huge black dog came bounding from the nearest farmhouse racing towards the garden. Clancy looked back and saw Chips clearing cabbages with a hurdling style unknown to the sporting world. He saw, however, that the dog was gaining, and he realized that he must make some move or they would both be in difficulties. Snatching out a bean pole he ran and menaced the barking animal, which immediately stopped, dropped tail and ears, and retreated.

"Ye poor misfit, ye have alarmed th' village," grated Clancy as they cowered among the vegetable rows. He had seen a farmer look from a barnyard, had seen faces at another home farther on. Then a woman waddled into view, coming from the yard that the dog had left. She headed directly towards the hidden men. spotted them, and made cautious signals. "She wants us to make a run for her house," said Chips, regaining his courage.

"Thin ye go first," suggested Clancy. "An' ye kin wave to me if iverything is Jake."

The little man hesitated. He looked at Clancy and then at the French woman, scrambled to his feet and hurried to the farmhouse. Clancy watched and saw him re-appear in a moment and wave him to come.

"Boche run." The woman pointed over the fields. "Sale Boche," she said fiercely.

Clancy nodded. "Come in here," piped Chips. "They got a good fire goin' an' coffee."

Clancy sat by the stove and looked around the room. A trim girl was serving them and several older women were watching. The retreat of the Germans was the topic of the day and the neighbours had gathered at each others' houses to discuss the move. They chattered and pointed at Clancy and Chips as they drank coffee and dried their clothes.

"Ask thim," said Clancy, "how we kin git away."

Chips had a meagre knowledge of French and the women a similar knowledge of English. It took time to get an understanding, then Chips looked mournful. "It's no use," he sighed. "We can't make it. They say th' only safe way is to go straight through a town that's above here. If we could git through that, it's all easy an th' other side, but..."

"How about th' other ways?" demanded Clancy.

"No good. Th' Heinies have men billetted everywhere. workin' battalions and all. She says we wouldn't stand ma chance..."

"Thin," said Clancy, "by th' crown av ould Ireland. I'm goin' through th' town."

"How?" faltered Chips.

"Ask yer friends," suggested Clancy.

There was a deluge of French, much head shaking, nodding, gesturing, then a big woman jumped to her feet and almost embraced Clancy. "Kape back," he growled, getting to his feet. "Are yez drunk or crazy?"

The women laughed and cackled and pointed. She caught the girl by the arm and stood her alongside Chips, who reddened and squirmed to escape. "They're bughouse," he said despairingly. "Don't let her do anything, Tim."

But the woman had turned to her neighbours, who suddenly understood her. They in turn clapped their hands and cackled as they surrounded the two men. Then there was a rush for an inner room and presently the waddling madame returned with an armload of capes and skirts and waists and articles of clothing that Clancy knew little about. "Gosh," said Chips. "Do you know what they're plannin'? They want you an' me to dress up in them rigs and try to git through th' town."

Clancy swore luridly, and burnt his mouth with hot coffee. "They are a bunch of cacklin' fools." he growled.

But the French women argued and explained, and Chips sputtered and interpreted as much as he could. "They say Heinie's lettin' th' French go and come without askin' questions. and that if we stay here we're liable to git caught, for there's Heinies in this village that's been here for six months an' know everybody."

"Th' divil with thim," said Clancy firmly. "Niver will ye git me in thim rigs. I'll take me chances in th' fields."

The debate continued with neither side gaining ground, and at length a supper of hot soup and dark bread was served. Reinforced by it, the Irishman decided that he would brave the Berlin Guards before subjecting himself to feminine attire, and as it grew dusk he sallied forth with Chips in tow. They made fair speed for an hour, and then the war seemed suddenly to shift nearer. They could hear the roaring of guns in the distance and see the reflection of flashes in the sky, then they were almost trapped. A party of Huns, badly disorganized, materialized out of the dark and passed within feet of them. Another column was glimpsed marching back through a field, and only a sustained sprint saved the fugitives. Once more they were headed by retreating Germans, and then the two men stumbled and ran in the darkness until they were back in the garden of the friendly woman. The big black dog barked once, then permitted them to reach the door.

Clancy walked right in. More women and several old men were present, and they were greatly alarmed. "Tell thim," ordered Clancy, "we're headed off, an' we want to kape under cover till daylight. We kin sleep in the cellar or in th' attic."

Chips explained and madame bubbled over with apprehension, then relented and hurried them upstairs. She escorted them to a closet-like room in the rear and there they lay and listened. From the cobbled roadway came the tramp of heavy feet. Trucks rumbled by, all kinds of wheeled traffic, and there were shouted guttural orders. Half an hour later some Germans came to the house. Clancy felt Chips shaking as they heard the harsh voices below. Then there was a grating and scraping of chairs. The unwelcome visitors had evidently come for a meal.

Clancy, listening to every sound, painfully aware of their helplessness to save themselves, made a decision. "Come daylight," he wheezed, "I'm puttin' on petticoats or anything ilse, and," he added threateningly, "ye'll be doin' th' same."

Chips made no answer.

At ten o'clock the next morning there was considerable traffic on the road leading into the town that had barred their way. One little procession was headed by a chic French girl who was leading a large black dog. The dog was drawing a cart in which sat a very large coarse-featured lady. Her dark-red countenance was partly hidden by her drooping bonnet, and only her bulging waist was visible. She was anchored in her seat by an array of farm produce. Back of her walked an old Frenchman, who looked as if he might be her husband.

The party crossed a bridge and sighted the distant street. "Stop th' baste," ordered the "lady" in the cart. "Me foot's asleep."

The chic damsel looked back, looked at the dog. "She" was walking well to one side of the canine. " How..," came her rather tremulous voice, "do you stop him?"

"Pull on th' rope," ordered Clancy from his seat in the cart. "Stop him. I'm tellin' ye." Never had he felt so helpless as when they had stowed him in the little vehicle, swathed in madame's raiment, and packed in by vegetables. But it was means of escape, and he bore it grimly. Now that his foot had gone asleep he had a chance to ease his feelings.

Chips, the chic young lady, had donned the girlish garments without making a single protest. Indeed he made a very nice-looking young lady, and as his hands and feet were small there did not seem to be a great risk in his part, unless he lost his bonnet. But Chips had not gotten over his terror of the big dog, and he refused to try further after the shaggy fellow resented the tug on his rope. "I can't stop him," he said plaintively. "Your foot'll be all right."

"I'll 'all right' you, me lad, when I get out av this mess," said Clancy in a blood-curdling manner, but he sat still, for what else could he do?

The Frenchman back of his cart grunted and talked to himself whenever they came to a crossroads, and Clancy was fearful that the old chap might betray them. The first street angled and cut off the view, but they sighted, a few blocks to the right, and partly hidden by a brick wall, a large group of German soldiers. Chips stopped suddenly. "Heinies," he gasped, and pointed.

"Kape that mitt av yours down," grated Clancy, "or I'll git out av this cart an' choke ye."

He was becoming very nervous. Perspiration broke out all over him. He wished he had not come in the cart. If the Germans captured them, both of them would be shot as spies. The dog, pulled back growled and headed onward, and Chips, springing forward to humour him, kept on. The big, pot-like helmets were bobbing beyond the wall as their wearers gathered in the square. They seemed to be massing for some purpose, and Clancy peered ahead, searching frantically for a side street which would allow them to escape the square. There was no such street in sight.

"Tim," faltered Chips. "We're goin' to get caught sure. Jist look at th' Heinies. I-I'm goin to beat it."

“If ye make wan step," said Clancy in a terrible voice, "I'll catch ye an' give ye over to th' Germans, an' they'll shoot ye fer a spy."

"But - but I can't," protested Chips. He tried to hang back on the rope, but the dog tugged on and the old Frenchman muttered.

They turned a corner. The square was not far ahead. But the people of the town were flocking out of their homes. There was a great cheering. The bell of the church began to ring loudly. "What in sivin divils?" said Clancy to himself.

He was bewildered, puzzled, scared stiff. Give him a rifle in his hands, a bayonet, and he would fight to the last, but, swaddled in the cart as he was, he was absolutely helpless, and felt it. "If iver I git out av this..." he groaned.

One more block. Chips was walking stiff-legged in sheer terror. The rope was taut and the big dog was pulling him along. The old Frenchman made throaty noises and came up and pushed on the cart to assist the dog. The shove set Clancy's heart jumping, but he dare not protest. He must now keep silent.

On and on, around the corner, then Chips started, staggered in amazement, stood and was tugged on, lurching like a drunken man. Clancy, his eyes distended under his bonnet, was also astounded. He could hardly realize their luck. Into the big square, marching like a band of school boys, came the Fifth Mounted Rifles. They were wild with hilarity, had flowers on their rifles and helmets, little flags tucked in their equipment, were shouting and singing. Before them, but now herded to one side, was a large group of German prisoners, those that Clancy had glimpsed, the ones that had so frightened Chips. Some of the soldiers had their arms locked in those of French girls. All were throwing kisses, calling and waving to women that lined the streets. The officers were as gay as the men.

Chips, pulled nearly off his feet by the dog, turned to Clancy, his face wreathed in smiles. "Hooray," he said "We're Jake. Let's pitch this gear and join th' boys."

Clancy had realized his position even as Chips spoke, and he almost had heart failure. Not for all the luck in the world would he be caught in such a predicament, he would never hear the last of it. Whatever else happened they must go on, and the chances were good. No one would obstruct their way, and everyone was too happy and excited to note their strange manner. "Kape goin'," he hissed, "or I'll cut yer heart out. Are ye a fool, man?"

Chips lost his grin. Clancy was in deadly earnest, and the little man knew what that meant. He hurried to follow the dog, and he kept his face averted and, smiled at no one.

"We have got the lousy Hun on the everlastin' run." sang a soldier who ambled across their path. "Say, Eddie, look at th' old lady here. Ain't that comfort for ya? I've a good mind to pitch her out an' take th' rig myself."

Clancy's jaw was set like iron. He never turned his head.

"Not for mine, Bill," came the rejoinder. "Did you ever see such a homely dial? Look at her old man behind, no wonder he's a sad-lookin' old frog. I'm goin' to hit up with the Jane that's leadin' th' dog."

"Suit yourself," said the singer," but them dogs is trained to protect these girls, I'll bet. 'We have got th' lousy Hun on th'..."

The singer was lost in the crowd. His mate took a few steps after Chips, then regarded the big dog more seriously, and stopped. Close back of Clancy the old Frenchman shouted shrilly and the dog stopped. The Frenchman came beside Clancy, rubbing his hands, smiling, clacking, gesturing. Wasn't it a bon war after all. Here were comrades and no danger - what more use of him or his dog and cart? Clancy surmised that this was what the Frenchman was saying, and he was at his wits end. Not for anything could he be caught now. Just ahead, looking their way was Sergeant Binns and Captain McKirk, the adjutant of the battalion. McKirk knew Clancy's record like a book, and would never believe anything he said. Furthermore the old chap was a stickler for propriety, and would have suspicions of how Clancy achieved his garb.

Clancy risked his voice once more, "Chips," he said, "git on with that baste if ye have to pull him. Niver mind this ould divil at all."

Chips, fright riding free on his features, strove manfully to obey. He pulled one way and the dog pulled the other. The old Frenchman got angry and cracked commands in a shrill voice. The dog obeyed. He leaped around, upsetting Chips, and almost upsetting Clancy. The Irishman made a lunge with his weight and maintained his cart, but the incident drew attention. Half a dozen soldiers rushed over and assisted Chips to his feet. One of them saw that the dog was unruly and, with a soldier's care-free way, released the harness. The dog bounded back to the old Frenchman who was protesting most vigorously.

Chips, luckily, had not lost his bonnet. He also had not lost his presence of mind. He bowed thanks to his assistants and walked on, letting go of the rope. He walked to a lane between buildings and disappeared.

Clancy, helpless to stop him, seethed and sweated, but kept his bonnet low. His fate was now in the hands of the mob. "For th' love a Pete," said one. "Did you ever see such a face? Lets move the old girl somewhere. She'll spoil the day if she sticks around."

"But what's this old guy sayin'?" asked another. "Him an' th' old girl's fell out, just listen to him."

"Say boys," said a third. "Let's have some fun. This old Jane's paralyzed or somethin'. Let's take her cart and all, and put her into old McKirk's billet."

"But she'll yell blue murder," said a more careful mate, "wait till th' officers are gone."

"Hell," objected the moving spirit. "That'll let old McKirk get there ahead of us. I'll bet she's dumb, lost her speech or somethin'. Let's try her."

Two of the soldiers took hold of Clancy's cart and moved it up the street. Clancy did not raise his head, but the old Frenchman nearly went wild. He caught hold of the back of the cart. "Get him away, give him some money or tobacco or something," said one of the men.

A soldier flourished a bundle of paper francs and the old man let go his hold, merely watching the direction they took Clancy. Up a side street, the soldiers walking about the old man like a body guard, then into a lane and the party stopped at a little building. A moment to observe the dangers near, then Clancy, cart and all, was hustled inside. There was a jabbering outside, then it faded and Clancy looked around. The soldiers were hurrying away, taking the old man with them. Clancy did not need two guesses to know why McKirk must be coming.

The Irishman was never in a more serious predicament. He could not imagine any person ever explaining matters to the adjutant. And what would happen to him... With a great surge he lurched from the cart, scattering vegetables about it, then leaped toward the door of an inner room. It was to be McKirk's sleeping room evidently, for his bedroll had been flung into it. There was a bed there, but no closet, no other exit except a small window. And then McKirk entered the outer room.

Clancy heard his heavy step, heard his gasp, and then the adjutant stood still, looking. In that scant time Clancy had a brain wave. He tore loose his big skirt, and stood in a pink frilled petticoat, the skirt loosely piled above his boots and puttees. His waist was loose over the top of the petticoat, and he pulled his bonnet down so as to hide the most of his Irish countenance.

McKirk took two quick strides and stood in the doorway. Clancy turned slowly toward him, without raising his head, shrugged his shoulders in a coy fashion, then peeped slyly.

The adjutant gasped and drew back. "You, you..." he exploded, then turned. "What a terrible depravity!" he cried, and burst out the door.

In three minutes Clancy had shed his borrowed rigging, and was thankful he had kept his khaki beneath his disguise. He opened the door and plunged out, enveloped in a sheet he had snatched from the bed. The men peering around the corner, yelled their amazement, and started to give pursuit. Clancy lost them in two lanes. He hurled the sheet into a tree and ran like a deer till he came to a rifle and equipment some celebrating soldier had discarded. These he salvaged at once, then he hurried to the town square. The first man he met was Sergeant Binns. "Where," asked the Sergeant, "have you been the last few days?"

Clancy knew how the veteran regarded him, knew the futility of trying to explain all that had happened. He winked and grinned. "I've been havin' th' time av me life," he said.

"You old heathen," said the Sergeant. "You're getting depraved in your old age. Have you seen anything of Chips?"

"No," said Clancy, "an' I'm lookin' fer him now."

"Send him to me when you find him, will you?" said Binns.

"I will," promised Clancy, with a grimness that the Sergeant could not understand, "whin I'm through with him mesilf."

L'ENVOI

After Cambrai the Dismounted Mudhounds had a comparatively easy time and therefore it seemed but the irony of fate that Clancy should get a bad leg wound a few days before the end. It was overhead shrapnel that caught him as he was "salvaging" a dinner of vegetables from a deserted garden, and he lay very quiet in the ambulance during his long trip down the line.

In England he became brighter, but when the Armistice celebrations were at their height he turned his face to the wall and was rude to the nurse who tried to make him smile. "The war's over, Clancy," she cooed. "Can't you sit up and cheer with the rest?"

"I cannot," he said. "Tis me burnin' Irish luck to be in this place at th' prisint, an' I could yell more if I was in a Heinie cage."

"This place!" she cried. "Why, every man here wants to celebrate. The Corporal next you has shouted his head off, and those two lads over there are delirious."

Clancy did not look. The Corporal was sporting an A.S.C. badge, and the two "delirious" ones had regimental numbers as long as a Brigadier's inspection. So the Irishman was quiet, and a sombre companion while he remained in the ward.

It was three years after the Kaiser's collapse that Tommy Binns, ex-Sergeant, heard that Clancy was engaged in some sort of construction work in Ontario, but it was not until 1925 that he located him, and he was amazed to see the Irishman looking prosperous. They re-lived a few of their front-line experiences and then Clancy entertained his guest with a lavish assortment of refreshments. As they absorbed liquids and fruit Clancy relieved his mind.

"Th' wans that seen it niver say nothin', an' th' bomb-proofers an' safety-firsts have niver stopped yappin' about it. There's wan at this hotel. He wuz with a labour outfit but he kin tell ye all th' tricks av bay'nit -fightin' and av th' way to use Heinie bombs. 'Tis instructive to Listen to th' gint, an' I got so ashamed av me ignorance that I took down me button."

"But - haw have you got on, Tim?" Binns could not understand how

Clancy had been able to be businesslike with contractors.

"Sure, now an' I could have been a sar'gint, if I could have kept me silf rispect," said Clancy slyly. "Ye see I kin handle men asily, and fer excavatin' cellars or movin' ould buildings, you can't bate this firm."

"Firm?" said Binns. "You never told me...?"

Clancy squirmed in his seat, then went to the door of his apartment and returned with a square-built, broad-faced man of blond appearance. "Sar'gint Binns," he said gravely, "meet with Sarg'int Miller - av th' Sixteenth Saxons."

"Saxons!" spluttered Binns. He took the man's hand, however, and responded to the warm grip. "Glad to meet you, Mister Miller," he said slowly.

"I am proud to meet a friend of Tim's," came the answer in correct but guttural English.

"Did you say a 'Saxon,' Tim?" queried Binns, bewildered.

"I did," said Clancy. "Miller's a Heinie, if ye will fergit th' wurrd, and he's th' greatest gint with figgers I've iver seen, an' a rale white man, an' th' biggest half av this firm, an' anyhow, me lad, if ye'll kape yer ears open an' read yer papers ye'll find there wuz more divils in th' brass hats an' th' big bugs with thim, than among th' boys at th' front-an' that goes fer both sides."

A Saxon! A Heinie! Timothy Fergus Clancy arguing in favour of a German ex-Sergeant. Binns gulped - and smiled.

"I agree with every word, Tim," he said warmly.

"Thin let's have a 'wet'," said Tim, and he raised his glass. "To ivery good German," he said huskily.

"To every good man who was against us," said Miller.

Binns held his glass the highest. "To all comrades of the trenches," he said, and at his words they stood to drink.

THE END

William Richard Bird (1891-1984)

Will Bird was born in Mapleton, Nova Scotia, May 11, 1891. He was the first son of Stephen Bird, by his second wife, Augusta (nee Bird), of Amherst, Nova Scotia. He was preceded by his two half-brothers, Harry (1885) and Hubert (1886), from his father's first wife. In 1893 a fourth Bird brother, Lew, was born.

In December 1895, with Augusta 4 months pregnant, tragedy struck the family when their father, Stephen died suddenly. Five months after Stephen Bird's death, Augusta gave birth to another son, a namesake for her late husband, Stephen Carmen.

Later that year Augusta Bird moved back to her hometown of Amherst bringing with her the 5 year old Will, Lew, the baby Stephen and the two sons from the late Stephen's previous marriage, Hubert and Harry.

The younger boys were educated in Amherst, at the High School and later Stephen went to work for the Canada Car Company. Both Will and Stephen competed in athletics, were keen baseball players and "red-hot" fans of both baseball and hockey. The two were very close, shared mutual likes and dislikes and "could read each other's minds".

With the outbreak of war in 1914, Stephen enlisted as a Corporal in the 25th Nova Scotia Battalion. Will also rushed to join the Colours but Stephen, using his influence, had Will turned down. Disheartened Will went to the Prairies to farm. In May 1915 the 25th Battalion sailed for England.

The 25th Battalion went to France in mid-September 1915 and occupied trenches at Kemmel, just south of Ypres, Belgium. On September 25th the inexperienced men of the 25th suffered their first fatalities. On their next tour in the trenches, just before 5 pm on October 8, 1915, the Germans blew a large, underground explosive charge beneath the 25th's frontline trenches. The explosion created a hole 65 feet by 35 feet and 25 feet deep. It killed 2 men outright, wounded 20, and 10 men were listed as "missing".

That same October found Will bringing in the harvest on a small farm in Saskatchewan, pitching sheaves into a wagon, when Stephen walked out from behind a farmcart! They did not speak and soon

Stephen vanished. Three days later Will received official notification that Stephen Bird, was missing, presumed dead in the mine explosion. His body was never found.

The well-liked Stephen had been popular amongst his comrades and one wrote to the Bird family after his death; "He had splendid courage and when urged to fall back a little further a few minutes before the explosion his reply was 'I am staying right here' ".

Another wrote, "He was a friend at all times and under all circumstances, no one need wish a better friend, we all loved him and we all mourn his loss." No one mourned his loss more than Will.

Will returned to Amherst and in April 1916 enlisted in the 193rd Battalion, Nova Scotia Highlanders. The 193rd Battalion was a locally-raised battalion and the men who comprised its ranks were all from the area and included Hubert Bird, Will's half brother. (The number block allocated to the 193rd Nova Scotia Highlanders was 901001 to 904000, Will Bird's service number was 901552).

In October 1916 the 193rd sailed for England. Upon arrival it was broken up for reinforcements and Will Bird and a number of his friends were shipped to France to reinforce the 42nd Battalion, The Black Watch of Canada, in the frontline. On January 5, 1917 the men from Nova Scotia joined the kilted Montrealers in the trenches in front of the infamous Vimy Ridge.

The 42nd had served in France since 1915 and had already fought in the Major battles of Mount Sorrel and the Somme when Will joined them in late 1916. Throughout the war the Black Watch fought with exceptional ferocity and success. By the end of the war 800 men had been killed and 2,000 wounded of the 5,500 men who passed through the ranks of the battalion. Shortages of reinforcements from Montreal brought many men from across Canada into their ranks and this is how Will Bird ended up with a Quebec Regiment.

Will Bird served with the 42nd Battalion throughout the war until demobilized back in Canada in March 1919. He was awarded a Military Medal for bravery in the capture of Mons, on the night of 10-11 November 1918, the last night of the war.

Will returned to Southampton, Nova Scotia and in 1919, married Ethel Sutton, his childhood sweetheart and had two children, Stephen Stanley in 1920 and Betty in 1923. The family moved to Amherst in 1923 and later to Halifax.

Like many veterans Will did not know which way to go after the war but through some good fortune and good writing found a career in journalism. During the 1930's his First World War memoir "And We Go On" was published, followed by a series of articles on visiting the old battlefields for Macleans magazine. The two publications brought Will into prominence in the burgeoning remembrance movement brought about by the aging veterans in the 1930's.

Will Bird was a prolific writer on many topics: fiction, non-fiction, books, magazines, articles, newspapers, columns and short stories. Over the years he became a literary presence in his native Nova Scotia.

The years took a toll on the many who survived the war. In 1939, Will's half brother Hubert, who had lost a leg at the Drocourt-Queant line, died. But the hardest blow came in 1944 when his son, Stephen was killed in Normandy. He was 24. Captain Stephen Stanley Bird of the North Nova Scotia Highlanders was killed in action July 8, 1944. He is buried in Beny-sur-Mer Canadian War Cemetery, France. Will often blamed his writing about his war experiences as a factor in his son's rush to enlist.

Time continued to take its toll and in 1977 his half brother, Harry died and in 1982, his beloved Ethel passed away. Will followed her in 1984.

Will Bird is survived by his daughter, Betty Murray, of Amherst and four grandchildren.